KATHERINE HASTINGS

Vinci Books

vinci-books.com

Published by Vinci Books Ltd in 2026

1

This work is a work of fiction. Names, characters, places and incidents are the product of the author's imagination or are used fictitiously. Any resemblance to actual persons, living or dead, places and incidents is entirely coincidental.

A CIP catalogue record for this book is available from the British Library.
Paperback ISBN: 9781036715854
The EU GPSR authorised representative is Logos Europe, 9 rue Nicolas Poussion, 17000 La Rochelle, France contact@logoseurope.eu

By Katherine Hastings

Immortal Hearts

Into the Light

Awakened Light

Eternal Light

The Wilder Widows

The Wilder Widows

The Wilder Widows: Wilder Ever After

The Wilder Widows: Walk on the Wilder Side

Door Peninsula Passions

The Other Half

The Other Room

The Other Plan

Rescue Ops Romance

Colombian Chemistry

Sicilian Savior

Russian Rescue

Daggers of Desire

In the Assassin's Arms

Beneath the Assassin's Touch

By the Assassin's Side

Also by Katherine Hastings

Riches to Ruinville

The Big One

The Arch Pirate

A War Within

Spectral Sleuths

Millie and Mabel's Afterlife Adventures

Immortal Hearts Series

Though each book can be read as a standalone, this series is meant to be read in order. While each book features its own love story and HEA, the books follow a continued timeline and pick up where the last one left off without an extensive history, as well as feature reoccurring characters.

Chapter One

CATRAIN

The waves lapped on the shore as I buried my toes deeper into the sand. Even though the sun had already slipped beneath the horizon, the darkening sky still held remnants of the orange and red hues left over from the sunset.

A sharp gust of wind blew my hair across my face, and I exhaled a sigh, knowing exactly what had caused it.

Or should I say *who?*

Thorne.

A vampire.

And my tribe's sworn enemy.

"So close," he said with a laugh as he plopped into the sand beside me. "I thought just maybe I could see a little more of the colors in the sky if I timed running out of my cave just right. Maybe tomorrow."

"No tomorrow!" I snapped and spun to stare at him. "You can't stay on the island anymore. You need to go home. Tonight."

His stormy-blue eyes lit up when they locked with mine, and I cursed the fluttering in my stomach they inspired.

Every time he looked at me, I felt my small world tip upside down, and it only righted itself when I looked away.

But breaking out of the hypnotic trance his eyes lulled me into was harder than it should have been. Instead of looking away, I stared deeper into them.

Again.

And I shouldn't. He was a *vampire,* and my tribe hated their kind for betraying us six centuries ago. Vampires were our greatest enemies, and we'd never allowed one to set foot on the island we'd hid on for centuries.

Then a couple days ago, vampires showed up begging for access to our island so we could heal Thorne's dying friend, Aiden. My mother's powerful magic saved his life. Though she'd normally have left a vile vampire to its fate, there was something different about Aiden. A kindness to him that I'd believed didn't exist in his species.

My mother had recognized it, too, and with my pleading to have mercy on him, she'd granted him immortal life along with his beloved, Emilia. The rest of their clan had taken leave the following morning, but Thorne had refused to follow, and much to our dismay, he'd spent the last three nights milling around the island learning about our tribe… and pestering me.

A crooked smile lifted his lip. "Ah, come on, Cat. You can't be sick of me already. We're just getting to know each other."

"Well, I *am* sick of you," I lied, as I sat up and crossed my arms. I wished it wasn't a lie, and I wished that I really did want him to leave, but as his smile grew, so did my desire to have him stay right here at my side.

If I was honest with myself, I'd admit that Thorne made me laugh harder than I had in my entire life. I'd admit that his stories of the outside world intrigued me, and I wanted him to tell me more and more. I'd admit that as much as it shamed me to have feelings for a vampire, I did.

But I refused to admit it and instead rolled my eyes and looked away. "I want you gone."

"Liar." He bumped me with his shoulder. "You like having me around."

"I do not." I pushed him back, but he didn't budge an inch. Maybe it was because he was a vampire and impossibly strong, but even without his special powers, with the size of his muscles, he probably wouldn't have moved even if he was a human.

"Liar, liar, pants on fire." He booped me on my nose, and I swatted his hand away.

"You're ridiculous. You're worse than a child." I smacked him on his shoulder as a little laughter escaped against my wishes.

"Ouch!" Dramatically rubbing the spot I'd just hit, he furrowed his dark brows. "That hurt."

Rolling my eyes, I shook my head. "It did not. You're a vampire, which means nothing hurts you. My ancestors saw to that when they created you to protect them. But maybe this would."

I arched an eyebrow and lifted my hand. My skin heated as I concentrated, and soon small flames appeared and flickered in my palm. Thorne's eyes illuminated in the glow, and it only seemed to accentuate the mischievous glimmer that never seemed to leave them.

"That's so awesome. That doesn't hurt you?"

I shook my head. "It's warm but not hot."

"Does it hurt when I touch it?" With no fear, he waved his hand over mine, grimacing when the flames touched his skin. "Yep. That hurt."

"The real question is, can it kill an immortal vampire?" Pursing my lips, I narrowed my eyes as my flame grew.

"Unless you've managed to harness sunlight, I doubt it. Regular fire stings a bit but doesn't kill original vampires like me. Your ancestors certainly tried to wipe us out with magic, but it didn't work. But that was then, so maybe it works now. Only one way to find out. If you really want me dead, have at it, Cat."

I held his gaze while he called my bluff, and with a huff, I clasped my fist and extinguished the flame.

The mischievous twinkle in his eye sparkled brighter. "See. I told you that you liked having me around."

"No, I don't. I come here every night for tranquility. Tranquility you continue to steal from me."

Every evening for years, I'd sneak away from my village and come here to escape the demands of my mother and our tribe.

A tribe that soon I would lead.

Spikes of anxiety poked me whenever I considered taking her place, but sitting in the familiar patch of sand each night helped me chase it away for a few blissful moments of respite. I'd shut out the world behind me, lean back, and stare across the lake separating me from a world I'd never seen. A world I'd only heard about through stories from a few of my fellow Pict tribesmen who'd been allowed to venture across the lake, and now from Thorne. I'd never been allowed to leave my familial island and surrounding magic had kept us hidden from intruders for centuries. Only a few rare outsiders had been allowed entry through the fog that blinded anyone who tried to find us.

Rare outsiders like the vampire staring at me right now.

"If you really wanted me gone, you'd have torched me with a fireball."

A strange thread of yearning wound through me. "Just because I'm not trying to incinerate you, doesn't mean I want you around."

"I'd argue it does."

We had a stare-off for a few moments before his smile coaxed out my own. "I hate you," I said with a chuckle.

"More lies," he teased. "So, what else are you going to show me tonight? I'll tell you more about the outside world if you show me another cool trick."

Ever since Thorne had arrived, we'd indulged in a little nightly magic. Since he hadn't dared head into the village with my mother and my tribe, he'd find me out here and pester me until he wore me down, and I'd show him some of my powers. While I did, he'd tell me about life on the other side of the lake. Hearing stories about all the unfamiliar lands, people, and customs infatuated me, and I couldn't even imagine what it would be like to experience it myself.

My need to hear more about the outside world quieted the dwindling good sense that whispered at me to send him away. "Fine. I'll show you how I do a locater spell, and you can tell me more about the city."

"Which one? There are thousands."

"Thousands?" My eyes widened.

"Thousands. More, actually." Thorne rubbed a hand across the stubble on his face, and his square jaw tightened. "How about I tell you about New York City. It's in a place called America."

"Is that far from here?" I asked while I smoothed the sand with my hand to make a place to perform my spell.

"Yes. It's across the ocean. And the ocean is like this lake, but so big that it takes months to sail across it."

"Months?" I choked on the word. "It takes months to cross?"

"Yes. Months. However, we have planes now that can fly you there in less than a day."

"I've seen things passing overhead and was told that people now fly in them." I gestured to the sky and shook my head. "Only birds belong in the sky."

His hearty laugh echoed around me and he nodded. "Humans are very driven creatures. They come up with new inventions every day. Planes are one of those inventions. I have a jet that lets me hop around the world after a quick phone call."

"And phones are the things you use to communicate with people far away?" I asked, still trying to wrap my head around that idea.

"Yep. I can place a call with a phone, and they will gas up my jet and be waiting."

I blinked as I tried to process it all. "I still can't comprehend the world you live in."

"And I can't comprehend that you can do magic. It's incredible."

I shrugged. "I only have some magic. Every member of my family does. The goddess blessed our bloodline with it."

"So, only your family can do spells?"

I nodded. "Yes. We can all harness nature to perform our spells… wind, water, earth, fire, and lightning. But only our leader gets full powers when they ascend. The leader of our tribe is all-powerful and can perform spells far more formidable than my little fireballs. I'll inherit them when I take over our tribe after my mother steps down and I ascend her throne."

"And when does that happen?" He drew a smiling face

in the sand next to the map I started drawing with my finger.

Anxiety twisted a knot into my stomach knowing my ascension loomed so close. "At the end of this year. We reign for fifty years and then pass on the honor to our firstborn child."

"Fifty years, huh? That's a long time."

Shaking my head, I placed the necklace my mother had given me on the sand map of our island. "It's how it's always been. Our tradition."

His tone softened. "And what happens if your leader dies before an heir is born? Who leads then?"

"The leader of our tribe can't die. While we reign, we're immortal. After we step down, our immortality passes to the new leader."

"Not too shabby," he said. "I mean, not as impressive as my six centuries of immortality and counting, but not bad at all."

Narrowing my eyes, I scolded him with a stare. "You only got your immortality from *my* people… and then you betrayed us."

"Ah, come on, Cat. That was a long time ago. Let's let bygones be bygones. Water under the bridge and all that shit."

My spine bristled. "I still hate your kind."

"My *kind,* but not me."

I caught his cocky grin out of the corner of my eye but refused to look straight at him before my eyes revealed the truth.

Ignoring his taunt, I held my hand over my mother's necklace.

"What are you doing?" he asked.

"A locator spell. This is my mother's necklace, and when

I perform the spell, the necklace will move on this map to wherever she is on the island."

"Seriously?" He leaned closer over the map.

"Just be quiet so I can concentrate."

"Sorry," he whispered.

Focusing all my energy onto the necklace, I closed my eyes and recited the words I'd learned from my mother long ago. The magic swirled inside me, charging me up with an energy that felt like vibrations beneath my skin. When I opened my eyes, I saw the necklace slowly dragging through the sand on its own toward the center of the island map. It stopped when it reached the drawings that represented our huts.

I pointed. "There. She's at the center of the village, likely in her hut."

"That's amazing." He shook his head. "Seriously. I mean, I'm a vampire and all, so I know magic exists, but I've never gotten to see it practiced until I met you. It's incredible."

"That's nothing." I shrugged and sat back. "My mother, now *she* has powers. Hell, I'm surprised she hasn't dropped a lightning bolt on your head since you've refused to leave. Though she told me today that you *must* leave tonight. I don't think she will overlook your presence out here anymore."

Thorne sucked the air through his teeth and then burst into laughter. "I'm not going to lie… I'm surprised too. She's certainly made it clear I've overstayed my welcome."

"We *all* think you've overstayed your welcome. Actually, there was no welcome to overstay." I arched a brow and he smiled wider. "Seriously. If you don't leave soon, she really will find some way to eradicate you."

He lay back in the sand and rested his head on folded

arms. When he closed his eyes, I took the opportunity to let my gaze explore all his impressive features.

Though I'd never seen anyone from the outside world other than his family, I couldn't imagine it was possible for someone to be more beautiful. Everywhere my eyes roved met perfection, from his dark hair to his masculine face with a straight nose and full lips. I wondered what he'd look like in the leather loincloth the men from my tribe wore. I could only imagine the muscles that lay hidden beneath his modern clothes.

As I worked my way back up his body, my gaze slid to a stop when it landed on the most incredible feature about him.

His eyes.

Deep blue and filled with such passion and intensity it took my breath away each time I looked into them.

And now they stared back at me filled with mirth.

"Don't let me stop you. You can keep checking out the goods." His crooked smile deepened his dimples as he waggled his eyebrows.

Heat flooded my cheeks as I quickly looked away. "I wasn't 'checking out the goods.' I was just looking for your most vulnerable spot so I can kill you with a well-placed fireball."

One eyebrow climbed. "Is that so?"

"Yes. That's so." I looked back at him, and his growing smile coaxed another out of me.

"Literally the worst liar in history. You're so busted." He laughed and I gave up my fight, covered my face and joined him.

"Don't feel bad. I've checked out your goods too. I dig all the tattoos."

"Oh, do you?" I asked, looking down at the tribal tattoos on my arms.

"I do. You're kind of a badass, Catrain. It's not often I'm intimidated." He propped up on his elbows. "Actually, I'm *never* intimidated. But when I first saw you standing on the beach with your spear and your tattoos, and all that face paint..." He blew out a whistle. "You scared the hell out of me."

"I did?" I smiled wider.

A quick puff of breath accompanied his nodding head. "Oh yeah. You looked like you could kick even my arse."

Pursing my lips, I raised my eyebrows. "Good. I glad I scared you."

"*I'm*. I am," he corrected.

I nodded in acknowledgment and repeated it. "*I'm* glad I scared you."

Part of our evenings involved Thorne helping me with my English. We'd been taught English since childhood from the few Picts who'd been allowed out into the world. They thought it was important we could all speak the language in the event our island was ever discovered. After years of speaking it, my English was fairly good, but Thorne had been teaching me how to make it sound a bit more natural. Though my native accent remained strong, I had quickly learned some of the more casual and correct ways of speaking the language.

"Perfect. You're a very quick learner, Cat."

"Thank you," I said while I watched him lower himself all the way back down again. I followed suit and mimicked his position and lay my head back on my folded arms and stared up at the darkening sky.

"I know you've been begging me to go, but I actually do have to leave tonight," he said quietly.

The words sucked the air from my lungs. I should have been celebrating the fact my family's greatest enemy was leaving my life, but instead, a pang of regret tightened up inside my stomach.

"Oh," I whispered.

"I can only survive on the hog's blood I've been feeding on for so long. I can feel my strength slipping away. We require human blood to survive, so unless you're willing to offer me a blood meal, I need to get back to the mainland to feed."

I crinkled my face in disgust. "I will *not* be letting you drink my blood. Disgusting."

"It's no more disgusting than you eating animal flesh. Unless you're a vegetarian, you don't have much of a leg to stand on."

"It's very different," I argued. "You drink *people.*"

He shrugged. "I do. But unlike the animals you kill for food, the people I drink remain very much alive. And most say the experience of being my lunch is euphoric. We could argue, in fact, that the real monster here is you."

I rolled my head over to face him, and when he turned his head, we locked eyes once again. My stomach tightened up and started those infuriating flip-flops that happened every time I looked at him.

"You really don't kill everyone you feed on? I've spent my whole life hearing of the horrors and brutality of vampires. That you slaughter innocents and kill at will."

Thorne gently shook his head. "I suppose when we first turned, we didn't have control of it like we do now. We did kill most of the humans we fed on because we didn't know another way. But we quickly learned to feed on them, erase their memory of it, and leave them alive. It's rare for a vampire to kill a human, and Lothaire, the leader of our clan and all the vampires, enacted a law that forbids it. Any vampire caught killing a human for pleasure is put on trial, and the crime is punishable by death. It's much easier to keep our existence a secret if we don't leave a trail of bodies in our wake, so the law was put into place centuries ago. Feed, erase, release. That's the way we function. And most of us have blood donors now or drink from a blood bag."

"Like Emilia?" I asked, my curiosity about his life deepening. "You said she started as Aiden's blood donor before they fell in love?"

"Yes." He nodded. "That's how they met."

"And you?" Pausing, I swallowed hard. "Do you have a… donor?"

The thought of him sucking on a woman's neck, or worse, falling in love with her, caused my stomach to churn in a much different way than his looks induced.

It twisted in jealousy.

"No. Not right now," he answered. "I've had donors before, but I travel too much these days. It's challenging to drag a human being everywhere I go. Instead, I live on blood bags and the occasional live meal when the opportunity presents itself and I have no risk of discovery."

Exhaling a breath of relief, I looked back up at the sky. "And you can live on these blood bags? Those don't hurt anyone?"

"Yep. A blood bag is just human blood that has been drained with a needle and stored. They do it willingly for medicine, and we buy them from the medical banks," he answered. "It's not nearly as good as fresh from the vein, but I'm no food snob like Aiden, so it suits me just fine. Portable, easy, and zero risk of detection."

Silence settled between us as I let the relief wash over me. He didn't have a woman waiting for him at home. A woman whose blood he would drink and maybe fall in love with like Aiden had done with Emilia. Then I cursed myself for caring.

He's a vampire and your enemy. Stop thinking about him like that.

"The fog that we came through when we came here… I haven't seen it since I arrived. Does that mean I can see the island if I come back?"

"No. The fog isn't visible from inside the island. It's a magical apparition to any trespassers. The minute you set foot off the island, it will engulf us once again."

His eyes searched mine. "So, if I leave, I won't be able to find the island again?"

I shook my head. "No. Not unless a Pict lifts it for you."

His eyes landed on me and my heart squeezed in my chest. "If I leave tonight, will you let me back in to visit you?"

I tried to assure myself I'd only imagined the weight of his gaze, but the look in his eye held a question far more complex than just his ability to return to the island.

I contemplated my words before I answered. I wanted to say yes, but I knew the reality of allowing him back… of allowing him into my life.

"No," I whispered. "I can't."

"Why?" He turned his head to look at me, but I kept staring at the sky. "Why can't I come back?"

"Because. You don't belong here."

"Catrain," he soothed. "Don't say that. I don't want to starve to death, but I'm not going to leave until I know I can come back to see you. Please."

I knew I shouldn't turn my head and look at him… shouldn't give in to the pull between us.

But I did.

When our eyes locked, I felt the earth beneath my body shift.

"Please, Cat." He reached out and brushed a braided piece of blonde hair from my face. "I know you're feeling this too. I can't explain it, and I'm not a guy who gets mushy with his feelings or goes chasing after some girl, but there is something going on between us. I know you sense it."

I opened my mouth to argue, but the look in his eyes stole away the words. His fingers brushed across my cheek and left my heated skin cooled in their wake.

"We can't," I finally managed to say, though the sentence lacked conviction.

The question swirled between us. "Give me one good reason why."

"Because you're a vampire and I'm a Pict. We're enemies."

"Fuck that," he said with a snort. "This isn't Romeo and Juliet."

I furrowed my brow, unsure of the reference. He noticed my confusion and shook his head.

"I mean, there's no sense in us paying for mistakes of the past. I like you, Cat. A lot. And that's not something I say to women often." He chuckled. "Okay, *ever*. But I do. And even though you threaten to kill me every day, I know you feel the same fucking way. I can hear your heart speed up when you see me. See your eyes light up when they look into mine. You may not *want* to have feelings for me, but you do. So fuck this old vendetta. Just let me come back and see you again so we can see where this goes."

I wanted to say yes. So badly. Every cell in my body begged me to agree. But even if I did, my tribe, and my mother, would never allow it.

And my duties would make any future with him impossible.

Though it pained me to utter the words, I whispered, "No. You cannot return."

Sadness filled his eyes before they lit back up again. "If I can't come back here, then come with me. Let me show you my world."

My eyes widened at the suggestion… and the idea of seeing everything I'd heard of with my own eyes. A world to be explored with Thorne at my side. It was more than I could have dreamed, but before I could give him the answer we both wanted, I remembered my duty… my destiny.

My heart sank as I shook my head. "I can't. My life is here."

"Cat." He leaned closer, and I felt his breath brushing against my lips. "Come with me. I don't want to leave you."

His cool fingers slid beneath my chin, and I didn't resist him lifting it up, guiding my lips toward his.

I couldn't. The pull was too strong to resist.

"Come with me," he whispered against my lips. His warm breath was a stark contrast to the coolness of his hand holding my face.

Desire like I'd never known sent my blood whooshing through my veins. Every nerve in my body fired at once, all screaming for me to kiss him. Every inch of my skin begged for his touch.

As his lips closed in on mine, I gave up the war waging inside of me. For just one moment, I wanted to be free to choose my own path. Free to follow my heart and go where my soul pulled me.

And I knew exactly where that was…

Right into his arms.

I closed my eyes and leaned toward him, but just before

I could touch his lips, the trees lining the beach rustled. Sitting up with a start, I pulled away from him and scanned the surroundings. One glance at my sand map showed the necklace moving toward us.

"My mother is coming," I whispered and scooted back. "You need to go."

"Catrain," he started and moved toward me, but I scooted back even farther.

"Go."

The trees parted, and my mother, Liùsaidh, appeared, her frail body leading a small group of my tribesmen toward us. Uradech, the largest and strongest warrior of our tribe, walked on her right, towering over her. My beautiful raven-haired younger sister, Alpia, walked on her left, clutching my mother's elbow in her hand. I tried to keep my calm while they approached, but with each step that brought my mother closer, my heart pounded harder in my chest.

She stopped, then pointed her staff at Thorne. "You go now!"

"Mother, it's fine. We were just talking."

She turned her intense stare to me, and I knew she could sense the attraction between us. It was palpable even without her magic to heighten her senses, but with her powers, we may as well have been locked in a kiss when she found us.

"Come, Catrain. Now," she demanded, tapping her staff into the sand at her side.

Thorne rose to his feet, and Uradech widened his stance. Even without the paint darkening his eyes, he looked positively lethal while he stared Thorne down. Long, blonde hair knotted in braids draped over his massive tattooed shoulders, and his expansive chest inflated with a low growl as his gaze burned through the vampire.

Thorne lifted his hands and smiled. "Now, now. I know I've overstayed my welcome, but I really appreciate you letting me stay and learn about your incredible culture. It's not often one gets to spend time on a magical island. But you don't need to worry. I'm actually heading out tonight," Thorne said, keeping his friendly tone.

"Go. Now." My mother narrowed her gaze and pointed across the lake.

"Liùsaidh, thank you so much for letting me stay. You've raised an incredible daughter. It was an honor getting to know her."

His compliment only caused my mother's eyes to narrow further. "I will not tell you again," she said. "This may not kill your kind, but I can make you wish you were dead."

Electricity crackled in her palms, and I knew she'd unleash hell on him if he didn't leave. Hosting a vampire, her greatest enemy, for several days had been difficult for her, but seeing him with her daughter, her heir, was more than she could handle.

I turned and whispered to him, "Thorne, you need to go."

"Come with me," he whispered back.

Those azure eyes pleaded with me while he stared into my soul. It was all I could do not to reach out and take his hand, launch into his arms, and run off into the world with him. I glanced over my shoulder at my tribe, and with tears stinging behind my eyes, I swallowed over the lump in my throat and stepped backward.

"Goodbye, Thorne." I continued stepping away from him with small, unsure steps.

"Please, let me come see you again," he said, starting toward me, but Uradech stepped forward and lifted his spear.

"I can't. There is a boat just down the beach. Take it and don't come back. Goodbye, Thorne."

I spun on my heel, walking back to my tribe, my deliberate strides pushing me away from the one thing in my life I'd wanted for myself… and the one thing I could never do.

To see the world with Thorne.

My tribe stared past me to Thorne with eyes filled with centuries of hatred. He called after me one last time, but I didn't look back. I couldn't. One last look into those eyes, and I'd never be able to do what it was expected of me… to stay here and honor my legacy.

When I reached my mother, I took a deep breath and turned around, taking my rightful place at her side. Lifting my chin high, I found the resolve to look at him one last time. Our eyes locked, and I struggled to force down the emotions ripping me apart inside. With a quick nod of his head, he accepted my wishes and bid me goodbye.

Before I could blink, he had gone.

Chapter Two

THORNE

After a lightning-fast sprint across the Scottish countryside, I arrived at our estate. I slowed to a stop in front of the towering stone castle and paused for a moment before going inside.

It had been several hundred years since I'd first stood at these doors and opened them. We'd taken the castle from a brutal laird who'd enslaved people to work the lands. Grizella, my brother Lothaire's wife, had been a slave herself centuries earlier. When she'd heard rumors of a laird abusing young women who lived as tenants on the estate, she investigated, finding a slew of cruelties happening under his care.

Laird Douglas harbored a thirst for suffering… and we happily gave him a taste of what he loved to dole out.

We'd marched right up to the castle door I now stood in front of and knocked, demanding an audience with him. When he'd arrived, Grizella had taken great joy in using our mind influencing to make him sign over his lands, granting independent property ownership and a chunk of his wealth to each slave we forced him to release, and each tenant who'd suffered at his hands. After he finished breaking apart his vast lands and giving every penny he owned to those he'd wronged, he signed over the castle and surrounding estate to us… and became the one slave left to care for it. Running Laird Douglas ragged became one of our favorite pastimes until he'd died from old age a decade later.

This castle became our primary residence for over a century. In the past fifty years, however, we'd visited it less and less, taking up in our other residences around the world instead. But since returning here a few weeks ago, I made a note to visit more and spend time in the Scottish countryside of my youth. I'd learned to hunt and fight on these lands, and each time I set foot on them, it reminded me of the warrior I'd once been… a warrior not unlike the ones who still resided on Catrain's island.

With a glance over my shoulder toward the island I'd never be able to return to… the *woman* I'd never be able to return to, I sighed and pushed open the huge wooden doors.

Warm light flooded the expansive old room, and I stopped and listened for voices. As vampires, we heard the world at the same volume as humans, but we could also focus our hearing, searching through the surrounding sounds and amplifying them to heights that allowed us to hear even a pin drop at a great distance.

I used that skill as I searched the house and listened for the familiar voices of my family. Though they weren't my family by blood, Lothaire, Aiden, Grizella, and Annella were my family by choice… a family I'd had for over six hundred years. I'd even taken their last name of Mackay after we'd turned.

I heard laughter coming from out back, so I walked

through the castle and pushed open the back doors. Lanterns swaying in the trees lit my way through the manicured yard to the pool by the gardens.

"On your mark, get set, go!" Annella yelled.

Emilia and Mark shrieked with laughter, and I saw the blur of movement as they raced around the gardens at vamp speed. They skidded to a stop side by side, toppling into a ball of tangled limbs as they collapsed onto the lawn.

It was strange to see Emilia moving with such speed—even though she wasn't quite as quick as Mark. I'd just gotten used to having him added to our vampire family, and now I would have to get used to seeing Emilia with the powers our immortality granted us. Mark had been my brother Aiden's assistant for years before we turned him recently at his request. Becoming a vampire had been his dream, and he thrived in his new life with us.

Emilia, on the other hand, hadn't wanted vampirism. Then a few days ago, when the choice came to become immortal to save her beloved Aiden's life, she'd taken it. Luckily for both of them, the transformation granted them a different kind of immortality… the original immortality we'd gotten six hundred years ago before the Pict witches cursed us. It didn't involve drinking blood or hiding from the sun but came with strength, speed, hearing, and all the other vampire perks.

"I kicked yo ass, hot mama!" Mark taunted, waggling his perfectly manicured blonde brows.

"Bullshit!" Emilia argued back.

The sight of them laughing and playfully swatting each other caused my lips to tug upward… something that normally came naturally to me. But as quickly as it started to come, it faltered when a vision of Catrain popped into my head.

Aiden crossed his arms and peered down at them. Though more clean-cut than me, he could have passed as my blood brother with our matching blue eyes and dark hair.

He raised an eyebrow. "Emilia would have won if you hadn't *cheated*. You had a head start."

Mark scoffed. "Cheater schmeater. Just because your half-vamp asses are still slow from whatever it was that witch did to you, doesn't mean you need to be all jelly that I'm faster than you. *Both* of you." He pursed his lips and flicked his wrist at them. "Haters."

Emilia tossed her arms around his neck. "I could never hate you. Never." Her chestnut brown hair cascaded around his face as she covered it with kisses until he broke down in laughter and wrapped her up in his arms.

I stood quietly watching them for a few more moments before Annella's impeccable senses picked up my presence.

Her head swiveled in my direction, and her face lit up when she saw me. "Thorne! You're alive! We were just saying we may need to go on a rescue mission."

"Oh, is that what this is?" I joked as I started toward them. "Training for my rescue?"

"Training? I don't need training to save your arse. I could save it solo with my eyes closed." Curling her full red lips into a smug smile, she flipped her long, auburn hair over her shoulder with a flourish.

"Indeed, you could." I walked to her side and placed a soft kiss on her cheek. Annella may look like a harmless, beautiful pixie, but she was as lethal as any of us. More lethal, if I was being honest.

"Welcome back, brother." Aiden pulled me in for a brief hug. "I was starting to worry that you hadn't made it home."

"Yeah," Mark chimed, widening his big brown eyes. "I saw that freaking Xena warrior princess on the beach. I was scared for you."

The mention of her caused a knot to twist up inside my stomach, but I forced a smile onto my face. "Catrain. Yeah, she turned out to be pretty cool."

Annella arched an eyebrow. "Pretty *cool*? She looked straight up ready to shank you when we left. I take it you won her over with your irresistible charm?"

I wished more than anything that I had.

"Well, she didn't kill me, so I suppose I did."

"And?" Aiden asked, expectant eyes waiting for more.

"And nothing." I shrugged. "We just became sorta friends. She showed me some of her magic, and I told her about the world out here."

"And that's all?" Annella goaded. "You lose your touch, stud?"

Chuckling, I shook my head. "Nah. She was cool. Really cool. Just the whole 'eternal enemies' kinda got in the way of anything more."

"Romeo and Juliet were enemies. They found a way." Mark furrowed his brow and lifted a finger. "Although, spoiler alert, they did die in the end."

His reference transported me right back to the beach when I'd said almost the same thing to Catrain. For a second, I could almost smell the scent of heather she'd used in her hair.

"I'm glad you're back," Emilia said, pulling me from my memory when she pulled me in for a hug. "So, tell us… how was it?"

"First, I need food. I've been living on hog's blood."

They all pulled a face, and then Mark whooshed off and returned a second later with a glass full of blood.

"A very bloody Bloody Mary," he said with a smile.

"Thank you." I tossed the blood down my throat. After three days of hunting and drinking from wild hogs, even though this was blood from a bag, it tasted as good as blood hot from the vein. "Wow. I needed that."

Almost instantly, all my strength returned. I hoped that maybe when I was back to full strength, the sadness I felt over Catrain would somehow disappear. Like perhaps it was just a symptom of the blood loss.

But I would have no such luck.

"Okay, now tell us all about the Picts. I'm fascinated." Emilia took my hand and led me over to the long table beside the pool. Small flames flickered from the rocks in the center, and two glasses of blood and two margaritas sat in front of the chairs. Aiden and Emilia took their seats in front of the margaritas, and Annella and Mark sat in front of the glasses of blood.

Emilia took a sip of her margarita and set down the glass. "It's just incredible the Picts still exist, so come on… tell."

Mark eyed up her drink, and Aiden noticed the longing glance. "Regretting living off blood?" he teased. "Wishing you could have a nice, cold margarita?"

Mark puckered his face and shook his head, but his gaze drifted back to the green frozen drink. "No. Not at all. I'll take the eternal beauty over a margarita, thank you very much."

Aiden teased him by taking a long, slow swig from his drink, finishing with a long "ahh" sound. Mark stuck out his tongue.

"What does that taste like? Compare it to something I'd recognize," I said. Since no humans currently knew what food tasted like six hundred years ago, I'd never been able to compare the flavors I knew to the flavors now. Since Aiden's transition back to our original powers and ability to consume food and drink , he could help me understand more about these strange drinks and foods humans insisted on eating.

"There was nothing back then to compare this to. Nothing." Aiden shook his head. "I'll just say, when we were all human, food tasted like shit compared to everything I get to eat and drink now. It's ridiculous what people have come up with."

"Really?" I shook my head. "That different?"

"I can see why Emilia didn't want to give it up. Food is incredible. And this margarita?" He lifted it in a cheers. "Worth giving up immortality for."

"Damn." I laughed. "Aren't you lucky you get both… immortality *and* all the food. How is it going? You have your full powers back?"

"Almost," Aiden answered. "It seems every day I get faster, stronger, and my senses pick up, but it's been kind of a slow start."

"Just like when we first turned, huh?"

I remembered the unfamiliar sensation of being immortal… the intensity of discovering our new powers and abilities. We'd raced each other across the countryside, then challenged each other to ax battles and wrestling matches… and even made a sport out of trying to shoot one another with a bow and arrow, only to be able to outrun the arrow and pluck it from the air and toss it back.

But as amazing as it felt when we first turned, it took a month before our abilities peaked. Every day we got faster… stronger… better.

"That's what Aiden has been telling me," Emilia answered. "He says it's exactly like when you first turned. I thought I was fast a couple days ago. But today I can move at almost twice that speed. It's incredible!"

"So, you like it?" I asked, curious about her transition.

"I *love* it." She beamed. "I've never felt more alive."

"And even at half-strength, I've never felt better," Aiden chimed in. "I have everything I've ever wanted. Especially my girl."

They leaned forward and kissed, and I tried to swallow my groan. Not that I wasn't happy for them, it just made me remember the girl I wanted to be kissing and referring to as *my girl*.

The girl I'd never see again.

"Sounds pretty amazing. I'm really happy for you both," I said. "Too bad the Picts aren't handing out immortality without all the downsides to everyone."

"Did you ask them?" Annella took a sip of her glass of blood then pushed it to me.

"I did." I laughed at the memory of Catrain's heated response. "She said something about me deserving the darkness I needed to live in." I shook my head, hoping to shake her out of my mind, then took a sip of the blood.

"Damn. That girl hated you!" Mark laughed.

"She hates all of us. We kind of screwed over her people."

"Well, they kind of killed a bunch of our clan," Lothaire said, and I turned back to see him and his beautiful raven-haired wife, Grizella, approaching.

"Lothaire." I smiled as I rose.

We shook hands, and he placed one of his huge mitts on my shoulder. His usually stern face softened slightly as he looked down past his beard at me. "Welcome back, Thorne."

"Good to be back."

A lie. I wanted nothing more than to be lying on a beach staring at the stars with Catrain.

Grizella kissed my cheek then slid into a chair beside Annella. Lothaire sat beside Aiden, and I sank back down.

"Look at this. All together again," Annella said. "It's been a long time."

"It has. And we have two new family members." Grizella gave a nod to Mark and Emilia.

"Aw, we're family, boo!" Mark reached over and squeezed Emilia's hand.

Tears welled up in Emilia's soft blue eyes. "I couldn't be happier to have you all as my family. Thank you so much for welcoming me."

"It's about time Grizella and I got another girl on the team. We'll be like sisters." Annella blew Emilia a kiss.

"Sisters it is." Emilia returned it then settled her head back onto Aiden's shoulder.

With the flames flickering between us, it reminded me of our childhood growing up together in Scotland sitting around our nightly bonfire. My mother passed away when I was born, leaving me with just a father to look after me… a father who resented me for my mother's death. He'd loved her with his whole heart and soul, and her loss had left him a broken man. Even though I understood his bitterness toward me came from heartache, it didn't ease the suffering of a boy desperate for his father's love… a boy who never got it.

One family in the clan noticed the way my father ignored me and cast me aside. The lonely boy left to wander alone.

The Mackay family.

They took me in, raising me and treating me as one of their own. Their father became the man who taught me right from wrong, and how to shoot a bow and swing a sword. Their mother was the gentle hand that dried my tears and always made sure I had a full belly. Aiden, Lothaire, Annella, and Caleb were the siblings I'd never had. We wrestled and played as children, and as adults, we fought side by side in battle.

My family.

We turned immortal together when the Picts bestowed the gift on us. Well, almost all of us turned.

We lost their parents and Caleb… a loss so devastating it could have destroyed us. But Aiden, Lothaire, Annella, and I bound ourselves together tighter… an unbreakable bond that would carry us through the centuries.

Lothaire eventually became our Chieftain and the ruler of all vampires. After Aiden retired a decade ago, I took his spot as Lothaire's right-hand man. It was now my job to handle rogue vampires and enforce his law. When clans rose up to unseat him, it was me that lead the charge to defend him.

But it wasn't my Chieftain I waged war to defend… it was my brother. My family. And I would give my life for any one of them.

"So, tell us, Thorne," Lothaire said. "How was it with the Picts?"

"I was just telling them about the experience. It was incredible. They are a fascinating people. It was remarkable to see it firsthand."

"And did they treat you well?" he asked, arching a brow.

With a shrug, I chuckled. "I spent most of my time in the cave or hanging out with Catrain. She taught me a lot and showed me some really cool magic. Her mother knew I was on the island, but I didn't dare push my luck, so I steered clear of the village and out of her eyesight. She didn't torture or try to kill me, so there's that. But they still harbor a grudge. A big one." I blew out a lengthy breath of air. "They put up with my presence begrudgingly for a few days, but finally had enough of me tonight and sent me packing. But I really learned some fascinating things while I was there."

"Yeah, like if Catrain's tattoos continue under that leather loincloth." Mark shimmied in his seat while waggling his eyebrows.

Everyone burst out laughing, and I felt the temperature of my cheeks rising.

"Holy shit!" Aiden laughed and pointed. "You're blushing!"

"I'm not blushing," I argued back while trying to suppress my smile. "I'm a man. We don't fucking blush."

"Then hand in your man card, baby, because you're as red as a freaking rose." Annella opened her palm.

Even the always stoic Lothaire and Grizella cracked a smile at my expense.

"So, you get a little tribal bow-chicka-bow-wow?" Annella waggled her eyebrows.

Shaking my head, I chuckled. "I did *not* get a little bow-chicka-bow-wow. It wasn't like that."

"Oh, I saw you looking at her." Emilia speared me with a knowing stare. "You had a *big* thing for Catrain."

I opened my mouth to argue, but she kept going.

"And who can blame you? She's stunning. Powerful. Smart. I'd think it was odd if you *didn't* have a thing for her."

"And scary," Mark added. "Don't forget scary."

Laughing, I raised my hands in submission. "Fine. If you all must know, yes… I have a thing for Catrain. No, we didn't hook up. And no, we aren't going to because her family basically wants me beheaded, and she needs to take over for her mother as the leader of their tribe this year. Even though nothing can happen between us, she's amazing." I stopped to look at Mark. "And yes, a little scary."

Everyone laughed again, but Emilia pursed her lips together and gave me a soft smile. "I'm sorry it didn't work out. I was really hoping it would."

I sucked the air through my teeth and shrugged. "Love is just not in the cards for me, I guess."

"Mark and I will take you out this week," Annella said. "Our single arses can commiserate together."

"You know what? I'll take you up on that. I could use a little time in the city after living on an island with no technology for the past few days."

"Party time!" Mark clapped.

"What? I'm not invited?" Emilia asked with a pout.

He crossed his arms and shook his head. "Nope, sorry, boo. Singles only this time. You couples can stay here in your happy couple bubbles while us singles go shake our asses at the club and break some hearts."

"Works for me." Aiden lifted her hand to his lips. Emilia lit up like a light, and I wondered if Catrain would light up the same if I kissed her hand.

Good God, man! Get your shit together!

I started to sound like a lovesick teenager the way I continued pining for the woman I couldn't have.

And the only woman I'd ever really wanted.

After centuries of casual flings and light-hearted affairs, Catrain was the first woman to really intrigue me in a way deeper than meaningless sex. She challenged me and pushed me. Her wit and intellect were as intoxicating as her obvious beauty. The connection I felt with her was something I'd never experienced before. A deeper connection than anything I'd ever known… an unexplainable pull that felt impossible to resist.

Though somehow, she'd managed to resist it when she'd sent me packing.

"How was everything while I was gone?" I asked, hoping to change the topic to one that didn't make my heart hurt. "Did you guys just hang around here and practice your new abilities?" I asked, directing the question at Emilia.

"Pretty much. Aiden and I hung out by the pool every day, then every night, these guys would help me hone my new skills. I'm getting good at focusing my hearing now. And soon, they will find me some humans so I can practice my influencing."

"You need to focus harder on your racing skills so I can get some competition around here. You know, cuz I'm *fast*," Mark teased. "Greased lightning."

"Give it a couple weeks and we'll be kicking your ass. And in the meantime, we have sunshine and margaritas to console us." Aiden waggled his eyebrows, lifted his glass and clinked it to Emilia's.

"Dick," Mark said, then burst into laughter as they each took a long, exaggerated swig.

"Well, I'm so happy to see everyone doing so well." I pressed my hands to my thighs and stood. "But I haven't had plumbing for days, and I could really go for a long, hot shower. You guys enjoy the evening, and I'll catch up with you later."

"We'll see you soon," Lothaire said as I started away. "Tomorrow, we need to talk about Clan Lennox. There is rumbling that Leeya and her brother Leith are considering making a move for power. We need to look into it and find out if there's any merit and squash their rebellion if there is."

"Leeya? Again?" Mark huffed. "I hate that crazy chick. Coocoo for Cocoa Puffs. Seriously."

"Me, too," Aiden grumbled. "I should have killed her when I had a chance."

Emilia shook her head and placed her hand on his. "You did the right thing letting her live. I don't want anyone dying on my account."

"Let's hope it was," Aiden said. "I warned her what would happen if she caused any trouble."

"Clan Lennox is always causing trouble." Annella glared. "I think it's time you let me loose on them to put an end to their rebellions once and for all. It needs to stop."

"We'll discuss it tomorrow," Lothaire said. "But I agree. They are pushing for a movement to allow the kidnapping and harvesting of humans. The idea is spreading, and they know I'm the thing that stands in their way."

"That's disgusting!" Emilia gasped. "Using humans like cattle?"

Grizella nodded. "Yes. There are vampires out there like Clan Lennox, who believe humans are nothing more than food. They don't care if they get discovered, because vampires united against humans could wipe out entire countries in weeks. But we believe in a quiet coexistence and never keeping humans as slaves. It's worked for centuries, so there's no need to change things now."

I nodded my agreement. "Then we'll make sure they remember who makes the rules. I'll meet with you tomorrow, and we'll make a plan to handle them."

Everyone said their goodbyes, and I started toward the house. Before I could reach the door, Aiden flashed in front of me and placed a hand on my shoulder.

"You sure you're okay, man? You don't seem like yourself."

I shrugged and gave a half-smile. "Yeah. I'll be fine."

"Is it Catrain?"

His astute observation only reminded me how much our bond meant to me. There was no hiding things from the man who'd been at my side since we were knee-high.

"I'm not gonna lie. I really had a thing for her, but it's just not going to work out."

He squeezed my shoulder. "Are you sure? It's not like you to give up on anything. The Thorne I know is relentless when he wants something that much."

Shaking my head, I let my shoulders slump. "Not this time. She's incredible, but she's fiercely loyal to her tribe, and there is no chance in hell they will ever accept me. It's just my luck the *one* girl in six hundred years to turn me into a lovesick puppy is the one girl I can never have."

"Hang in there, buddy. You never know. It could still work out."

I patted him on the back. "Doubtful since I'm never allowed on the island to see her again, but I appreciate the sentiment."

We clapped each other on the back, and then I walked around him and headed into the castle. Maybe, just maybe, a hot shower could wash away the feelings for Catrain that seemed to amplify by the second.

Chapter Three

THORNE

I stretched and pushed out of my bed, grateful for another day's sleep in it. It had been two weeks since I'd been back from the Pict island, but after those three days sleeping on a cave floor, I didn't think I'd ever stop appreciating this cushy bed.

Though I didn't miss the cold, hard floor of the cave, I did miss Catrain… even more than I ever imagined I could. Every day I woke up hoping the ache I felt for her would soften, but every day it only seemed to deepen. Parting with her left me with an agony I'd never experienced… an agony so deep I found myself wishing we'd never met.

But then I'd see her face in my mind, and the thought of never knowing she existed, or never having her in my life, pained me more than the thought of never seeing her again. It was a dizzying mix of foreign emotions determined to drive me mad.

After focusing my hearing to have a quick listen through the household, I heard Aiden and Emilia outside after likely spending a day in the sun.

Aiden in the sunshine. It still seemed surreal to imagine him out there soaking up the rays.

I still couldn't comprehend what it would be like to enjoy the sunshine again. It had been so long since I'd seen it that I could barely remember what the world looked like bathed in light. Aiden had explained to me how incredible it was to step out into it for the first time in centuries, and I had to admit his new abilities left me slightly jealous. Of course, I was happy for him, but as my oldest friend and confidante, I hated that I couldn't be part of his new journey.

Since I wasn't lucky enough to walk in the sun without bursting into flames, I waited a few moments to ensure the last of the light evaporated before getting dressed and heading downstairs to the kitchen. When I arrived to get some blood from the fridge, Grizella had beat me there.

"Evening, Thorne," she said, offering me the freshly poured cup.

I kissed her on the cheek. "Thank you. Sleep well?"

She smiled. "As long as I'm with Lothaire, I always sleep well."

"You two haven't spent a night apart in a few hundred years."

"Longer." She smirked. "So, yes, I slept well like I always do."

"As did I," Lothaire said as he entered the kitchen. He stopped to press a kiss to Grizella's forehead before grabbing a blood bag for himself. After he split it between two glasses, we walked to the sitting room and sat down by the fire.

"Any movement on Clan Lennox?" Lothaire asked me as I sipped my blood.

I shook my head. "Nothing yet. I've got people investigating their movements and reporting back. So far, no word about an actual move on us."

"Good," Lothaire said. "Hopefully, they've come to their senses."

"Let's hope so," I agreed.

Since taking over for Aiden as Lothaire's enforcer, I'd been surprised by how quiet the other clans had been. Years of squashing any revolts with enough brutality to cripple them for years had served as a warning to any that followed. It seemed I'd done my job well the last time someone dared to challenge Clan Mackay because no vampire had risen against us since. It'd been so long, in fact, I worried I may need to practice my fighting techniques to ensure my skills didn't suffer from my time off.

"Evening, everyone," Emilia said as she entered hand-in-hand with Aiden. Their skin looked kissed by the sun, and I felt the pang of jealousy once again that they had the freedom to enjoy it.

We greeted them as they settled onto the loveseat.

"How was your *day?*" I asked, emphasizing the fact they got to have one while the rest of us slept.

"Great," Aiden answered. "We went for a horse ride through the countryside, and I showed Emilia some of the places we used to explore as kids."

"Did you show her the view from the cliffs?" I asked, remembering fondly how we used to love to sit on them as kids… and how we'd all taken turns jumping off them when we'd first become immortal.

"He did." Emilia grinned widely. "So beautiful. I grew up in Milwaukee. The little park a few blocks away was about as close as I got to nature every week. I can't imagine getting to grow up running around the countryside like you did. You were all so lucky to have such a beautiful country to explore."

"We were," Lothaire agreed. "I'm glad you get to see our home."

"Me too."

"It's your home now too." Grizella smiled with more warmth than usual. It wasn't that she was cold or uncaring, but she kept her emotions close to her chest and only offered them freely to Lothaire.

Emilia's smile stretched across her face, and she settled back against Aiden's chest.

"Where's Mark?" Aiden asked as he closed his arms around her.

"I'm not sure." I shrugged. "He and Annella went to the city clubbing last night. Something about Ryan Gosling being in town?"

"Oh, God," Emilia said with a laugh. "Are they still trying to seduce him? Poor guy."

"They have a bet to see who he falls for first." Aiden chuckled. "Though I'm quite certain he loves his wife and they are both going to be losers."

The front door opened and slammed, then Mark appeared in the living room. "Seriously. I just ran from freaking Glasgow in like, fifteen minutes. I dare any of you to beat me in a race."

"Give us a couple weeks to get our speed back up and you're on." Aiden smirked.

"Any luck with Gosling?" Emilia arched a brow. "Or have you finally accepted that you're just not his type?"

"Ugh. I give up. Gosling's straight as a board. There's no other explanation because if he was even a tiny bit gay, he'd have been all over this last night." He waved a hand over his body before collapsing in a chair. "I don't feel too bad though, because Annella struck out too. It's over. We need to move on. Maybe we should try for Chris Hemsworth. Rarr." He swiped his hand through the air like a claw.

We all laughed at Mark, ever our entertainment, and I shook my head.

"Sorry, Mark. Gosling's a straight married man, and I'm pretty sure Hemsworth is too. Maybe set your sights on someone else next time. Someone who at least plays for your team or isn't madly in love with their spouse."

"Valid. But it was worth a try. Though I guess it doesn't matter because I met the *cutest* boy last night. *And* he's a vamp! What are the freaking chances? We danced all night, and he was the absolute best kisser. The *best.* And he's a ginger. A hot Scot if you will." He waggled his eyebrows.

"Atta boy!" Emilia cheered. "I want all the details."

"He looks like Jamie from *Outlander.* Swear to God! Ugh." He bit his closed fist. "So fucking hot. Annella's gonna be so jelly because she was eying him up too, but lucky for me, he didn't swing her way. Where is she? I've got to tell her what a good kisser she missed out on." He looked around.

"I don't know," Aiden said. "She's not back yet."

Mark's brows pinched together. "She's not?"

Lothaire picked up on the worry in his tone and sat forward. "No, she's not. Why does that worry you?"

Mark's brow furrowed deeper. "I'm pretty sure she said she was heading home when we split up at the club."

"Pretty sure?" I asked, my own worry starting.

Mark shook his head. "No. Sure. She definitely said she was heading back before sunrise. I crashed at the apartment in the city with Gregor."

Worry lines creased in Aiden's brow. "Well, she didn't come back."

"Let's not panic," I said. "We all know Annella. Maybe she met some guy on her way out of the club. It wouldn't surprise me one bit if she pops through that door any minute and tells us all about the new hottie she spent the night with."

There was a universal agreement throughout the room, but worry still weighed heavily on us. It *was* like Annella to hop off with someone she just met, but it *wasn't* like her not to let us know she wasn't coming home.

"Try her phone," Lothaire said to Mark.

Mark took out his phone and pressed the screen then held it to his ear. After a few seconds, he shook his head. "Straight to voicemail."

Emilia sat up out of Aiden's arms. "Maybe her battery died?"

"Maybe. Or maybe she lost her phone?" Mark said.

Lothaire looked the least convinced, and I hated to admit the knot in my stomach telling me something was wrong had me as worried as he looked. Annella was tough, tougher than all of us despite her tiny innocent appearance, but that didn't mean she was invulnerable.

The large knocker slammed against our front door, and we all spun to look. Lothaire flashed to the door and opened it, and we all walked up behind him.

A timid-looking vampire stood in the doorway, shaky hands holding an envelope. "I'm sorry. Please don't hurt me. I'm not any part of this, but they made me. Said they'd kill me if I didn't deliver this to you today."

"Who?" Lothaire growled as he ripped the envelope from the young vampire's hands.

He didn't answer, instead, flitting away before Lothaire had the chance to read the words.

"What does it say?" Grizella asked, leaning over his shoulder.

Darkness clouded Lothaire's eyes as he read the letter, and I could feel anger like I hadn't felt in centuries pulsing off him in waves.

"Lothaire. What's wrong?" I asked, stepping forward.

"They have her," he ground out.

"Who has her?" Aiden asked, his eyes flickering with concern.

Lothaire lifted his head and narrowed his amber eyes. "Clan Lennox. They have Annella."

"What?" Mark gasped. "What do you mean?"

"They've taken her hostage. They said they will kill her at week's end if we don't give them what they want."

"What do they want?" Emilia asked, her voice quaking with fear.

There was a long pause as Lothaire tightened his fist and crumpled the note into a tight ball.

"My head."

"What?" we all echoed at once.

Grizella stepped forward in front of Lothaire. Her confident eyes shone true fear for the first time since I'd met her. "What do you mean your head?"

"I mean, Leith Lennox wants to take power, and they've required my death by Friday night, or they will kill Annella in my place."

"Then we have to find her!" I shouted, rage making my blood boil inside my veins. "And kill every last one of those motherfuckers."

Aiden stepped to my side. "I'm with you."

"And me." Mark joined us.

"We don't even know where she is," Lothaire said. "And I'm not willing to risk her life for mine."

"Lothaire!" Grizella took his hands in hers. "You are *not* going to die. We *will* find another way."

He took her face in his hands and kissed her gently. "We will try. But if it comes down to her or me, I will sacrifice myself to save her. She's my little sister."

"You can't die," Grizella begged with a wavering voice. "I love you. Please. You can't leave me, Lothaire. You can't."

"We aren't losing either one of you!" Aiden roared. "We will find Annella, and I will rip out Leith's throat with my fucking teeth after we do."

"And Leeya's," Emilia said, straightening up tall. "I never should have stopped you from killing her. This is all my fault."

"It's not your fault." Aiden slid an arm around her shoulder. "Clan Lennox has been looking for a chance to take us down for decades. If I'd have killed Leeya, he just would have used that as an excuse. This was coming no matter what. But it ends now… with their blood on our fangs."

"I just can't believe they got the jump on Annella. She's stronger than every one of them," I said, still trying to wrap my mind around the fact that Annella had been captured.

"They must have ambushed her in a large group. It's the only way," Lothaire agreed. "She's tough, and because of that, I know she's okay… for now. But we're going to keep her that way. No matter the cost."

The weight of his words settled over us all.

"The note says they want my head on a pike at the summit of Ben Nevis as proof of my death. Let's see to it the only heads on pikes are theirs when this is all said and done."

"Hear, hear." I tightened my fists. "Every last Lennox."

"So, how do we find her?" Mark asked.

"We start by mobilizing every single one of our contacts. Someone must have heard something or seen something," Aiden said.

Lothaire gave a sharp nod. "Everyone start making calls and reach out to every last clan. Make it clear that anyone found withholding information will be considered a traitor and meet the same fate as Clan Lennox."

As I started going through my mind trying to think of who would be most likely to have the information on Annella's whereabouts, a beautiful face popped into my mind… the face that hadn't vacated it since I last saw it almost two weeks ago.

Catrain.

"Wait." I raised my hand. "I have an idea."

They all waited while I lifted my head and passed a glance at all of them. "Catrain. She can perform locator spells. If they'll let me back on the island, she can perform a spell and tell us exactly where they're holding Annella."

"She can do that?" Emilia asked.

"Yes. I saw her do it. All I need is one of Annella's personal effects."

"I thought you said they wouldn't let you back on the island," Aiden said.

"They did, but maybe I can convince them to part the fog one more time. It's worth a try."

"Do it," Lothaire commanded. "Do whatever it takes."

I gave him a nod of solidarity before flashing up to Annella's room and grabbing her favorite earrings. Tightening my fist around them, I took a moment to process the danger she was in… and the danger I may be in if I returned to the island again.

But I didn't care. If it meant the chance to save Annella, it was worth the risk.

And it was worth the risk to see Catrain one more time.

Chapter Four

CATRAIN

"I have heard your argument and will consider it," my mother said to Athdar.

"Thank you, Liùsaidh." He bowed his head and backed out of the hut.

When the door closed, my mother and I sat in the empty room on our wooden thrones. My mother's towered over mine, which was at her right hand… my place until I took over for her at the beginning of the new year. Soon it would be me sitting on the tall throne, and someday my child would be at my right hand.

The transfer of our power was a tradition that went back over a thousand years, and they had groomed me since birth to take my place as the leader of our tribe. An honor I tried to remind myself every day to be grateful for, and not the burden I always felt it was.

My mother turned and looked down at me. "When it is your turn to sit here, you will be the one making decisions when your people come to you. Be fair, but not weak. Sometimes what they want is not what they need. It is important to know the difference."

"Yes, Mother," I answered.

"It's a big responsibility." Lifting her weathered hand, she pointed a finger in my direction. "They will be depending on you."

"I know, Mother." I lowered my eyes and bowed my head. "I will do my best to lead them."

"I know you will, child. The Goddess will guide you." She reached down and lifted my chin with her hand. Wise old eyes stared back at me, and her thin lips drew up into a slight smile. "I'm proud of the woman you've become. You will lead them well."

"Thank you, Mother." I smiled back.

I hoped she was right. I hoped that I had the skills to protect and guide our tribe. It wasn't the life I'd have chosen for myself, but I respected our traditions and could only hope I was up to the task. Not that I had a choice. In less than six months, it would be done.

"That was the last tribesman to be heard today," my sister said as she stood from her chair in the corner.

Even though as the oldest, I would inherit the throne, Alpia sat in for all our meetings and my trainings. Years from now, after my mother passed on, Alpia would become my adviser. She would replace my mother as the person I turned to when I needed to work through decisions, but in the end, once I ascended, the decisions would always be mine.

"Go work on your spells, and I'll see you for dinner." My mother nodded toward the door.

"I'll see you soon, Mother." I rose from my throne, kissed her hand, and then walked out of the hut, giving Alpia a brief nod as I passed. The cool evening air chilled my exposed skin. I wrapped my arms around my shoulders and walked to my hut to grab a fur blanket before heading down to watch the sunset from the beach.

With the fur wrapped tight around me, I passed through our village toward the path to the beach I walked every day. Members of our tribe bowed their heads as I walked by, and I greeted each one with a smile. Even as a child, it had been tradition to honor the heir to the throne with great respect, but it had also made me isolated from the very tribe I was supposed to lead.

As a child, instead of being invited to join in on the games the children had played, they stopped and bowed their heads when they saw me. As an adult, conversation stopped when I entered the dining hall, and no one ever invited me to sit with them. Their respect was my loneliness, and it wasn't until Thorne arrived that I'd found someone that treated me like a person and not a queen.

He laughed with me. Teased me. Listened to me. Excited me.

For the first time in my life, someone saw *me*.

We'd only spent three days together, but it was the best three days of my life. And when he left, it only illuminated the loneliness I'd felt all along.

I felt more alone than ever now.

But I had no choice except to embrace my fate and the duties that lay ahead of me.

Cool sand squished between my toes while I walked down the beach. I made it to my favorite spot, then settled into the sand beside the water. I was just in time to see the orange orb before the last sliver slid beneath the horizon. When it disappeared, I closed my eyes and waited for the gust of wind I knew deep down wouldn't come. Waited to hear Thorne's voice and laughter when he joined me on the beach. But it had been over two weeks since the day we'd said goodbye, and it was time for me to accept I'd never see him again.

I heard footsteps behind me, and for a split second, my heart jumped in my chest, thinking somehow, someway, he'd found his way back to me. But when I turned around, it was my sister making her way toward me.

"Need some company?" she asked.

I shrugged and turned my attention back to the colorful horizon. "Sure."

Alpia sat down beside me and dug her toes into the sand. "It's chilly tonight."

I looked over and met her blue eyes that looked like mine. Aside from our hair color difference, her dark to my light, we couldn't have passed for twins, but we certainly looked like sisters. "Here, share my fur."

"Thanks." She scooted closer to me and pulled a corner of the fur over her shoulders. "You never miss a sunset, do you?"

I twirled one of the braids that dangled around my face. "Very rarely."

"Why is that?"

"I don't know. I just like them I guess." I shrugged. "It's peaceful and beautiful. I like looking out at the horizon… wondering what it's like out there."

"What's the point? We'll never go there. Our life is here."

Even though I was out in the open air, her words make me feel like the world around me closed in. "I know better than anyone that my life is here. I've heard nothing but that since the day I understood words. I don't need the reminder."

"I didn't mean it like that," she said, her voice softening.

"I just mean, there's no sense in staring out at the horizon every day torturing yourself. I know you want to see it, and I know taking over for Mother isn't the life you want, but it's your duty… and one you should be so grateful for. It's an honor to lead our people."

"Could everyone stop telling me that?" I grumbled. "I *know* it's an honor. I've heard nothing else my whole life. And I'll do what's necessary to maintain our traditions, but it doesn't mean I need to like it. It doesn't mean I can't wonder what else is out there."

"I'm sorry I offended you," she said meekly. Just hearing her concede so quickly made me roll my eyes—another curse of my position.

Even though she was more than capable of going toe to toe with me, and likely winning, like everyone in the tribe, she wouldn't dare argue with me. Even when they were in the right, and I was in the wrong, tradition dictated the leader and the heir to the throne should never be questioned. They all agreed with everything I said and jumped to appease my every desire.

Everyone but Thorne at least.

I missed his brazen attitude and the way he called me out. Admittedly, the first time he had, I'd been shocked. No one had dared to speak to me like that before. But after the shock wore off, it had invigorated me to have someone to banter with… someone to speak to me openly and honestly. It was refreshing, and remembering our conversations made me miss him even more.

"Don't apologize," I said on a sigh. "You're right. I should be more grateful."

"I just don't want to see you unhappy forever." She stroked a hand down my hair, and I pursed my lips and smiled. "I love you, Catrain. I know you're going to make an excellent leader. I just hope that someday you'll stop staring out at the horizon, wishing for a life that will never be yours and embracing the wonderful one you have right here."

Her words hit home harder than I expected.

She was right. Instead of embracing my destiny, I spent all my time wishing for a world I would never see, and now a man who could never be mine.

"Thank you, Alpia. I needed to hear that."

"Good. I just want you happy, sister."

"And I want you happy, too. And speaking of your happiness, when are we going to find you a man to marry? Got your eye on anyone?"

Her sun-kissed skin deepened to a crimson red as she shook her head. "No. Of course not."

"No one?" I bumped her with my shoulder. "Come on, there must be someone."

She shook her head harder. "No. No one."

"What about Culloden? He's handsome." I waggled my brows, but she just laughed and crinkled her nose.

"No. Definitely not Culloden. He's got the brains of a trout."

"Gawen?"

"No! Definitely not!" She pulled a face and shook her head. "I'd rather marry a vampire than him!"

My face dropped at the reference, and her laughter stopped when she saw it.

"What? Are you okay?"

"Uh, yes. I'm, uh, fine."

But I wasn't. After a life of thinking vampires were the lowest of the low, the vilest creatures on this planet, I'd met one.

And he was anything but.

Alpia chewed on her lip for a moment and then whispered, "What was he like? That vampire who was here. Was he awful? You two spent a lot of time together."

I exhaled a sigh and considered my words. Tell her the truth about how amazing he was and risk her discovering my unquenchable feelings for him, or lie and confirm the stories we'd heard about vampires all our lives?

"He wasn't as terrible as I expected," I said, keeping it vague.

"What was he like? Tell me more. I still can't believe we had a *vampire* on or island."

Dragging my fingertips through the sand, I drew a spiral. "Well, he was kinda funny."

"Funny? A *vampire?*"

I nodded. "Yeah. A funny vampire. And he was really curious about our tribe and our traditions."

"Probably so he could learn more about us to come back with his clan and kill us all."

Chuckling, I rolled my eyes. "That's not what he was doing. He was legitimately curious."

"So you think." She raised her eyebrows and pursed her lips into a tight line.

"Thorne wouldn't hurt us. I'm certain of that."

"Well, I, for one, am glad he's gone. I didn't sleep a wink knowing that he was prowling around the island."

I wanted to defend him more, explain to her what an incredible man lay inside the body of a vampire, but it didn't matter. We'd never see him again and talking about him only ripped open the crack in my heart I already struggled to heal. Everywhere I looked, I saw his face. The skin on my cheek still tingled from his touch. I heard his laughter and voice in my mind each time the world around me quieted.

"Catrain," I heard a deep voice echoing around us.

I furrowed my brow and looked behind us, but no one was there. I waited for a moment, then decided it must have just been the wind.

"Catrain."

There. I heard it again.

My heart stalled out for a beat. It sounded just like…

Thorne.

"Did you hear that?" I asked Alpia.

"Hear what?" she said, stopping to listen.

For the love of the Goddess. I'd officially lost my mind. Now I wasn't just remembering Thorne's voice… I actually heard it.

"Nothing," I answered, struggling to slow my heart down after thinking for a moment that Thorne had returned. "It was just the win—"

"Catrain!" he called, and this time it wasn't a soft echo. It was a shout.

"I heard that!" Alpia said as she looked around. "Who is that?"

My mouth went dry while I searched for the answer to her question. Finally, I coaxed the word out of my mouth. "Thorne."

Her eyes widened as she looked at me. "The *vampire*? Where?"

He called again, and I knew it came from the lake. Thorne wanted entrance to the island… entrance only my mother or I could give him.

"Catrain!" he shouted, and I heard the desperation in his tone.

I jumped to my feet, but Alpia grabbed my wrist and stopped me from sprinting off.

"What are you doing?" she asked as she tried to tug me back down. "You're not going to let him in, are you?"

"I have to. He needs something. I can feel it."

"Catrain! You can't! He could be here to kill us all! Please don't do it!" she begged, but I shook my wrist free from her grasp.

"He won't hurt us. You have to trust me."

"Catrain! Please!" Thorne shouted again.

"Don't do it!" Alpia reached for me again, but I turned on my heel and sprinted across the sand. It flew up behind me as I bolted down the beach, my powerful strides driving me closer and closer to the voice I never thought I'd hear again.

When I reached the beach where we'd first met, my breath hitched in my chest when I saw him. The protective fog visible from the outside of our island concealed me from him, but I could see him floating in his boat; the moonlight illuminated his beautiful eyes searching the emptiness while he called my name.

"Please, Catrain! I need you!"

I didn't care that my mother would be furious with me when she found out.

I didn't care that it was forbidden to let him in.

All I cared about was helping him… seeing him again. At that moment, nothing else in the world mattered to me but Thorne. I lifted my hands while I closed my eyes. Concentrating hard, I chanted the words my mother had taught me, and I used my powers to lift the fog keeping him at bay.

I opened my eyes and watched his face as he looked around him, and I knew my chant had worked. Even though I couldn't see it, I knew the fog was disappearing. A moment later, his searching eyes slid to a stop when he saw me.

"Thorne," I whispered. "You came back."

Chapter Five

THORNE

When the fog parted, and I saw Catrain standing on the beach, I struggled to take my next breath. Not just from the shock that she'd actually answered my call, but because even my most vivid memories hadn't retained just how beautiful she was.

She looked exactly like she had the first time I'd seen her on this beach. She looked powerful, confident, and wild. Her leather clothes left most of her tattooed skin exposed, giving me unchecked views of her muscular legs and tanned, toned abs. The breeze lifted her long blonde hair and the braided knots keeping it out of her face.

But her eyes drew my attention the most. They were a blue so light they almost appeared translucent, and the contrast of the black paint surrounding them made them look even lighter.

She was the most stunning woman I'd ever seen in my six hundred years on this earth.

The last of the fog drifted away as I tried to regain my

senses. After what felt like an eternity floating in my boat staring at her, I finally grabbed my paddle and pushed my boat across the water and onto the sand beach. Catrain stood unmoving while I climbed out.

As I approached, my heart pounded so hard in my chest I was certain she could hear it. "You said you wouldn't let me back in." I smiled. "Liar."

"Thorne. You shouldn't be here," she said with her thick accent.

"I know." I reached out for her hands, but she stepped back and glanced over her shoulder. "I'm sorry, but I had to come back."

"If my mother finds you here, she'll kill you."

"She can't. I'm immortal." I grinned wider.

"Thorne." Worried eyes searched mine. "She'll find a way. You really shouldn't have come back."

"I know," I said, exhaling a sigh as I remembered the reason I was here. "And even though I intended on breaking your rule and coming back to see you anyway, this isn't a social call. It's an emergency. Annella's been kidnaped, and I need your magic to locate her. Please, Cat. They're going to kill her."

"Annella? Your vampire friend?"

"Yes. And she's more than a friend, she's my family. Will you help me find her?"

She pursed her lips tight, and after a few moments, she shook her head. "I'm sorry, but I can't help you. I can't get involved in vampire affairs. My mother would forbid it. You really should go."

"Catrain, it's Annella. You met her. She's kind and sweet, and she really liked you. And she needs your help."

"I can't."

Even while she said no, I could see the conflict brewing in her eyes. It wasn't *her* saying no; it was her loyalty to her mother controlling her decision.

"They'll kill her if Lothaire doesn't kill himself, so I need you to help me find her. Please, Cat. I can't lose *either* of them. And Lothaire will sacrifice himself for Annella in a heartbeat."

She chewed on her lip as her worry lines deepened.

"Cat." I stepped forward and took her hands in mine. She tried to pull away, but I held onto them anyway. When I felt her soften, I gave a gentle squeeze. "I know your tribe hates us. I know that you've spent your whole life hearing that we're nothing but monsters. But you've met us now. Me, Annella, Lothaire, and Aiden. We're all vampires. Do we seem like heartless, bloodthirsty monsters to you?"

With a deep sigh, she shook her head. "No. None of you seem at all like I expected vampires to be."

"We're good people. And Annella and Lothaire are the best of us. We're out of options. Please help them… help me."

Those intense eyes softened as she nodded slowly. "Okay. Fine. But we need to do this quick before my mother finds you."

"Thank you!" I reached forward and pulled her into my arms for a hug. Her body stiffened for a moment before relaxing and pressing against me.

I held her a few moments too long before releasing my grip around her.

We both stepped back as I cleared my throat. "Sorry."

"It's fine," she answered as she dropped her gaze to the ground. "Did you bring something of hers and a map or something I can use to locate her?"

"Yes and yes," I said, then flashed to the boat to retrieve

the duffle bag and flashed back. "Here are her earrings and here is a map of Scotland. I brought several other maps in case they took her out of the country, and several maps of some bigger cities so you can get me a more accurate location if she's in one of them. But let's start with this one."

"Lay the map on the sand."

I grabbed the large paper map and unfolded it, holding the corners tight so the breeze didn't whisk it away.

She opened her hand. "Give me an earring."

I pulled them from my jeans pocket and handed them to her. We both kneeled beside the map, and Cat placed the earring in the center. I watched with bated breath while she closed her eyes and held her hands over it. She chanted quietly while I stared at the earring, waiting for it to start moving to the location where Clan Lennox held Annella.

The location that would be a bloodbath when we got done with them.

But the earring didn't move.

Catrain closed her eyes tighter, her chants growing louder as she continued trying.

Nothing.

"What's wrong? Why isn't it working?"

She stopped chanting and sat back on her heels. "I don't know. It should have moved. Are you sure this is her earring?"

"Yes. They're her favorite ones. She's had them for over a century."

She furrowed her brow and stared back at the map. "Then it should have worked."

"What does that mean? Why can't you locate her?" I asked, then swallowed hard. "Does that… does that mean she's… dead?"

"No," she answered quickly, but then I saw the uncertainty in her eyes. "I… I don't know."

"You don't know?" Panic caused my voice to jump an octave. "Have you ever not been able to locate someone?"

She held my worried stare while she shook her head. "No."

"So, she could be dead," I whispered, barely able to say the words.

"That's not necessarily what it means. Maybe it doesn't work on vampires?"

I perked up. "Okay. Good point. Here." I slid my ancestral ring off my finger and placed it in her hand. "Try me."

Catrain handed me back the earring and placed my ring in the center instead. I shifted back and forth nervously while she performed her spell.

When my ring slid north on the map, my heart plummeted to my feet. "It works on vampires."

Catrain stood quickly and took my hand. "It doesn't mean she's dead."

"What else can it mean?"

An iron grip of fear squeezed my insides.

Annella dead? No. No way.

Not only was it impossible to imagine a world without her, it was impossible to imagine someone being able to kill her. Annella was fierce and strong. And why would they risk killing her if Lothaire's death is what they wanted?

"It can mean a lot of things," Catrain said, tightening her grip on my hand. "Don't lose hope. I feel in my gut that she's still alive."

"You do?"

"Yes. I do."

"Thank you for trying, Cat."

"I'm sorry it didn't work. But you need to go now. My

mother certainly felt me lift the protection spell and will be here soon."

"I appreciate you letting me come back and wish I could spend more time with you. But I don't want to get you in trouble, and I need to go find Annella." I squeezed her hands and stepped into her space. "Please tell me you'll let me come back and see you again after we save Annella. Maybe talk to your mother and make her see that I'm not the monster she thinks I am."

"Thorne." She closed her eyes. "You can't come back."

"No, he cannot," Liùsaidh said, startling us both.

When I looked to the trees lining the beach, I saw Liùsaidh and Cat's sister, Alpia walking toward us, with a dozen warriors behind them.

"Mother." Catrain dropped my hands and stepped back. "I'm sorry. He just needed my help."

"We will not help vampires again," she scolded, stabbing her staff into the sand.

"It was just this once," Catrain said. "Annella was kidnapped, and he needed me to do a locator spell. That's all. It didn't work, and now he's leaving."

She looked at me and gestured for me to get into the boat.

"It will not work because she is not on island. The magical barrier prevents magic from leaving."

"What?" I asked, stepping forward, but Catrain stopped me with a hand on my chest. "So, it won't detect anyone off the island? She's not dead?"

Liùsaidh rolled her eyes. "Not likely. You are impossible to kill."

Catrain spun back. "She's right. I can't believe I didn't think of it, but the barrier that protects us would stop my magic from crossing it. That means I can't perform the spell to find her unless I'm on the other side."

"It will work if you cross the lake?"

"I think so," she said, excitement brightening her eyes.

"Please. Cross with me." I reached out my hand, but she just glanced at it before looking back to her mother.

"Catrain, please. You can't let them die. I need your help," I begged.

"You leave now." Liùsaidh pointed her staff at me. "Do not return."

Catrain looked at her mother and then lowered her head. "I'm sorry, Thorne. I hope you find her."

"Cat," I said on a sigh. "Don't do this. You have a choice. You're not a prisoner here, are you? You can leave and come back to your tribe."

"I shouldn't. My place is here."

"Shouldn't but not *can't*. Just for a few minutes. Just ride in the boat with me until your magic works and then perform the spell on the map. I'll bring you back straight away." I lifted the map off the ground and held it up for her. "It will just take a few minutes, and you can save Annella. Please."

I saw her contemplating it, but before she could answer, the map ignited in my hand. "What the hell?" I dropped it into the sand and watched it dissolve into ash.

"Catrain will not help you. You go. Now." Liùsaidh stood taller, and I knew then the cause of the flames.

"You've got to be kidding me," I grumbled, then smiled at Liùsaidh and pointed at my duffle bag. "Nice try, but I have other maps. Come on, Catrain. We can still find her."

My duffle bag burst into flames, and I clasped my hands onto my head. "Are you fucking kidding me?"

Anger roared inside my chest. I spun to face Catrain's

mother, clenching my fists while I glared. The look in my eye caused several of the giant tribesmen behind her to step forward, lifting their spears. The biggest one that I'd seen around the village, and a few days ago on the beach, lowered his head and growled.

"You see," Liùsaidh said. "Vampires are bad."

"Mother!" she snapped. "You are being unreasonable. He has done nothing to you, and you have just taken his best chance at finding his friend. If someone had kidnapped me, wouldn't you want help finding me?"

She didn't answer, only lifting her chin higher.

Liùsaidh and I stared at each other for a moment before I turned back to Catrain.

"Come with me. Get on this boat, come to my castle and perform the spell there. I promise I'll bring you back safe and sound. This is *your* decision… not hers."

We both glanced at Liùsaidh, and then Catrain took a deep breath. She spun on her heel and marched up to her mother, squaring up with her.

"I am an adult, and I am going to rule this island next year. You do not have the power to stop me, and I *am* going to help him find her. You may not like it, but that's your problem, not mine. I love you, and I love our people, but I will not be a prisoner here. I am going to the mainland, and I will return when I am done."

"Catrain," she started, but Catrain just lifted her hand and stopped her.

The powerful woman I'd gotten to know now stood on the beach, and not the obedient daughter she turned into every time her mother came around.

And she'd never looked hotter.

"I will return," she said one last time, then turned and

strode toward me. "Get in the boat," she whispered as she marched past.

"Seriously? You're coming?" I asked, still struggling to process she'd actually agreed.

"Hurry up before I change my mind."

I didn't hesitate even another second. I flashed to the side of the boat and held it while she climbed inside. Once she sat down, I pushed it into the water and hopped onto the bench across from her. Catrain sat proud and immobile while I paddled us away under the glaring gazes of her tribe.

After a few moments, a thick fog crept across the lake, and I watched while her island and her tribe disappeared. The minute they were gone, I looked back at her and saw the terror filling her eyes.

"Are you sure about this?" I asked as I padded.

She shook her head. "No."

"I'm so sorry you had to leave under those circumstances, but I really appreciate you helping us. It means the world to me. It was good to see you stand up to your mother."

"What did I do?" she whispered to herself. "What did I just do?"

She continued repeating the same words over and over while she stared at her feet.

"Are you okay?" I asked, slowing down my paddling.

"No! I'm not okay! I just disobeyed my mother, my leader, and abandoned my island. What am I doing out here? I've never been this far out before! What am I doing?"

The panic in her voice sent it up a few octaves higher than normal, and my heart squeezed in my chest.

I slid the paddles over my lap and leaned forward and took her hands. "Do you want me to take you back? I can. I don't want you to do this if you don't want to. You have a choice here, and I want you to know that."

"A choice?" she asked, her worried eyes meeting with mine. "I don't even know what that means. I've never had a choice in my life. Ever. I just do what's asked of me."

"Well, you have a choice now. If you want to go back, I'll turn around right now. But if you want to go forward, I promise I'll keep you safe and bring you back the minute you want to return. The *choice* is yours, and I'll understand if you want to go back."

She chewed on her lip while she glanced back over her shoulder at the island we could no longer see. After a few moments, she took a deep breath and shook her head. "No. I can help you find her."

"Are you sure?" I asked again, wanting to be certain she knew that for the first time in her life someone wanted to know what *she* wanted.

She nodded. "Yes. I'm sure. I will live on that island for the rest of my life, and I've always wanted to know what's out there in the world. This is my chance, my one chance, to see it before I rise to power and can never leave again."

"So, we're doing this?" I arched a brow and struggled to suppress the giddy grin starting on my lips.

"Yes." She smiled back. "We're doing this. Keep going."

Our grins grew to match as I slipped the paddles back into the water. "You're gonna love it out here."

"And you'll keep me safe? If something happens to me, my mother *will* find a way to decimate you all."

Keep her safe. From looking at her, no one would ever think she needed *anyone* to protect her. A fearless warrior. A powerful witch. But in her eyes, I could see the wariness as I took her toward a world she'd never seen.

And never in my life had I been more driven to protect

something as I was to protect Catrain. I would never allow harm to come to her.

"I promise you I will get you back home safe. You have my word."

She snorted. "The word of a vampire. Never thought that would be something I'd have faith in."

The air between us thickened. "But you do? Have faith in me?"

She held my gaze for a moment before nodding. "I do."

Hearing those words set my world on fire, and I couldn't contain my grin. "My, my. Did the Pict just admit she trusts a vampire?"

"Don't push it," she warned, but I saw the playful twinkle in her eyes.

"I wouldn't dream of it."

We shared a smile, then I paddled faster and pushed the boat across the lake. When we landed on the other side, I saw the unease return to her face.

"Well, this is it." I hopped out of the boat and tugged it up onto shore. "First steps onto the mainland. You ready?"

She looked at my extended hand, then took a big breath and grabbed it. With one tentative step, she placed her foot onto the ground.

"Congrats. You're officially out in the world."

Her face lit up as she lifted her other leg over the edge of the boat and stood. "Wow. I'm not on the island."

"Nope." I smiled. "How does it feel?"

"Strange." She looked around at the rolling fields surrounding us. "And big."

"You haven't seen anything yet. Wait until you see our home. It's beautiful. Been in the family for centuries."

"How do we get there?" she asked.

The second she said it, I slumped my shoulders and

laughed. "Shit. I wasn't planning to bring you back with me, so I didn't bring a ride. I ran here."

"So, we run back?"

"No. It will take me minutes but you hours. Longer even. And if I try to carry you, the speed will make you sick. I don't want your first minutes on the mainland making you puke."

"So, what do we do?"

What *did* we do? I was about to offer to run home, grab a map and run back, but then I realized it would mean not getting to show her any of our world… and not getting to spend the time with her I so desperately wanted. Even though I knew I could keep it from her, I decided it wouldn't be right to lie.

"Well, it will only take me a few minutes to run home and a few minutes to run back. I could go there, grab the map, and come back. Then you can go right back to your island."

"Oh," she said, the disappointment heavy in her voice.

"*Or* you can wait here for just a bit. There are a few farms I passed on my way here. One is just a few miles away. I can run to it, grab a vehicle, and come back to get you. We can take the vehicle back to the estate."

"Vehicle?" she asked.

"Yes… it's… how the hell do I explain this?" I scratched my scruffy chin while I tried to think of a reasonable comparison. "You know what? Why don't I do that? When I get back, you can decide if you want to ride back with me, or just have me bring you the map and take you home. How does that sound?"

"Okay," she answered.

"Just sit here right by the boat, and I'll be right back. You'll be safe here. I promise."

Those blue eyes of hers filled with worry, but she nodded anyway.

"Don't worry, Cat." I placed a hand on her shoulder. "You're gonna love it out here, and I'll take care of you. I promise."

She pressed her lips together and smiled.

With one last look into those eyes I never wanted to stop staring into, I turned and flashed off toward the farm.

Chapter Six

CATRAIN

I sat at the edge of the lake with my knees pulled up under my chin. It had only been about ten minutes since Thorne had left, but it felt like hours. On my island, I was confident and strong. Fearless. Capable. A born leader. But over here on the mainland, I felt vulnerable and unsure. The foreign feeling unsettled me, and I hoped Thorne would return quickly and bring back the security I felt at his side.

I still couldn't believe I'd done what I'd done.

Disobeyed my mother.

Left my island.

Left my island with a *vampire,* no less.

It seemed impossible that I'd made the decisions that brought me here to this moment, but the fact I still sat on the other side of the lake and could feel the grass beneath my feet confirmed my new reality.

My whole life I'd imagined what lay past where my eyes could see, and now I was here. It terrified and excited me all at once.

A strange noise ruptured the silence around me and sent

the birds in the tree overhead fluttering away. I furrowed my brow while I listened to the sound growing louder and louder. I'd never heard anything like it, and my heart started pounding as it continued intensifying.

I jumped up from where I sat and slid behind the boat, pressing low to the ground while I waited. My instincts sent me reaching for my spear, then I cursed myself for leaving it on the island. With no spear or bow, I had no weapon to defend myself. The wooden boat paddle caught my eye, so I reached forward and grabbed it, pulling it into hiding with me behind the boat.

When the sound that buzzed like a giant bee grew even louder, I gripped the paddle tight and prepared to battle. Thorne wasn't here to protect me, so I'd need to remember the training I'd spent most of my life perfecting and hope my magic worked the same on this side of the lake. I channeled the magic inside my body, ready to unleash hell on whatever threat approached.

"Catrain? Where are you?" Thorne called over the now-quieting buzz of the giant bee. "Catrain?"

The buzzing disappeared, and I peeked my head up over the edge of the boat. Thorne stood beside a strange object as he continued calling my name.

"There you are. I thought you'd run off." With a relaxed smile that didn't allude to any danger nearby, he walked toward me.

"What was that noise?" I stood up slowly, still clutching my paddle.

He took one look at it and laughed. "I'll give you points for quick thinking. That paddle would have made a nice weapon."

I tossed it aside. "My spear would be better."

"I'm sorry I scared you. It didn't even occur to me you wouldn't understand the noise of a dirt bike."

"A dirt bike?" I asked, furrowing my brow.

"Yes. That is what this is." He pointed to the strange object. "It's our ride back to the estate. I grabbed it from the farm."

"Did you steal it?"

Twisting his lips, he hesitated, then answered, "Um, borrowed. I'll bring it back to them."

Narrowing my eyes, I placed a hand on my hip. "My mother says vampires hypnotize people and steal."

He rubbed a hand behind his neck. "Well, that part of the rumors about us is true."

I furrowed my brow.

"*But* we try to only steal from shitty people. We take their money, their homes, and the things they don't deserve. My family doesn't use our powers to take things from good people."

"No?" I asked, searching his face for lies.

"No. I promise. And I will bring this bike back to them. I didn't steal it. Borrowed."

"Okay." I crossed my arms. "But stealing is punishable by death in my tribe."

"*Borrowed.* Don't kill me." He grinned, then waved me to come to his side. "So, this is a dirt bike. I'm going to sit here in the front, you're going to sit on the seat behind me and hold on. It will drive us across the countryside to my home."

"I sit on it?" I stared at the contraption and couldn't begin to imagine how it worked.

"Yes. Have you ever ridden a horse?"

I nodded and stood up proudly. "I've ridden the island ponies many times. Almost every year, I win the tribal race."

"This here?" He tapped the dirt bike. "Exactly like

riding a pony. But it's motorized and faster. You're going to love it."

I tipped my head while I examined it and contemplated going back to the safety of my island, but the excitement in Thorne's eyes encouraged me to stay here and learn a little more of his world.

"Okay."

"Okay." He smiled widely, then straddled the dirt bike and patted the seat behind him.

I climbed on tentatively, then settled onto the seat. When my thighs closed around his body, a shiver of excitement snaked down my spine.

"Hold on tight around my waist," he said as he glanced over his shoulder.

I did as he asked, and when my body pressed against his back, that shiver returned and intensified. My hands touched his rock-hard stomach as I pulled myself closer to him, and I struggled to keep my breathing steady.

"You hanging on?" he asked as he did something with a small jagged metal object.

"Yes." I squeezed him tighter, and I felt that now familiar flutter inside my stomach he always seemed to cause.

"When I turn this key, it's gonna get loud again, but that's just the sound a dirt bike makes, so don't be scared. Just keep holding tight to my waist when the dirt bike moves, and if you need me to stop, just yell. But you're gonna love this. Trust me."

I couldn't even imagine how this thing worked, but I nodded anyway. My heart pounded against my ribcage… excitement about what would happen mixed with excitement to have Thorne in my arms.

The dirt bike started making that noise again, and it

startled me at first. I could feel vibrations between my legs, and the sensation only amplified the ones Thorne had already started there.

"Hang on, Cat!" he called over the noise.

The dirt bike started forward, and I shrieked.

"You okay?" he asked as we crept forward.

After exhaling a breath, I gripped him tighter. "I'm okay."

"I'm gonna go a little faster. Just keep holding on. I won't let you fall."

I did as he said and tightened my grip around him. The dirt bike took off, and the wind whipped against my face as we reached speeds even my fastest race pony would envy. I'd never felt more exhilarated in my life as we flew across the moonlit field.

"You doing okay?" he called back.

The huge smile plastered on my face made it difficult to answer, but I finally managed to shout back, "Yes!"

"Having fun?" he called again.

"Yes!" I shouted louder.

I heard his laughter as the dirt bike picked up even more speed, though I found that increased pace impossible to comprehend. It bumped and bounced as we hit ruts on the ground, and each time it did, I laughed even harder. I hadn't even been on the mainland for twenty minutes, and already I was having more fun than I'd ever imagined possible.

The scenery streaked by as we drove across the moonlit countryside. Despite the darkness, I could still make out enough of my surroundings to be in awe of the world around me. It seemed to stretch on for eternity, and everything looked so different from the small world I'd known my entire life. It invigorated me even more. The intoxicating combination of having Thorne in my arms, the feelings of speed as we raced along, and the excitement of seeing this unfamiliar world nearly took my breath away.

After we had raced on for a while, Thorne drove the dirt bike up a long sloping hill and slowed to a stop when we reached the top. A stone building so large it seemed impossible it existed sat at the top of the next hill on the horizon.

He pointed to it. "That's our home. Castle Mackay."

"That's a *home?*" I asked in disbelief.

"Not exactly a hut, huh?" He smiled back over his shoulder.

"No. Not a hut at all."

"We're almost there."

The dirt bike grew louder as he twisted the handle, and I knew by now that meant to hold on. Gripping him tight, I pressed against his back as we surged forward. The dirt bike crossed the space to the castle with speed even faster than we'd hit before. I'd never felt more awake or more alive than I did as we raced across the field with my hair flying wildly behind me.

We wound up a long stone path until he pulled up in front of the castle. My eyes widened as I took in the sheer size of it up close.

"Welcome to my home." Thorne swung his leg over the front of the dirt bike and stood up. He held out his hand and helped me off. My legs wobbled when I stood, and it caused me to a stumble a step. Before I could wobble even once more, Thorne snaked an arm around my waist and held me tight against him.

"Careful, there. The vibrations can do strange things to your legs. They'll feel better in a minute."

It wasn't the dirt bike making my legs weak now. As he held me in his arms, I felt boneless and dazed. When I looked up into his incredible eyes, my body slackened even more.

"You okay?" He brushed a piece of hair from my face. Concern brewed inside his eyes as he held me suspended in his embrace.

I tried to answer him but struggled to form words. It wasn't just being in his arms that made speaking difficult, though it did. It was that my lips were dry and sticking to my teeth. I ran my tongue over them and swallowed before answering back.

"I'm okay. Thank you."

The mischievous sparkle lit back up in his eyes. "Are your teeth dry because you couldn't stop smiling back there and the wind dried them up?"

The smile I'd worn the entire ride returned, and I laughed. "I think that's exactly what happened."

"Fun, right? I take it I can add dirt biking to your list of things you like in the real world?"

I nodded, and my smile stretched wider. It was the first time in my life the muscles in my face felt strained from overuse. I'd never smiled so much in my life. "It was amazing. I never knew such a thing could exist. Humans really are quite inventive, aren't they?"

He scoffed. "Oh, you haven't seen anything yet."

My eyes widened as I tried to comprehend something more incredible than a dirt bike.

"Come on inside. We'll find my family and figure out where Annella is. Your legs okay to walk now?"

Even though I didn't want to pull back out of his arms, I convinced my body to straighten up. The wobbling in my legs had subsided, and I could stand up on my own. "I'm okay."

"Then come on in."

We walked side by side to a huge wooden door. Thorne pushed it open and stood aside while he let me go in first. I stuttered to a stop at the entrance. It was almost more than I could process.

The sheer size of the room dwarfed anything I'd ever been in, and it overwhelmed me with its bright, colorful decorations. Beautiful artwork covered the stone walls, and the strange candles that didn't flicker with flames illuminated the entire room. I'd heard stories of electricity and modern décor, but I'd never imagined it would all be so magnificent.

The door closed behind me, and Thorne stepped to my side. "This way."

I followed him through the castle while I struggled to keep my jaw shut as I took it all in. Every room we went through looked different from the last and was filled with strange objects I wondered about. Maybe once we found Annella, Thorne could take the time to show me what everything was.

As we walked through another large room with a roaring fireplace, I heard the din of arguing voices coming from the next room.

"I will *not* let her die!" A baritone voice shouted, and it rumbled right through my gut. "She's my little sister, and it's my duty to protect her!"

"And you're my *husband*, and it's your duty to stay with me! I am immortal for *you*. What the hell am I supposed to do if you're gone? Have you thought about that? It will kill me. You dying will destroy me."

Thorne looked over at me and grimaced before whispering, "Things are a little stressful right now. Please forgive them."

I nodded my understanding before we reached the door separating us from the room.

"I don't know what to do, Grizella! Of course, I don't want to leave you, but I can't just let her die. No one knows where she is, and we are running out of time. It's an impossible situation."

"No, it's not," Thorne said as we entered the room.

I stepped behind him, surprised by how timid I felt again… and how protected he made me feel. Everything was so new and overwhelming, and walking into a room full of vampires wasn't doing anything to ease my anxiety.

"Thorne," a voice I recognized as Aiden said. "Glad you made it back, brother. Please tell me Catrain was able to locate her."

"She was not. It turns out she can't locate people outside the barrier around the island unless she's outside the island as well."

"Well, fuck," the deep voice I now recognized as Lothaire said. "We're out of options. No clan has any leads on Annella."

"Not out of options," Thorne said as he stepped aside and slid his arm around my waist, pulling me up to his side. "She couldn't do the spell there, so Catrain has come here to perform it."

Swallowing hard, I stood up straight and looked across the shocked faces of the immortals I'd seen once before on our island.

Aiden looked to Thorne and arched an eyebrow as a smirk started on his face.

"Catrain!" Emilia shouted and raced toward me. I wasn't sure what to expect with the speed that she approached, but before I could respond, she threw her arms around my neck and wrapped me up in a warm hug.

"Thank you! Thank you, thank you, thank you. We appreciate you coming to help us so much."

"You're welcome," I answered as I patted her back. Hugging wasn't a usual part of my culture, and it felt awkward at first, but after a moment, I smiled and returned it.

Aiden approached behind her and slid his arm around her waist when she released me. "I can't believe you left the island to help us. Thank you, Catrain."

I gave him a brief nod and a small smile. "I'll do my best to help."

Lothaire came up with the beautiful woman and the blonde man I'd evicted from the island when they'd first arrived. He reached out his hand and offered it. I took it tentatively, his giant hand encapsulating mine with a squeeze.

"Welcome to our home. You have my eternal gratitude for doing this, Catrain. I'm not sure if you remember us all, but I'm Lothaire. This is my wife, Grizella, and our friend, Mark. Then you know Emilia, Aiden, and of course, Thorne."

He gestured to each of them as he went around the room, and they all greeted me with a warm smile. There weren't blood dripping fangs and snarls like I would have once expected upon seeing a vampire. Instead, they looked like just a beautiful, nice family.

"It's good to see you all again," I said.

"It's really nice to meet you, Catrain," Mark said as he stepped forward. "And I'm a hugger, so get your cute ass in here."

Before I could respond, he wrapped his arms around me and lifted me up into the air.

"You're so tiny!" he laughed as he set me back down. "Like a tiny little lethal warrior pixie. I love it!"

"Don't squish her with your new powers, Mark," Thorne warned as I slid out of Mark's embrace. "He's a new vampire, and sometimes we don't realize how strong we are."

"I'm not gonna squish her." Mark rolled his eyes. "I mean, I'm hella strong, obvie." He flexed his impressive bicep. "But, I would never hurt our little Catrain."

His mannerisms and enthusiasm caused me to chuckle as I stepped back from him.

"I promised to return Catrain safe and sound," Thorne said as he passed a stern gaze across his family. "That means everyone here will protect her with their lives. Is that clear?"

"Of course," Grizella said, and everyone nodded in agreement. "We just appreciate you coming here. We can't lose either of them, so we really need your help."

Lothaire and Grizella exchanged a glance, then he slid his enormous arm around her shoulders.

"So, how does the spell work?" Aiden asked.

Now that I felt safe around them, I was comfortable enough to talk. "I'll need a map and her earring. We'll place it on that table, I'll perform my spell, and it should tell us where she is."

"I'll get a map," Grizella said before flashing out of the room, only to return a few seconds later. "Here."

She placed the map on the large wooden table in the center of the room and spread it out.

"Do you have the earring?" I asked Thorne as I walked over to the table. He stayed inches from my side each step of the way and pulled the green jewel earring out of his pocket.

"Here you go."

"Thank you." I placed the earring on the center of the map, closed my eyes, and began chanting.

"It's working!" I heard Mark squeal as I kept up my spell.

"Holy shit. It is," Thorne said. I felt his body press closer to mine, and his close proximity made it hard to keep up my concentration.

"It stopped!" Emilia said.

After opening my eyes, I looked to see the earring had moved south on the map.

"She's in Edinburgh." Lothaire jabbed his finger at the location.

"That was amazing, Cat." Thorne turned to me and took my hands in his. "You're amazing."

The simple words felt anything but with the way he looked at me when he said them.

"So where in Edinburgh would they keep her?" Grizella's question pulled me from the trance Thorne's eyes had lulled me into.

"We can ask our contacts if they have any idea where they would hide," Aiden said.

"No." Thorne broke our eye contact and looked up. "We can't take any chance they know we're coming. If there is a leak in our loyalties and they find out we know where they are, they could run… or worse. Since we have it, I think we need to keep the element of surprise on our side."

"But then how do we find her?" Lothaire asked. "Edinburgh isn't a small city."

Thorne turned back to me. "If I get you another map, a smaller one, can you perform the spell again and help me narrow down the location?"

"Yes," I answered.

Thorne flashed out of the room and returned holding a

map of Edinburgh. He pushed the other map off the table and handed me the earring. Once again, I performed my spell, and when I finished, we all stared at the earring sitting on the lower left of the map.

"So, she's on that block?" Aiden asked, and I nodded.

"Yes. That's in New Town."

"Then we go to Edinburgh, and we hunt her down," Lothaire growled.

"But what building?" Aiden said. "We don't know how many of them are guarding her or on lookout, and if we have to go building to building, we'll be seen before we can get her out safely. We need a better plan."

They started to argue amongst themselves, each tossing out different plans only to be deterred by another argument. As their voices rose with the panic palpable inside them, I lifted my hand and stepped forward.

"Since you don't know what building she's in, or what they have for forces, what if I go with you? They won't recognize me as one of you, so I can get close and use my magic to find out exactly where she is."

"It's too dangerous," Thorne said quickly. "You should stay here where it's safe."

"Let's just hear her out." Lothaire gestured for me to continue.

"When I'm close, I can perform a spell that will guide me right to the building she's in and tell me exactly where she is inside of it. Then you will know right where to go."

"Cat." Thorne slid his hand onto my shoulder. "She's in a big city, and you've never even been to a small one. I can't just have you wandering by yourself down the streets, especially into an area with dangerous vampires. They aren't like us. These are the monsters you've learned about. It's just not safe."

"I came here to help." I stood up tall, remembering who I had been raised to be.

A warrior. A leader. Fearless.

"I can do this."

Worry filled Thorne's eyes as he stared into mine. "If you do this, then you need to do exactly as I say, and if anything, *anything*, feels off, you need to say so. I'll be nearby listening and watching you, and I'll get to you in seconds."

"Are you really sure you want to do this?" Aiden asked. "I appreciate the offer, but Thorne is right. It could be dangerous, and a city is a lot to process if you've never even been off your island."

My heart stuttered, but I willed it to stop. "You'll show me what I need to know about the city, and I will find her."

They all exchanged a look and then turned to Thorne for his final decision.

With a heavy sigh, he looked at me. "Okay. But you have to stay safe."

His concern for me warmed me from the inside out, but I knew I could help him find his friend. Even though I felt fear deep down in the pit of my gut, knowing I could help Thorne helped me squash it down.

I lifted my chin high and looked across the family staring intently at me. "Then it's settled. We go to this Edinburgh."

Chapter Seven

THORNE

"She's ready!" Mark called from the top of the stairs, then flashed down to the foyer where we all waited. His palpable excitement had him looking ready to jump up and down at any moment.

"What the hell did you do to her?" I arched a brow.

When we'd decided last night to take Catrain to the city with us, Mark was the first to point out that she couldn't exactly blend in wearing her leather clothes and war paint. A makeover had been in order, and he'd jumped at the chance.

Now he prepared to unveil her big transformation. I couldn't wait to see her again… or what she looked like in modern clothes. Since I couldn't be out in the daylight, I hadn't seen her since she went to bed last night. Aiden and Emilia had entertained her all day, and though I appreciated them keeping her safe and occupied, I hated to miss a minute of seeing Catrain explore this world.

Tonight, when I'd emerged from my room, Mark had already rushed off to get her ready for our expedition. Even though it'd only been an hour since I'd awakened, it was another hour I'd missed spending with her.

Now the anticipation of seeing her again had me as excited as Mark… though I held my enthusiasm on the inside.

"You are gonna love it. Love. It." Mark pursed his lips into a self-satisfied smile and gestured for me to watch the top of the stairs. He looked at all of us and crossed his arms. "She started out looking like a wicked hot Lagertha from *Vikings,* and now she looks like she belongs on a Paris runway. May I present the new and ever-so-beautiful, Catrain!"

She appeared at the top of the stairs, and I had to clutch the table beside me for balance. It wasn't that she was more beautiful, she'd been stunning before, but it was a different kind of beauty descending the stairs.

Instead of knots and braids twisting up her hair, soft, blonde waves fell around her face. Dark, smokey eyes replaced the war paint that once surrounded them, and tasteful makeup accentuated every incredible inch of her face. The leather clothing exposing all her tanned skin had been swapped out for fitted ripped jeans and a soft black shirt draping off her shoulder that showcased some of the black tattoos snaking around her arm.

Then there were her lips. Red. Sexy. Plump.

And unbelievably kissable.

"Told ya," Mark whispered into my ear, having taken notice of my slack jaw and stunned appearance.

I didn't even attempt to argue with him because words refused to form.

"Damn, girl!" Emilia whistled. "You look amazing. Mark is the master of makeovers… I should know."

She gave him a hip bump and he took a bow. "I'm an artiste."

"You truly are," Grizella said. "She looks wonderful."

"How do you feel, Catrain?" Emilia asked as Catrain approached us.

"Different." She paused and glanced down at her clothes. "But good."

"You look incredible," I finally managed to say.

A shy smile drew up the corners of those impossibly luscious lips. "Thanks."

It was impossible not to stare at her, but I caught Lothaire and Aiden's smirks from the corner of my eye and knew I looked like a lovesick fool. Clearing my throat, I tried to find the senses her transformation had stolen from me. "Well, we should probably get going. We've got to get to Edinburgh, rescue Annella, and get back before dawn."

"So, this will work? I can walk in the city like this?" Catrain asked, her eyes searching all of us then landing on mine.

"Yes. You'll blend in just fine. But I want you to be sure you want to do this. You don't have to."

"I'll be okay," she said confidently. "I want to help. I liked Annella."

"We'll all be watching you closely, but hidden," Lothaire said.

"I won't let anything happen to you." As I said the words, a primal protective rumble coursed through my body.

I couldn't. Never in my life had I wanted to protect something more than I wanted to protect Catrain.

"I'll call the helicopter," Grizella said.

"What's a helicopter?" Catrain asked as Grizella lifted her phone to ear, something else we'd had to explain to

Catrain last night. She'd been mesmerized watching us call each other from different rooms and had laughed when I'd held my phone up to her ear so she could hear Emilia talk.

"We could all run to Edinburgh much faster than the helicopter, but since you can't, we'll take a helicopter. It will fly us there fairly quickly."

"Fly?" Her eyes widened. "In the sky?"

"Yes, fly. Remember I told you about the planes people fly in? This is kind of like that."

She shook her head back and forth. "Only birds belong in the sky."

"Catrain, I promise you'll be safe," I soothed, but she just shook her head harder.

"No flying."

I was about to try more reasoning with her, but I saw the fear inside her eyes. "Okay, no problem. No flying. We'll just drive there."

"Do we have that kind of time?" Aiden whispered. "It will be a three-hour drive,"

"Not the way I drive." I grinned. "We'll take the Bugatti. And it's got the option to go light tight if we get delayed. I can just park it until the sun goes down, and I won't light up like a candle. It only seats two, so you guys run there, and Catrain and I will be there soon."

"Are you sure?" Lothaire asked.

"I'm sure. Just get to the outskirts of the area, take position, and wait. We don't want to risk being seen."

"We'll see you there."

They all gave me a quick nod before disappearing out the door in a flash, leaving Catrain and I standing alone in the foyer.

"What is a Bugatti? Like a dirt bike?" she asked.

My smile stretched wide as I shrugged. "Kinda. It's a

car. A very fast car. If you liked the dirt bike, you're going to love the Bugatti."

"But no flying?"

"No flying."

She gave a sharp nod and walked toward the door. I couldn't help but sneak a peek at her ass in those jeans. The way they hugged her admirable curves almost dropped me to my knees.

"Ready?" She turned back.

I lifted my eyes before she caught my stare. "I was born ready."

As we walked around the estate to the garage that housed our collection of cars, Catrain told me a little of her day with Aiden and Emilia. They had taken her for a walk around the property and introduced her to margaritas by the pool… something Aiden and Emilia did together every day.

"And what did you think of your margarita?" I asked as I pushed the buttons for the alarm code at the garage.

"It tasted funny. Sour. Salty. But I liked it." She smiled widely. "Do you like margaritas?"

I sucked the air through my teeth. "Can't say I've ever had one. Unlike Aiden and Emilia, I'm still living on a blood diet."

She wrinkled her nose. "Oh yeah. Yuck."

I shrugged. "It keeps me alive. Did you eat any good food?"

"Oh, yes!" Her eyes lit up. "Emilia went somewhere and came back with something called McDonald's. It was incredible! I've tasted nothing like it."

Once again, I wondered what food tasted like. I'd stopped caring about food centuries ago, but lately, seeing Aiden enjoying every bite with such enthusiasm and hearing how much Catrain enjoyed it, I grew more and more curious what all the fuss was about. But there was no sense in wondering, since a blood diet remained the only item on the menu for me… and I happened to enjoy every drop of my sustenance.

After pulling the keys to the Bugatti out of the safe, I led her over to the sleek black car.

"This is a car," I said as I opened the door. "It's kind of like the dirt bike, but we sit inside instead of on top of it. You sit there."

She looked at the seat I pointed to, and after a moment, she slid inside onto the smooth black leather. When I closed the door, she disappeared behind the opaque black glass. I hurried around the back of the car, then opened the driver's door and climbed in.

"Normally, I would tell you to strap on your seatbelt," I said as I pointed to mine. "But since I'm a vampire, on the off chance I miss a turn, we're better off having you loose, so I can whisk you out of the car before we wreck."

She stared at me and furrowed her brow. I realized nothing I said made any sense to her.

"Never mind," I said with a laugh. "Just sit back and enjoy the ride. If you liked going fast on the dirt bike, you're going to love this."

Catrain didn't look frightened this time when I started the engine. Instead, she looked excited. I pressed my foot on the gas and rolled out of the garage, then turned on the radio. She tipped her head and looked around, listening to the sounds, then smiled.

"That's the radio. We'll go over all the music options on our way there and find out what kind you like. You ready?"

"Ready." Her eyes sparkled with excitement.

I stepped on the gas, and she squealed with delight as I

hit over a hundred miles an hour in a matter of seconds. The car handled every twist and turn of the roads as we hit top speed on our way to Edinburgh. Catrain's eyes never stopped searching the moonlit countryside as she pointed out all the wonders we saw along the way.

Everything to her was new. Exciting. It made me smile seeing how much she enjoyed herself out here in my world even under the cover of darkness.

When we got into Edinburgh, she stared in awe at all the buildings and lights. I'd seen the world transition slowly from a life similar to hers to the one I lived now… fast cars, private jets, and all the technology that had become second nature had happened over time. I couldn't even imagine what it would be like to have skipped the last six centuries and just appeared in the world today.

"It's beautiful," she said as I steered the car down the streets toward our destination.

"It is a lovely city."

"Are all cities this big?" she asked as she tipped her head and looked up at the buildings we passed by.

"Actually, this is a small city."

She spun in her seat, and those wide eyes met mine. "Small?"

Laughing, I turned the car onto the next street. "Yes. It's really a pretty quaint large town. The big cities are filled with skyscrapers so tall you can't even see the tops and more colorful lights than you can imagine."

"I *can't* imagine it." She blew out a breath.

"This is a good starter city for you. Someday, I'll take you to New York. Now *that's* a city."

The minute I said it, it felt like I'd been kicked in the gut.

There was no *someday* with Catrain. After we found

Annella, she'd go back. Back to her island, her people, and out of my life forever.

I looked over at her and tried to calm the sadness consuming me from the inside. There was a reason I'd never fallen for a woman in six hundred years. I'd seen what my father went through when he lost my mother… seen the monster that heartbreak had created. When Aiden met Isobel and fell in love, and Lothaire found Grizella, I started to wonder if maybe I could find someone and be happy… that maybe my aversion to heartbreak was irrational and unfounded.

Then I'd seen what Aiden went through when he lost his wife… a pain I didn't think he'd survive, and a pain I never wanted to risk. To give someone my heart, my whole heart, was a chance I'd never been willing to take, filling my days with fun flings and casual hookups instead.

But tonight…

Tonight, I'd have ripped my heart out of my chest and handed it to her on a platter if it meant convincing her to stay.

My phone rang and startled us both. I pulled the car to the parking spot on the side of the road and answered it.

"Lothaire, we're here."

"I know. I'm looking at your car."

I lowered my head and looked out the windows, scanning the area for my family I knew were nearby, but saw no signs of them.

"We're spread out around the surrounding blocks. I don't think you should drive any closer. You're just over a block away now."

"I can see it from here. I can stay in the car and keep an eye on her from here."

"Is she sure she wants to do this?"

I looked over at Catrain, questioning my decision to let her put herself at risk. But she was right. It was her decision, and after a life of being told what to do, I wanted her to have control over every move she made… even if it terrified me to send her down this street alone.

"She's ready."

"Good. We'll be waiting. As soon as she locates the building, have her keep walking, and we'll meet her two blocks down. She can tell us then which one it is. Any sign of trouble, and we'll all move in."

"It's a plan. Good luck," I said before hanging up.

"Everything okay?" she asked.

"Yes. They are all ready. I'll be right here in the car behind you, watching and listening. I can hear extremely well, so all you have to do is whisper you need help, and I'll be at your side in a second. I won't let you out of my sight."

"I can take care of myself." She smiled as she lit up a little fireball in her hand.

I laughed. "I know you can. But there are some nasty vampires on this block. They aren't like my family. *These* are the monsters you've heard of all your life, and I don't want you to get hurt. So just walk down the street using your magic to figure out which building she's in, then *keep walking,* and Lothaire will meet you up the road two blocks."

"Okay. I'll see you when I'm done."

We stared at each other for a moment, and my gaze slid down to her lips. It was almost impossible to keep myself from reaching across the car and pulling her in for a kiss I'd never want to come up from.

Instead of doing what I wanted, I just smiled and said, "I'll be watching you. Be careful."

Catrain smiled back, then turned to the door. After a moment, she turned back. "How do I get out?"

"Oh, shit," I laughed and pointed to my door handle. "Just pull on that metal thing."

She gave it a tug, and the door opened, causing her to smile wide.

"Be safe," I whispered as she climbed out.

When the door closed and separated us, I considered racing out to her side to walk beside her. But everyone in Clan Lennox would recognize me in an instant, and I'd blow our entire plan. Instead, I sat poised and ready to act while I watched her out the front window.

Catrain strolled down the street looking more natural than I'd expected. If she was in awe of her surroundings, she hid it well. She'd told me how she'd perform the spell as she walked, and that it didn't require any obvious magic. All she needed to do was hold Annella's earring in her hand while she chanted, and it would gently pull her where she needed to go.

My heart pounded in my chest as she got a full block away. I knew I could make it to her in under a second, but there were also vampires around here who could do the same. And a beautiful woman walking alone on a street was an easy target for any man with loose morals… especially a vampire lacking them.

Which described every member of Clan Lennox.

"I'm close," I heard her whisper. "It's pulling me to the left. I think it's this building across the street or the next one."

I wanted to tell her not to get any closer and to keep walking, but she couldn't hear me like I could hear her.

Instead of continuing straight, she crossed the quiet street and moved closer to the three-story stone buildings lining the road.

"Dammit, Cat," I whispered under my breath. If she

thought Annella was in one of those buildings, then it also meant the vampires would be nearby. "Don't get close to them."

Catrain kept walking until she made it to the sidewalk on the opposite side of the road. "It's this building here," she whispered as she passed by.

I held my breath while she kept walking, glad she followed our instructions to locate the building and keep moving. But as she moved passed the building, a tall, dark-haired man stepped out in front of her.

"Hey, beautiful," he said as she kept moving.

I reached for my door handle, prepared to flash to her side and rip out his throat if he dared lay a hand on her.

Catrain ignored him and side-stepped his large frame. Instead of letting her go around, he spun around and stepped behind her.

"I'm okay, don't come," she whispered, and I knew it was for me.

"What?" the man asked.

"Nothing. Leave me be," she said as she kept walking.

I practically shook in my skin wanting to race to save her, but I heard her once again.

"Stay. Put. I'm okay."

"Are you talking to me?" he asked.

"No. Go away." Her small hand closed into a fist, and I watched intently, prepared to make my move the second she needed me.

Was this a Clan Lennox vampire? A shady human? Unfortunately, vampires couldn't detect one another. We didn't have beacons over our heads declaring our condition. Unless we chose to show our true nature, vampires smelled, looked, and seemed entirely human. And even if we could sense one another, the distance to the one following Catrain would be too great to know for sure. I watched him closely for any signs he was one of my kind, knowing if he was, I'd have little time to respond if he decided to make a snack out of her.

The man lifted a hand and placed it on her shoulder. Every nerve in my body fired, and I prepared to fly out of the car to her side. Then I heard her voice.

"I've got it."

A second later, I saw the sparks flicker in her hand, and she spun around and placed it on his chest. The force of the shock sent the man flying backward, and he landed on his arse with a pained cry.

Even though she couldn't see me, she still looked in my direction. I saw the proud smirk start on her lips as she stared at my car.

"Well, I'll be damned." I laughed as she took a step closer to the man.

"Do not touch," she said, pausing between each word for added effect before turning and sauntering away.

My phone rang, and I pressed the button and put it up to my ear.

"Anything?" Aiden whispered.

"Yes. She's passing in front of the building now. She said Annella is in there."

"Good. Get her out of there before something happens and then let's make a plan to get Annella out."

I snorted. "Something already happened, but she's fine."

"What happened?" he asked, his voice heavy with concern. "Is she okay?"

"She's okay, but the dude she just laid out with a lightning bolt may not be." I laughed.

"What?"

"Some stupid horny human tried to lay hands on her. She lit him up."

"You're sure he's human?" Aiden asked.

"If he was a vampire, he'd already be up and ready to… oh shit."

The man leaped back to his feet with stealth no human could possess. In less than a second, three more vampires appeared at his side.

There was no way to keep up our plan of a stealth rescue mission now that Catrain was in danger.

"Vampires! Move in!" I shouted and dropped the phone on my seat.

I arrived at Catrain's side before the vampire she'd assaulted could finish the grab he'd made for her hair. She shrieked when I snagged her around the waist, and as she spun around, her eyes widened at the sight of the four vampires who'd appeared behind her.

"Get behind me!" I shouted as I shoved her back, then popped my fangs and snarled.

The vampires standing across from me looked shocked to see me standing there, but only for a second. Their stunned expressions twisted into anger as they glared.

"Thorne," the tallest one growled.

It took me a second to remember his name, but I recalled seeing him at clan meetings in the past.

"Hello, Brodric," I said on a snarl. "I'd think long and hard about your next move. This won't end well for any of you if you don't back the fuck up and tell me where Annella is."

I could see him contemplating his decision… weighing the options between disobeying Leith or fighting an original vampire. It was well known in vampire circles that Clan Mackay, the original vampires, possessed significantly more strength and speed than vampires turned by others. With each following generation of vampires, their strength and speed decreased… the magic inside them diluting. And there wasn't a vampire on the planet who didn't know my reputation for being Lothaire's enforcer and my famous and lethal skills. I hoped that he'd remember my undefeated status and run for his life while he still could.

My hair blew in a sharp breeze, and my family appeared at my side.

"Think long and very fucking hard," Lothaire said as he stepped forward, going nose to nose with Brodric. "Your next move may be your last if it's not the right one."

The energy surged between us as the tension rose. I could hear Catrain's quick breathing behind me, and I hated that I'd brought her into this dangerous situation. Part of me wanted to run her off to safety and return to fight, but the other part of me knew not to let her out of my sight. Even though she was a capable warrior, and obviously her magic had some effect on vampires, it was still too risky to leave her unattended.

"Just stay back, Catrain," I whispered to her as I prepared for the fight I knew was coming.

Movement in the window above caught my eye, and Aiden's head flashed toward it. "Leith and Leeya! Third floor!" he said.

"Go for Annella!" Lothaire roared. "They'll kill her!"

Aiden, Emilia, and Grizella bolted inside, leaving Lothaire, Mark, Catrain, and me to face off with the four vampires still standing on the street.

Lothaire moved first, launching at Brodric with a roar. They disappeared into a blur of movement as I attacked the man in front of me who'd tried to touch Catrain. He went down with my third blow, and I gripped his head and tore it from his body before it even hit the ground. It felt primal and good to annihilate the man who'd dared try to touch my Catrain.

As I spun to my feet to make sure she was still safe, I saw Mark was on the ground with his fangs sunk into the throat of the third vampire. Since an original vampire had turned Mark, he'd inherited almost all our strength and held his own quite well.

Though we'd told him how to fight and taught him that vampires could only die from the loss of their head, this was his very first battle. I remembered well from my first battle how quickly your training could fly out of your head in the heat of the fight.

"Get the head!" I reminded him.

"Look out!" Catrain shouted, and I spun to see the fourth brute of a vampire lunging at me.

I braced for impact, prepared to counter-attack the minute he collided with me, but a bright blue burst of sparks landed square in his chest and sent him flying backward. The minute his body hit the ground, I was on him, and his head rolled down the sidewalk a second later.

After a quick look back and a nod of thanks to Catrain, I spun to see Lothaire landing a final blow into Brodric's face. With a rumbling growl, he tore off his head and rose. Blood dripped from his hands as he spit on the corpse. "Fucking prick."

"I got one! Did you see me? My first vamp fight, and I was like a vampire ninja!" Mark shouted proudly, then stopped his air chopping and pulled a face. "Ugh. I got his blood in my mouth. Vampire blood tastes like shit."

He spit it out on the sidewalk and wiped the remnants from his face.

"Everyone okay?" I asked as I took a quick survey. "Catrain? Are you hurt?"

"No. I'm okay," she said, though the ashen color of her face said her body may be okay, but her mind may need some time to process.

Lothaire took no time to regroup. "Annella. We need to go in and help—"

Movement at the front of the building caught our eye, and we spun to see Leith, Leeya, and a huge Scottish vampire with shaggy red hair emerge. They froze for a second when they saw us, but then bolted away in a blur.

"Should I go after them?" I asked, prepared to run and annihilate the fuckers who'd taken Annella.

"No. We'll deal with them later. We need to find Annella." Lothaire barely finished his sentence before he shot inside the building.

Mark stood stunned, staring at the place Leith, Leeya, and the other vampire had been before rushing after Lothaire.

"I'm staying with you," I said to Catrain, though I desperately wanted to help my family. There was no way I would leave her unprotected with Leith and Leeya nearby. I pulled her against my chest and wrapped a protective arm over her shoulder as I listened closely inside the building, hoping I didn't hear any sounds of battle.

"I found her!" Emilia shouted.

I held my breath, waiting to hear if Annella was okay.

"She's alive! I've got her!" Emilia called.

"Thank God," I breathed into Catrain's hair as I pulled her in tighter. "You did it. You saved her."

"I just showed you where she was. You guys saved her."

"You did more than that. Your little lightning bolt sure

helped out." I looked down at her and arched an eyebrow. "Just don't ever use that on me."

The visibly shaken look on her face softened as she smiled. "Then don't give me a reason to."

I pulled her tighter against me as I laughed. "I'll try not to piss you off."

Lothaire appeared in the doorway holding Annella in his arms. She looked so tiny and fragile against his massive chest… a far cry from the fearless warrior we'd always known her to be.

"Is she okay?" I asked as they walked out. "Please say she's okay."

"She's fine," Lothaire said, clutching his little sister tighter to his chest. "They had her under UV lights to weaken her, but she'll be fine soon."

"We need to get her home." Grizella stroked Annella's long, auburn hair.

"You guys go. Catrain and I will drive back and meet you at the estate."

Aiden had his arm around Emilia's waist as he walked toward me. "I'll get rid of the bodies, and then I'll be behind you."

"We'll see you all at home." I clapped Lothaire on the shoulder as he walked by. "Just take care of Annella."

Mark followed behind him, his normally playful eyes solemn and heavy.

"You okay?" I asked him.

Instead of the cocky answer that usually accompanied anything Mark said, he just nodded his head. Before I had time to press him, Lothaire announced it was time to go.

"We'll see you soon," I said and watched them flash away. Aiden grabbed a body from the street and disappeared toward the ocean.

Catrain and I stood alone on the street, and even though I knew Leith and Leeya were probably running for their lives and a hundred miles away by now, I didn't want to take a chance. "Come on. Let's go."

Catrain didn't say a word as I guided her back to the car. What could she say? Everything she'd been told about vampires had just come true right in front of her eyes. She'd be begging me to bring her back to her island tomorrow, and the thought of parting with her tore apart my soul.

But I'd made her a promise to bring her back as soon as she was ready, and even though it would kill me to say goodbye, I would respect her choice.

For once in her life, she deserved to have one… even if it meant an eternity of missing her for me.

Chapter Eight

CATRAIN

"If it wasn't so close to sunset, I'd teach you how to drive," Thorne said as we wound down the roads close to his home.

"Me?" I laughed. "I don't think so."

"Oh, come on. You're a badass, Catrain. If ever there was a woman who belonged behind the wheel of a Bugatti, it's you."

The thought of driving made me smile, or maybe it was the compliment he'd just given me.

"You laid a vampire out on his arse with a touch. You can handle driving a car."

"Are most other vampires bad like those tonight?"

He shook his head. "No. Most vampires follow the rules Lothaire has laid out for them. Each clan of vampires has their own leader, like Leith leads Clan Lennox, but Lothaire leads them all. He's like the King… or like your mother to all vampires. The clan leaders report to him and enforce his rules within their clans."

"But they don't all follow the rules?" I asked.

"Most do. Don't kill humans and don't get discovered

are the big rules, and vampires coexist with humans fairly well. But every century or so, a clan tries to take power. This time it's Clan Lennox. They want a world where humans can be harvested and kept like cattle for feeding."

"Disgusting," I said, the thought churning my stomach.

"It is. And Lothaire has dismissed their pleas to have the rules changed to allow them to do so. They got fed up and tried to use Annella to get Lothaire out of the way so they could take power and change things."

"You can't ever let them take over."

He chuckled. "We won't. Our family is far more powerful than them. We've handled every other clan rebellion for centuries, and we'll handle this one too. Lothaire is our leader, and he'll remain that way for eternity."

"Good. I like Lothaire."

"Me too. He's a good man. He'd do anything for any of us, including give his life to save his sister. Thanks to you, though, that didn't need to happen. Grizella never would have recovered. None of us would have."

"Was she immortal when she met him?" I asked, wondering more about the connection between Lothaire and his stunning wife. It was as strong as the one I'd seen between Aiden and Emilia… and one I was glad I didn't see between Thorne and someone else.

"She wasn't. It was a few hundred years ago when he met her. She'd been taken as a slave, and Lothaire caught sight of her and tried to purchase her."

"He wanted to *purchase* her? Humans can be sold?" I asked, shocked to hear a man who seemed as honorable as Lothaire would partake in such disgusting practices.

"They used to be able to," he answered. "Luckily, humans have adapted, and times have changed."

"Good. That's awful."

"It was. And for the record, Lothaire didn't want to own her. He wanted to free her. But someone else wanted to purchase her badly and stole her from Lothaire. She ended up on a ship sailing away."

"But he saved her?"

"Yes," Thorne said with a smile. "He saved her. After one look into her eyes, he was in love, and nothing would stop him from being with that woman. We ended up on a journey to the Ottoman Empire to rescue her, but in the end, Lothaire succeeded. They've been together ever since."

"Well, it certainly seems to have worked out for them. They are very much in love."

Thorne snorted. "That's an understatement. You'd think after all these years it would have dwindled some, but not for those two. Each day it seems they love each other more."

I swallowed hard before I asked the next question. "And you? You've never… met a woman you wanted to make immortal?"

The car swerved and hit a bump on the side, but Thorne quickly righted it. After a long pause, he shook his head. "I haven't. It seems that love like that wasn't in the cards for me. After watching my father lose my mother, and then Aiden lose his wife—"

"Aiden had a wife?" I interrupted.

"Oh, yes," Thorne confirmed. "And he loved her with all his heart. But she wanted to remain mortal, and he lost her to old age. Nearly killed him. And after that, I decided I wasn't up for having my heart ripped out of my chest. Forever is a long time to long for someone." His voice drifted off as his eyes flicked to me.

I felt equal parts relief and sadness as I stared into them.

Relief that he'd never met a woman to love, and sadness at his long, lonely existence.

Not that it differed much from mine.

Love wasn't an option for the heir to my mother's throne, and I'd never even considered the notion…

Until now.

"So that's my story," Thorne said as he turned his gaze back to the road. "Just a six-hundred-year-old Scottish warrior who now drives a sports car instead of a battle steed. I'd say it's an upgrade." He arched an eyebrow and looked at me. "Though, you should have seen me in my battle gear. I had hair halfway down my back, and war paint like yours. I bet we could have made a hell of a team back then."

The thought of him charging into battle with his long hair and exposed chest made my heart race… then one glance over at him proved the modern version beside me produced the same effect.

Thump, thump, thump, thump, thump.

When his lips pulled up into a smug grin, I had no doubt his exceptional hearing had picked up on my primal desires. Grateful he decided not to call me out on it, I sat quietly as he hit the gas and pushed the car up the last hill to the estate.

Thorne parked the car, and we hurried inside since the sun would rise soon. My mind still reeled from everything I'd seen and done tonight.

Riding in a car. Seeing the city. Fighting the bad vampires.

Spending a night with Thorne.

It was all a blur my brain struggled to process. Until yesterday, my life had been days filled with more of the same.

The same island. The same people. The same routine.

Practice my magic. Practice my fighting. Sit with my mother while I learned how to rule our tribe. Watch the sunset. Go to sleep.

Every. Single. Day.

I'd never felt so awake and alive as I had since I'd left my island with Thorne, but now that Annella had been found, I would have to go back. The thought of leaving this world, of leaving Thorne, made my heart feel as heavy as a boulder.

"Is she okay?" Thorne asked as he rushed into the living room.

Annella lay on the couch with her family sitting around her.

"I'm okay," Annella said, her voice still weak.

"Thank God," Thorne breathed as he dropped to his knees by her side, taking her hand in his. "We were so worried about you."

It was strange to see the vampires so kind and caring. The soulless monsters I'd believed them to be wouldn't be capable of such warm emotions. Though the vampires I'd heard about definitely existed, and I'd met some of them tonight, Thorne's family was nothing like the stories I'd been told since childhood.

"I'm not that easy to kill." She lifted her lips into a feeble smirk. "I am still wicked pissed those arses got the jump on me, though."

"How did it happen?" Thorne asked.

"They got me alone outside the club and hit me with a big arse UV light. It weakened me, and when they flipped it off, before I could get my strength back, eight of them took me down with chains. So fucking pissed," she said, the strength returning to her voice.

"Well, it makes sense they needed a UV light and chains to take you down," Lothaire said proudly. "At full force, you'd have annihilated all eight of them in seconds."

"Your damn straight I would've." She narrowed her eyes and pressed her lips into a tight smile. "And I intend to do just that as soon I feed more and get my strength back. Clan Lennox is as good as dead."

Grizella flashed off and returned with a blood bag. Annella smiled and sipped on it, crumbling it up and tossing it with the others on the ground.

"More?" Grizella asked.

"No. I think that's got me filled up again. I'm almost ready to bring the pain to Leith and Leeya."

"We'll handle Clan Lennox soon." Aiden placed a hand on her leg. "They'll be in the wind for a while, I'm sure, but when they surface, we'll take care of them. Let's just focus on getting you back to your old ass-kicking self for now."

"I still can't believe they got you down," Emilia said. "I haven't known you long, but all I've heard since I've met your family is that Annella is unstoppable."

"It was planned. An organized assault," Annella said. "They won't be so lucky next time."

Mark stood up, placing his hands on his head as he paced.

"What's wrong?" Emilia asked him.

He let out a lengthy sigh and turned to face everyone. "This is all my fault."

Lothaire furrowed his brow. "Why is this your fault?"

Mark chewed on his lip and looked down at the ground. "Do you remember the hot Scot I told you about? Gregor? The ginger I met that night?"

They all nodded.

"I saw him with Leith and Leeya. He was the third

vampire outside the building. He used me. It was all a setup to separate Annella and me. I'm so sorry, Annella. I'm so sorry." He dropped to her side, and tears glistened in his eyes as he took her hand. "Can you forgive me?"

"Mark," she said softly. "This is *not* your fault. This was a well-orchestrated plan, and you couldn't have known that Gregor was a plant. *I* had no idea either."

"I never should have split up with you," Mark said quietly. "This wouldn't have happened if I'd have just kept my damn pants on."

"Hey." She smiled. "I saw Gregor that night, and let's be honest, if he'd have swung my way, I'd have been the one ditching you to be with him."

Mark and Annella laughed quietly together.

"He was really hot," Mark said, finishing with an exaggerated pout.

"They didn't hold back when they sent in the decoy." Annella waggled her eyebrows, then slid a hand across Mark's cheek. "Don't blame yourself, okay? I go out by myself all the time. We're vampires, for fuck's sake… it's not like we need to travel in a pack for safety. This was one isolated incident. And I'm fine now. Gregor, on the other hand? He's mine this time… and he's not gonna have as much fun with me as he had with you."

"There's our Annella," Aiden said as he laughed.

"If you guys don't mind, I'm really tired. I think I'll head up to my room and get some sleep. The sun will be up soon."

"It's been a long night. We should all get to bed." Lothaire slid his arm around Grizella's shoulders. "We'll get some rest, and tomorrow we'll start asking around and trying to locate Leith and Leeya."

"Sleep well, everyone," Aiden said. "Emilia and I may skip poolside margaritas in lieu of sleep as well."

"I could use a nap," she agreed, then she stopped and looked at me. "Will you be okay out here alone if we sleep for a while?"

I nodded. "I think I'm going to go to bed myself."

"If you need anything, just knock on our door." Emilia pulled me in for a quick hug before all the vampires headed off to their rooms, leaving me and Thorne alone.

"So," he said as he glanced out the window. The dark sky had started to lighten into a deep shade of blue. "You sure you're okay alone today? I wish I could spend the day with you, but it wouldn't be real fun watching me incinerate into a pile of ash."

I laughed and rolled my eyes. "Probably best if you stay out of the sun."

"I'll be up as soon as it sets."

"I've been up all night, so I think I'll be sleeping like a vampire all day."

"I bet. You must be exhausted."

"I am," I sighed.

Thorne rubbed a hand behind his neck and glanced down at his feet. "So, now that we found Annella, does that mean that you go back tonight?"

The silence settled between us while I thought about my options. I didn't want to leave. I'd never had so much fun in my life. Every second I spent with Thorne made me question my destiny to rule my island, but each time his eyes started to seduce me into thinking of throwing it all away, I remembered my responsibility to my people.

My duties. My destiny.

"I should go back," I said, though the words lacked certainty.

After a long pause, Thorne exhaled a sigh. “Why rush? I know you need to go back, but maybe you could stick around for a few more days. You’re going to spend the rest of your life on that island, why not use this time to explore a little before you return?”

I wanted to say yes—more than anything, I wanted to say yes. But I knew the longer I stayed, the harder it would be to go back.

“My mother is probably worried,” I said as I looked out the window. “She’s also probably furious. The faster I get back, the less angry she’ll be. I hope.”

He nodded his head, but I saw the disappointment in his eyes. “I suppose.”

“I do wish I could stay, though,” I said. “I’m having a lot of fun with you.”

“Yeah?” A small smile lifted up those lips I wanted to taste. “I’m a good host? I mean, other than almost getting you killed by vampires, of course.”

Laughing, I shrugged. “Even though it sounds like I’ve only seen a sliver of the world, what you’ve shown me has been incredible. I’m just glad I got to experience it. Even if just for a day.”

“Me too.” He smiled for a moment, then it faded. “I understand you can’t stay. I’ll bring you back as soon as the sun goes down.”

I nodded, unable to find any other words that didn’t come out as *I want to stay*.

Thorne glanced at the window again. The sky had lightened even more. “Well, I guess then I should get to my room. If you decide to get up during the day, just stay in the castle for your safety. I don’t think Clan Lennox will come here, they’re stupid but not *that* stupid, but just to be on the safe side.”

"I won't go out alone. I promise."

"Good."

The awkward silence settled between us as we stood staring at each other.

"I guess this is goodnight," I finally said.

"Good day, actually," he joked.

"You're right. Good day."

Another stretch of silence passed between us.

"Just think about staying. Sleep on it. You've spent your whole life following a well-laid path, and I want you to really weigh your options today. Think it through. Choose what *you* want to do."

What *I* want to do? It was so hard for me to comprehend a world where I got to choose my fate, but I loved how much Thorne left me to make my own decisions.

"I'll think about it."

"Yeah?" he asked, smiling.

"Yeah. I've got a lot to think about."

We both looked out the window and saw the strip of orange sky starting on the horizon.

"That's my cue," he said, then started out of the room.

I watched him go, taking my time to appreciate his muscular body as he walked away. When he reached the bottom of the stairs, he stopped and pressed his hand onto the banister and paused.

"Fuck it," he said.

Before I could blink, he was back in front of me, his eyes boring into mine.

"If you're going to make a decision, then you need all the facts. And the fact is that I'm fucking crazy about you, Cat. Think about this when you're deciding."

He slid his hands along my face, and his lips crashed into mine. I gasped from the exquisite pleasure and pain of his passionate kiss. From the second our lips touched, my body was no longer my own to command. My desire for him took over, and I wrapped my arms around his neck and gave into the kiss I'd craved since the first time I'd seen him.

A kiss I needed more than I needed the air I could no longer breathe.

My primal need for him ripped through me as his tongue slid into my mouth. Emotions I never knew existed inside me unleashed as his rough hands cupped my face, and he deepened our kiss.

With a whoosh, he sent me backward, and my back slammed into the wall. His large body pressed into mine as he pinned me against it, his fingers sliding through my hair as he pulled my lips tighter to his.

I clung to his back as I struggled to stay upright from the power of his kiss. A kiss I never wanted to end. The feelings for him it awakened inside me were a force of nature I had no power or desire to control. With every touch of his lips against mine, my unquenchable desire for him grew inside me like a fire I could never put out.

His lips softened against mine, and I whimpered as he gently pulled them away. Heavy breaths lifted his wide back as he kept me pinned to the wall with his hypnotic stare.

"I hope this gives you a reason to stay," he whispered against my lips before he vanished from my arms.

Rays of sunlight crept into the room and warmed my skin as I stood alone, panting against the wall. I touched my swollen lips as I tried to process what had just happened.

I'd kissed a vampire.

And I'd never wanted anything more in my life than to do it again… and again… and again.

Chapter Nine

THORNE

I paced inside my room, waiting until I felt the sun set. Anxiety tore apart my insides while I wondered what decision Catrain had made.

Would she stay? Would she go? Desperation to know the answer stole my sanity.

After that kiss we'd shared last night, I couldn't imagine she'd be able to go.

It had been transcendent.

Over the centuries, I'd kissed my fair share of women, but what I'd felt this morning when her lips touched mine eradicated every woman who'd come before her. Nothing I'd experienced in my immortal life had come close to what I felt when we kissed. It awakened something inside me I didn't even know had been asleep. She'd lit a light inside of me burning so bright it illuminated every dark crevice of my soul, erasing all the insecurities I had about my capabilities of loving a woman.

And now that it had woken, I knew I'd never get it to rest again.

My already powerful feelings for Catrain had amplified to unimaginable depths when I'd seen the desire reflected in her eyes. Felt her hands clawing at my back. Tasted the passion on her tongue. When she matched my lust with her own, it was like a dam broke open and transformed the sleepy lake behind it into a raging, powerful river.

A dam I'd never be able to repair.

Or want to.

I felt the sun go down, so I shot out of my room searching for Catrain, desperate to hear her say, "I'm staying" and terrified to hear her say, "I have to go" instead.

But one way or another, I needed to know. No matter what, my world would change tonight. I'd either have a chance at having an amazing woman at my side, or I'd be spending an eternity pining for the woman I could never have.

After a quick listen, I heard movement in Catrain's room. I rushed up the stairs and stopped at her door, pausing to take a deep breath before I knocked.

"Come in," she answered.

I pushed open the door with a warm grin, but my smile dropped when I saw her back in her tribal clothes.

"Oh," I said quietly. "I guess this means you're leaving."

It felt like chewing on glass having the words *you're leaving* pass through my mouth. Even though I'd entertained the idea she may go, deep down, I didn't believe she would. Not after what I'd felt in her kiss this morning.

But the look in her eyes confirmed my worst fears without her having to utter a single syllable.

"I understand," I said, even though I didn't.

She stepped toward me, then stopped. "It's not that I want to go back."

I nodded but glanced away. It hurt too much to look at her.

"I wanted to help you find Annella… to see your world, but my place is on my island with my people. They need me."

"I'll take you back whenever you're ready." I turned out of the room.

"Thorne," she said, and I stopped. "If it was up to me, I would stay. I just want you to know that."

I paused in the doorway and gave a quick nod, but I couldn't look back. "I'll see you downstairs."

Defeat shoved my shoulders down as I walked down the stairs. Aiden passed by on his way to the kitchen as I came down, and my oldest friend stopped and backed up when he saw me coming.

"You okay?" he asked as he furrowed his brow.

"Not in the slightest."

The lines on his forehead deepened as I walked toward him.

"She's leaving. Now," I said on a sigh.

"Damn. I'm sorry to hear that." He pressed a hand onto my shoulder and squeezed. "I thought for sure you'd charm her into staying."

"You and me both, brother. You and me both."

I wasn't in the mood to talk, and Aiden could tell. He stepped aside while I made my way to the living room to wait for Catrain to come down.

The next ten minutes I sat slumped on the couch felt like an eternity. All I wanted was for her to stay, but now that I knew that she was leaving, I wanted to get it over with as quickly as possible. The longer I had to sit here and picture saying goodbye, the more the ache in my heart grew to unbearable pressure.

I heard her footsteps coming down the stairs, so I blew out a big breath and tried to force the look of despair from my face. If this was the last night she would see me, to hell if I was going to leave her with the memory of a love-sick wounded man.

"You ready?" I plastered a fake smile on my face.

Catrain looked around the room and nodded.

"Everyone," I called loudly, knowing they would hear me no matter where they were in the castle. "Catrain is leaving if you want to say goodbye."

Within seconds they all appeared, and one by one, they hugged her and said their goodbyes. Annella gave her the biggest hug, thanking her for saving her life.

"You're welcome. I was happy to help. You have a wonderful family who loves you."

"Don't I know it," Annella said as she released Catrain from their hug. "And we're a lot of fun. I wish you would stay and spend some more time with us."

"I wish I could too." Catrain pressed her lips into a tight smile.

They waved goodbye from the entryway as I led Catrain out to the garage. We walked quietly to the doorway, and I punched in the code.

"Are we taking the fast car again?" she asked.

Laughing, I shook my head. "We're going cross-country, and the Bugatti isn't made for off-roading. Plus, I've still got to return the dirt bike. I don't want you to kill me for stealing," I joked. "We'll just ride it back, and I'll drop it off on my way home. Sound okay?"

Her eyes lit up. "I love the dirt bike."

"Then dirt bike it is."

We walked over to the little blue bike, and I kicked the footstand up and rolled it out of the garage. After I climbed on, I gestured for Catrain to do the same. When she slid on behind me and her body pressed against mine, I had to choke down my outward groan. It'd been torture having her wrapped around me the first time we'd ridden this bike, but at least that ride had been filled with excitement and anticipation. This ride would be filled with nothing but dread and despair.

Her arms tightened around my waist, and I closed my eyes for a beat as I exhaled a long stilling breath. I twisted the handle and sent the dirt bike surging forward. We skidded out along the driveway, and I steered it into the fields surrounding our estate, picking up speed as we hit an open stretch and headed toward her island. When we reached the turn I'd usually make to take her home, I glanced to my left and slowed the bike down to a stop.

"I'm taking a little detour," I called back over my shoulder.

"What's a detour?"

"It means we're making a stop before I take you home."

"A stop where?"

I smiled. "You'll see."

Before she could answer, I shot the bike forward and turned west. We bumped along the countryside as I guided the bike over the rolling hills separating us from our destination. Catrain held on tight around me, and for a moment, I questioned my decision to extend our journey… and my torment. But there was something I wanted her to see before she resigned her life to the island and her people.

I gave the bike a little extra gas to get up the long sloping hill I'd galloped my horse up hundreds of times centuries ago. When we reached the top, I slid to a stop and killed the engine.

"We're here." I swung my leg over the front of the bike

and hopped off. Our eyes connected for the first time since we'd left the estate, and my heart squeezed in my chest that this would be one of the last times I'd look into them. Ignoring the pain searing through my soul, I held out my hand and braced for the agony of her touch. "Come on."

Chapter Ten

CATRAIN

I took his hand, and it was all I could do not to fall back into his arms and annihilate him with a kiss like the one he'd given me last night.

The one I'd spent all day thinking about. Over and over and over again.

Instead, I shoved my urges aside and let him guide me off the bike. We walked side by side until we reached the edge. When I looked out, my mouth slackened as I stared out over the endless moonlit water.

"This is the ocean." He stepped to my side. "I wanted you to see it once."

"It's… it's incredible," I breathed. It was the most amazing thing I'd ever seen. I'd thought my lake was beautiful, but this ocean took my breath away. I peeked over the edge and watched the giant waves crashing against the wall below.

"It goes on so much farther than your eyes can see. It's endless."

"I can't believe such a thing exists."

Thorne sat down and kicked off his shoes, so I lowered myself beside him, pulling my knees up to my chest. We sat silently, listening to the crash of the waves against the rocks down below and watching the ripples of moonlight flickering across the surface of the water.

"We used to come here as kids." He plucked at the blades of grass.

It was almost impossible for me to picture such a powerful man as a small child. I imagined him with his big blue eyes filled with mirth, a mop of shaggy brown hair, and a smile that never left his face.

"We'd dare each other to jump, but of course none of us did because as a human, the drop would have been fatal."

"It's a long way down." I peered over the edge again.

"When we turned immortal, one of the first things we did was launch ourselves off this cliff. It was incredible to free fall into the water below."

"I can't imagine how that would feel. Like flying, I suppose."

"It did feel kind of like flying. It was much more fun the second time, though. The first time, we knew we were immortal, but it was new. So we weren't sure *how* immortal yet. There was still a moment of terror on the way down that we'd all just jumped to our deaths. But when we all popped up in the water unscathed, you'd never seen bigger smiles on anyone's faces. We raced back to the top and leaped off again and again."

"So, you've all been together since the beginning?"

"Yes. They've been my family for over six hundred years. Well, they aren't my family by blood, but we're closer than most families who are."

"And you were the first vampires?"

He nodded and picked up a stone, then tossed it over the edge. "Yeah. We were the first."

"So, what happened?" I picked up a stone and did the same, watching for a few seconds before I saw it plunk into the churning water below. "I've always heard that you were granted the gift to protect my people, and you betrayed us and refused that protection, then found a way to keep your immortality. That's why you've been cursed to stay out of the sun. Now that I've met our family, I'm having a hard time imagining you betraying us. Why did you?"

He exhaled a long sigh and tossed another rock off the edge. "We didn't betray you. Things didn't exactly turn out as planned. Your leader at the time, the one who offered immortality, speed, strength, and all the perks of being an immortal in exchange for our protection of your tribe, didn't tell us that only *some* of us would survive the transformation. More than half of our clan died, including my own father as well as Aiden, Annella, and Lothaire's mother, father, and brother... who were also like family to me."

"Oh, Thorne. I had no idea." I spun to look at him and saw the sadness flooding his eyes. "That must have been awful."

"It was a nightmare." He blew out a puff of air. "Only some of us awoke, and when we realized half our clan was dead, including our Chieftain's beloved wife, you can imagine the fury we felt toward your tribe."

I didn't answer, instead, looking back out over the ocean. How could I? There were no words I could use to justify that tragedy. My people had destroyed his clan... something I'd never known. No wonder they refused to help us after. In fact, if it had happened to us, I'd have slaughtered every last person responsible.

"Honestly, there'd been talk of eradicating all of your

tribe with our powers as punishment for the deceit. But cooler heads prevailed, and instead of killing your tribe, we'd refused our protection. Even though we felt this was a kindness, your leader at the time considered it a betrayal and argued he'd never promised some of us wouldn't die."

"This is not at all how I heard the story," I admitted. "It seems they left some of it out… like that half of your clan died. I'm so sorry, Thorne. I can't imagine what you all went through."

"We all lost people we loved. But we moved on, we had to, and even though your leader tried to remove the gift, we found a way around that by consuming human blood. It allows us to utilize their life force of sorts. So, he cursed us with the sun instead. Your people fled, and we never knew where you went. In fact, we thought all this time the Picts eventually went extinct."

"We've been on that island for centuries. And I'm sure we'll be there for centuries more."

"Centuries hating vampires… the very ones that got betrayed." He arched an eyebrow.

I gave him a sheepish look. "When I return, I swear that I will tell them the whole story. I'll tell them you aren't the monsters we've been led to believe."

"Well, not *all* of us, at least. Just like any people, there are good and bad of both."

"Yes. This is true."

"You think once you set your mom straight, she'll let me come visit?"

With a snort, I shook my head. "Not likely. Her hatred for your kind runs deep."

"Her *misguided* hatred," I argued.

"Misguided or not, my mother doesn't change her mind. About *anything.*"

He clucked his cheek. "So, that's a hard no to me visiting the island?"

"I think I can safely say it is."

"So, back to the lonely island for you. I can't imagine living on an island day in and day out. It must get so boring."

I shrugged it off, but inside I felt the searing pain of my reality. "It's all I've known."

"Until now." He waved a hand over the views that stretched out before us. "Now you've seen a tiny part of the world. Think you can go back to your island and still be satisfied?"

After a long moment of silence, I shook my head. "It's not about me being satisfied… or happy. It's about my destiny and commitment to my people."

"God," he said, exasperated. "I get that you want to fulfill your duty or whatever, but Christ, Cat… enough of the martyr 'for the good of my people' shit. This is *your* life. *Your* choice."

"And I've made it!" I shouted back. "I've made my choice, and it's to return."

"No. You've made your *mother's* choice. *Your* choice would be here to stay longer. I know it would. For being such a badass, you sure do have a problem standing up for yourself."

My eyes saucered as my blood heated to boiling. "Just because I'm going back does not make me weak. In fact, it makes me *strong*. I'm strong enough to deny myself everything I want for the good of others. I'm sorry that you see that as a weakness."

He let out a heavy sigh. "I didn't mean that. I know you're strong. I know why you're doing what you're doing, but I don't have to fucking like it."

"No, you don't. It doesn't affect you."

His eyebrows shot to his hairline, and he snorted. "Doesn't affect me? Wow. Guess that answers that."

I knew instantly what he was talking about and immediately regretted my choice of words. "That's not what I meant."

Thorne just shook his head. "Apparently, that kiss this morning meant more to me than it did to you. I thought we had something between us… something rare, special. But the fact you don't think your decision to return affects me means that what I'm feeling is one-sided. Message received. I'll get you back to your island. You can get on with your life, and I'll get on with mine."

"It did," I whispered. "It did mean something to me, but it can't. *We* can't."

"Why?" He turned toward me, and his gaze drifted to my lips. "So what if I'm a fucking vampire and you're a Pict. Just because I've been your enemy for centuries, doesn't mean it has to stay that way. We can figure something out."

I swallowed hard as I shook my head. "I can't be with you."

"Give me one good reason why."

With a long exhale, I dropped my eyes to the ground. "Because I'm betrothed to another."

"What?" he choked out the word.

"Uradech, the warrior you saw on the beach. I've been betrothed to him since I was born. It's a pact in our tribe and a commitment I cannot deny. It's tradition and my duty to marry him before I take my position as the leader of our tribe."

He pushed off the ground and stood, and I reached for him. "Thorne. Wait."

Instead of stopping to talk to me, he just strode off toward the dirt bike. I jumped up and trotted after him, grabbing him by his muscular bicep and tugging him to a stop. "Please stop and talk to me."

"Why?" He spun around, and those intense eyes bore into mine. "You've made it pretty fucking clear that I'm not a factor in your decision. And you know what? I would be less pissed about it if it was *your* decision. But it's not. You're gonna marry that fucking oaf of a dude and take over for your mother, and no matter what I say, nothing is gonna change that. So, why bother talking about it anymore? I think it's bullshit that you're not even allowing yourself to consider another possibility… a possibility that includes me."

He stepped closer and leaned down until I could feel his breath on my face. I swallowed hard as I glanced at his lips.

"If you tell me right now that what *you* want is to go back to your island, marry that fucking oaf, and lead your people, then I'll throw you on the back of that bike and bring you home right now and not say another word."

He leaned closer.

"But if you think you could, even for one *second,* think about making the choice *you* want, then stay here and think about it. Don't rush back. Think about a life where I'm in it."

His face drifted even closer to mine. My lips parted in desire as I remembered the feelings he'd awakened inside me with his kiss.

"Tell me you don't want me. Say it, and I'll get out of your life for good."

His lips ghosted mine, and I closed my eyes while I struggled to dig deep inside for the resolve to do what I must.

Tell him no.

"For the first time in your life, do what you want to do." His lips almost brushed mine.

"Tell me, Cat. Do you want me or not?"

The breeze barely fit between our lips as he moved them even closer to mine. I inhaled his breath as I searched for the strength to tell him no and turn away. But instead, I leaned forward and pressed my lips against his, moaning into his mouth as I threw my arms around his neck.

With one powerful pull, he yanked me against his body, leaning me back with the force of his passion. His strong hand slid across my face, sliding into my hair and pulling me deeper into his kiss.

A kiss I never wanted to end.

Desire obliterated my senses as I slid my hands underneath his shirt, letting my fingers free to trace the chiseled abs I'd been so desperate to touch. Thorne moaned when my fingers worked their way across all the rock-hard planes of his body and up to the bulging muscles of his chest.

The world around me spun for a moment, and I wasn't sure if it was really happening or just the result of every last one of my senses exploding from the way my body felt beneath his touch. But when I felt the cool grass underneath me, I realized he'd lay me down with his remarkable speed. Our lips broke apart, and as he hovered over me, I panted for breath as I looked up into his eyes.

"Is this what you want?" he asked with an intensity in his eyes that rattled me down to my core. "Am *I* what you want?"

My head nodded even though I hadn't made the choice to answer yet. My mind may have known that he could never be mine, but my heart and my body wanted to claim him as my own and never let him go.

"Yes. I want you. Please," I heard myself begging.

Those blue eyes lit up with lust and desire, then he lowered himself back to my lips. His soft, sensual kiss brushed across them before he slid his tongue along my swollen lips. A strong hand moved to my hips and slid along my body, grazing up the heated skin of my torso. Inch by inch, he moved up my body to the breasts that rose and fell with my quickened breaths.

His full lips drifted from mine, and I whimpered as they moved to my neck. Gentle kisses peppered my skin as he worked toward the hand now sliding beneath my leather top. When his fingers brushed across my hard nipple, I bit my lip to muffle my cries. It tightened even more as he worked it between his fingers before moving his hand to the leather strings keeping it closed. With speed I couldn't process, he unraveled the ties securing my top. It fell open, and the cool breeze brushed over my exposed skin.

Thorne sat back and stared down at my body. Everywhere his eyes roved seem to ignite from the heat of his gaze. Desperate to see what lay beneath his clothes, I lifted my hand and whispered beneath my breath. The soft breeze blew harder as inch by inch, his shirt crept up his body as I guided it with the power of my magic.

Thorne looked confused as he glanced down at his rising shirt, then smiled when he figured out what I was doing and lifted his arms. With the flick of my wrist, it moved the rest of the way up his body and dropped on the grass beside him.

"Awesome." He chuckled as he glanced at the crumpled blue shirt, but I was too busy staring at his perfect physique to take notice of it.

Every inch of his body swelled with muscles, and deep lines formed the chiseled abs I'd felt with my touch. His chest muscles bulged in all the right places, and they flexed as he lowered himself back down to me.

"I need you, Cat," he whispered into my ear before his lips brushed against it.

My skin ignited when his lips touched my neck, his descending kisses leaving burning trails as he made his way to my breasts. I moaned as he took one in his mouth while his fingers drifted up my thighs below the leather loincloth separating us. When he slid them along my wet, heated skin, I bit my lip and stifled my cry.

"No one can hear you out here," he whispered.

I released my lip and cried out loud as he slid his fingers into me. They worked inside my body in time with his lips on my hardened nipple. My body started trembling, and I felt the magic swirling and intensifying inside me. Sparks flickered across my skin, and Thorne slowed down his movements while he watched them crackle across my body.

"Do I need to be worried you're going to incinerate me?" he asked as he kept rubbing me where I needed him most.

"I don't think so," I panted, but in reality, I didn't know. This was my first time with a man, and I'd never had such a powerful, uncontrollable reaction with my powers. "But I'm not controlling them right now."

Thorne skimmed his finger across the bundle of nerves between my legs that screamed for release.

"Fuck it. I'll take my chances."

When his fingers drove back inside me, I pressed my head back into the grass and screamed his name. I quaked and quivered with the power of my release, and the magic inside me coursed through my body, exploding into a blue light that illuminated my skin and filled the surrounding darkness.

As I tried to catch my breath and find my senses, I looked to make sure Thorne was all right, and I hadn't accidentally harmed him. When his mischievous smile met my worried gaze, I exhaled a breath. "Thank the Goddess. You're okay. I don't know what happened."

Thorne let out a proud chuckle. "What happened was fucking incredible. Your orgasm literally exploded. Like, *literally.*" He laughed. "Does that normally happen?"

A soft blush crept along my cheeks as I shook my head. "I don't know. I've never had one."

His eyes widened. "Never?"

"No. We save ourselves for our wedding night."

A worried look crossed his face. "Shit. I'm sorry. I didn't realize—"

I stopped him with a hand and shook my head. "Don't be sorry. I wanted this. I don't care about saving myself… I want you. *All* of you."

He saw the meaning in my eyes as I coaxed him back to me with a hand behind his neck. When his lips collided with mine again, I released all the duties and expectations that had been held over me my entire life. For just this one night, I wanted to do exactly what I wanted with my life.

And I wanted Thorne.

All of him.

I worked along the fastenings of his pants and pushed them down over his hips. When I glanced down and saw his naked body between my legs, my heart rattled faster against my ribs.

"Are you sure?" he asked between kisses. "We don't have to do this."

"I'm sure," I whispered against his lips.

With a quick movement, he pulled something from his pants pocket and slid it over his rock-hard cock. Another quick movement shoved his pants all the way off, and he lowered himself between my legs. I felt him press against my entrance as he held my stare. With a long, slow push, he slid himself inside, and I gasped as he moved past the resistance.

Thorne held still as I adjusted to the unfamiliar sensation. I'd never felt more connected to anyone in my life as he started moving inside me. Pleasure replaced the fleeting pain, and it got my magic churning inside me once again.

His lips found mine as he pushed deeper inside, and I gasped from the pleasure I'd never imagined. Our sweaty bodies connected as I wrapped my arms around him and held onto him tight. The magic inside started swirling beneath the surface as I rode the wave. The sparks traveled through my skin and onto his, and he quickened his pace while I clung to his muscular back.

I screamed his name again as I reached the heights he'd taken me to before, and I felt his body stiffen and tighten as the blue light enveloped us. When the glow around us faded into dark, Thorne collapsed against my body.

"Holy shit," he mumbled against my skin. "That was incredible."

"It was," I whispered back, still buzzing from the feelings he'd created in me. "It was so much better than I'd expected."

I'd been told what to expect for my duties as a wife and to conceive an heir, but they'd made it sound like a chore and something to be endured.

This was anything but a chore or something to be endured. What I'd experienced with Thorne had been bliss like nothing I'd ever imagined.

And I wanted to feel it again, and again, and again.

"Are you sure you're okay?" he asked as he pressed

himself off me and collapsed onto his back. A strong arm slid around my shoulders, and he pulled me up against his muscular chest.

"I'm better than okay," I answered as I stretched my naked body along the length of him.

He pressed a kiss to my forehead and enveloped me in his arms. "I've never experienced anything like that in my life."

"Me neither."

"Now I'm definitely not letting you go back. Sorry. You're trapped here." He laughed.

The reality of my situation settled into my stomach like a punch to the gut, and now I wondered how I'd ever be able to go back… to leave him.

"Thorne—" I started, but he stopped me.

"Not yet. Let's not talk about it yet. Just lay here with me for a while and let me enjoy this time with you."

"Okay," I said and laid my head against his chest. He stroked my hair as I tried to enjoy being in the moment with him… tried to push aside the words I still needed to say.

I still have to go.

Chapter Eleven

THORNE

It wasn't just the crazy light show that had made sex with Catrain so incredible, although that had been beyond amazing to see her body glowing blue with her passion. It was that I'd never connected with another human the way I'd connected with her. I'd thought our kiss had been transcendent, but that was nothing compared to what it felt like to be inside her body.

Inside her soul.

I finally understood what Aiden and Lothaire felt for Emilia and Grizella. Finally grasped the depths that a man could love a woman… and love her I did. Though I had only known her a short time, there was no doubt in my mind that the feelings pumping through my heart and my body were love.

True, primal, irrevocable love.

As she lay there on the side of the cliff in my arms for an hour, I tried to quiet the voice in my head wondering if what had happened would change her mind. Wondering if it still meant I'd be saying my goodbyes and sending her into the arms of another man before the sun rose. But instead of asking, I just held her tighter and tried to enjoy the moments she belonged to me.

The waves crashing along the rocks below were a soft melody blended with the breeze wafting over our naked skin. I felt her shudder, and I closed my arms around her tighter before realizing it may be me making her cold. My skin didn't radiate warmth like the heat coming from hers.

"Are you cold?" I asked as I pushed a piece of hair from her face.

"A little," she answered back, and I felt another shudder.

"I'm sorry. I forget my skin is cool to you. Hold on." I flashed to my discarded clothing, dressed and flashed back, handing Catrain her clothes. "Here. Yours won't do much to keep you warm, but my clothes should shield you from the coolness of my skin."

I watched her naked body disappear beneath the leather pieces and groaned when the last of the ties had been fastened. After she dressed, she rubbed her arms across her bare skin.

"I guess the fact I make you cold with my touch can go into the cons list for reasons you should go, huh?" I joked.

"I don't mind. It's just cold up here with the breeze coming off the water."

"Hold on. I have an idea." After flashing away, I reappeared holding an armful of kindling. I stacked it into a pyramid at her side, then gave it a nod. "Do your thing."

With the flick of her wrist, she produced fire in her hand and lit up the sticks. The flames grew quickly, and she rubbed her hands over them.

"Better?" I asked.

"Much. Thank you."

I sat down and pulled her down between my legs. She

settled back against my chest, and I wrapped her in my arms and rested my chin on the top of her head.

"Do you get cold?" She peeked up over her shoulder.

I shook my head. "No. Granted, I haven't headed to Antarctica and stood naked in their seventy below temps, but generally not. I don't get too hot or too cold."

"Another perk of immortality," she said as she settled back against me.

"Yeah, I suppose it is. Now, if we could just get rid of the pesky curse of the sun, then I could really get down to enjoying my eternal life."

"Do you miss it?"

"The sun?"

"Yeah. Have you really not seen it in over six hundred years?"

With a lengthy sigh, I nodded my head. "Yep. The day we got the curse was the last time I saw it. Honestly, I don't remember anymore what it feels like to have the sun shining on me."

"Would you want to?"

I furrowed my brow. "Have the sun on me? Yeah. Definitely."

Catrain pulled out of my arms and spun around to face me. "I can do that, you know."

My eyes widened. "You can lift the curse? Are you serious?"

"Well, not quite. I don't have my mother's powers yet. If I did, I could lift your curse. But for now, I can enchant your ring to combat the sunlight curse."

She pointed to the family heirloom I'd worn for six hundred years. It was a pewter band engraved with my clan symbols surrounding a polished rock sitting prominently in the center. It had been my father's and passed down through the generations. When he died during our transition, it became mine. I'd worn it every day since.

"My magic isn't strong enough to make it permanent, but I could give you roughly a week of protection from a curse... including the one that keeps you out of the sun."

My heart sped up in my chest. "Are you serious? You can make me sun-proof for a week?"

She smiled and nodded. "Yes. And when I take over for my mother, I can remove the curse on you and your family for good. Make you all able to live forever in the sun. It's the least I can do after what happened to your clan."

My mouth fell open as I tried to process the information she'd just given me. Having the curse removed was a dream for all of us, but then I realized the price it would come with.

"But that means you're going back," I said with a swallow.

Catrain pursed her lips into a thin line as she sighed. "I have to."

It wasn't surprising news, but it gutted me none-the-less. Instead of letting my anger and sadness overwhelm me again, I just nodded.

Her small hand wrapped around mine. "This isn't what I want, I hope you know that. But it's what I have to do. You would sacrifice for your family, wouldn't you?"

I lifted my eyebrows as I sighed. "I'd give anything for them. My happiness, my life… anything."

"Then you understand. It's the same for me. But I want you to know that when I take my mother's place, I'll remove the curse on your family. You suffered greatly with what your clan endured, and it wasn't fair to curse you for not holding up your end of the bargain. But only your family…

I wouldn't dare lift it on all vampires after what I saw in the city."

I was as elated to hear I'd be able to walk in the sun as I was devastated that it meant it was because Catrain had to return to her people. But instead of pressuring her and begging like I wanted to, I just smiled.

"It would be an incredible gift, Cat. Thank you."

"For now, give me your ring." She opened her hand.

I slid it off my finger and placed it in her palm. She encased it in her fist and closed her eyes, then began chanting. When she finished, she slowly peeled open her fingers, and the gray stone had turned a deep shade of blue.

"When the color wears off, so will the spell that protects you."

"So, you're saying as long as this ring is blue and I'm wearing it, I can be in the sun?"

She nodded.

Laughing, I arched a brow. "You sure? Because if you're wrong, I'll light up like a candle."

She smiled. "I'm sure. Just don't go in the sun if the color fades."

"And I get about a week?"

She nodded again.

"Then stay." I reached out and took her hands in mine. "Stay for one week. We'll see the world in the light and experience it together. When the color starts to fade, I'll bring you back and deliver you to your island as promised."

She chewed on her lip as she looked everywhere but my eyes.

"One week, Cat. You owe it to yourself to experience the world with me just a little."

Her gaze finally lifted to meet mine. "Okay," she said quietly.

My eyebrows shot to my hairline. "Okay? Seriously? You'll stay?"

Her shy smile grew. "One week, and *only* one week. Then I need to go back."

"I'll take any amount of time with you I can. A week is better than the hour it's going to be when the sun comes up and I'm supposed to have you back already."

"One week." She lifted a finger. "I can't be gone any longer."

"One week," I repeated, then leaned forward and scooped her into my arms. With a soft kiss, I sealed our deal.

I loved how her body responded to my kisses, and how she leaned into my touch. I knew it would be torture saying goodbye, and an eternity of hell living without her, but I would try to forget the pain I'd be in next week and just enjoy every second of her touch, her kiss, and her laughter.

I pulled her into my lap and took her again on the cliff, our bodies connecting, again and again, ending in those explosive blue lights she emitted at the height of her pleasure. When we were done, I pulled her back in my lap and watched the sky lightening as the sun started its ascent for the day.

"You sure I'm not going to go up in flames?"

"I'm sure," she said, then twisted her lips. "And just in case, you can dive off the cliff and hide in the water, right?"

Laughing hard, I nodded. "I suppose I can. On the off chance I go up like dry timber, just push me over the edge and wait here until the sun sets. I can't die, so I'll hold my breath and spend the day sitting at the bottom of the ocean, cursing your faulty magic."

Her laugh matched mine as we sat together and watched the orange glow of the sky growing brighter by the minute. I couldn't remember a time I'd felt as nervous as I did awaiting the arrival of the sun I hadn't seen in centuries.

As the sky lightened even more, Catrain squeezed my hand and rested her head on my shoulder. "Now it's my turn to show you something new."

When the first sliver appeared on the horizon, I held my breath and awaited the searing pain that would follow. But the pain never came, and I struggled to exhale when I saw the sun lift from the water and illuminate the darkness around me. It felt like it'd been asleep for centuries and finally awakened after a long slumber.

The beauty of the world in the light stole my breath away. The rich colors of the green grass and the flowers surrounding us looked so different than the darkened hues I'd become accustomed to. The sky, no longer black and speckled with stars, glowed with soft blues that got richer by the second. As the sun continued lifting, the first warm rays stretched across the land, and when they touched my skin, I opened my hand and felt their warmth for the first time in centuries.

"Incredible," I whispered as I stared at the soft glow on my skin. "I'd forgotten how amazing the sun felt."

"I'm so glad I could do this for you."

"So am I. And I'm glad I'm not sitting on my arse at the bottom of the ocean."

Catrain tossed back her head in laughter, and I joined her.

"Me too," she finally said between laughs. "I'd have hated to see your face after twelve hours of sitting under the waves."

"When I came out, I'd have looked like a prune." I laughed harder, but as she furrowed her brow, I realized she'd never seen one. "Never mind. An analogy for another time."

I pulled her in for a kiss and then pressed my forehead against hers. "Thank you for this."

"Thank you for showing me your world."

We broke apart, and I sat back. Now that the sun had risen more, I saw the highlights in her hair catching the rays, and the way her blue eyes sparkled in the light. I'd thought it impossible she could be even more beautiful, but in the sunlight, she looked like the Goddesses she worshiped.

"So, one week, huh?" I asked as I rubbed my stubble.

"One week. What are we going to do?"

I waggled my eyebrows and watched the pink flush creep across her cheeks.

"*Besides* that." She laughed.

"Well, I hadn't gotten that far. But I have one idea to get us started."

"Oh yeah? What's that?"

I glanced over to the dirt bike. "Now that it's light out and we've got time, what do you say I teach you how to drive it?"

Her eyes lit up as she nodded quickly. "Yes!"

After giving her a quick kiss on the nose, I stood up and held out my hand. "Try not to kill me."

"You're immortal. Don't let me kill myself." She arched an eyebrow.

"Valid. And I won't. I'd never let anything happen to you." I slid an arm around her shoulder and guided her over to the bike.

After a tutorial on how to turn it on, stop, go, and balance, I climbed on the bike behind her. She felt so small as I leaned forward and wrapped my arms around her to grab ahold of the handles.

"You ready?" I asked, and I could feel the excitement radiating off her.

"Ready."

"Put your hands on mine, and we'll do it together. Once you have the hang of it, I'll sit back and enjoy the ride."

The dirt bike chugged when I started it up. Catrain and I squeezed the handle together, and she squealed when it started forward, wobbling back and forth. I laughed as I put my feet on the ground and ran along to steady us, but soon she found her balance, and I lifted my feet and rested them on the pegs. After another minute, I slid my hands off the handles and gave her full control.

"You're doing it!" I shouted as we picked up speed. Her blonde hair drifted behind her, and it smelled so good I didn't even mind it smacking me in the face.

"I am!" She laughed louder and gave the bike more gas.

Of course, my fearless Catrain would opt for breakneck speeds her first time driving a dirt bike… or anything, for that matter. But I knew I would have plenty of time to save her if her trial run ended up with a crash, so I let her go faster and faster until we hit top speed racing across the countryside.

As we drove along, this time, it was me being mesmerized by the sights around me.

Beautiful.

I'd forgotten how gorgeous the countryside looked in the daylight. Everything seemed to sparkle in the sunlight, and now that I'd gotten a taste for it again, I couldn't imagine going back into the dark. The vibrant colors were as seductive as the woman driving me past them.

When we arrived unscathed back at the estate, I had to

reach forward to help Catrain remember how to stop before we collided with the garage. The dirt bike skidded to a stop, and I hopped off and helped her to her feet.

"You kicked ass, Evel Knievel!"

"That was incredible! I felt so powerful being in control!"

"You are powerful," I said as I pulled her into my arms. "You're powerful enough to control this vampire, and there isn't another person on the planet that can say that."

Her eyes sparkled with that seductive twinkle that nearly took me to my knees.

My hearing picked up on laughter by the pool, and I knew, as always, Aiden and Emilia were already out there enjoying the sun. With a smirk, I waggled my eyebrows and took Catrain by the hand. "Come on. Let's go say hi to Aiden and Emilia."

We walked hand in hand across the estate to the back of the castle where the pool sat in the gardens. Grinning widely, I approached Emilia and Aiden's lounge chairs. Their slack jaws mirrored one another as they slid their sunglasses down in unison.

"What the fuck?" Aiden said as he stared at me.

"Thorne! You're in the sun!" Emilia gasped.

I tugged Catrain against my side. "Got room for two more? And maybe some of that sunscreen humans are always going on about? I may not turn into ash in the sun now, but it's been centuries since my skin has seen the sun. I don't want to burn."

They looked at each other and burst into laughter.

Aiden blew out a breath. "I have no idea how you're doing this, but welcome back to the light, brother."

I pulled up a lounge chair, yanked off my shirt, and

pulled Catrain down into my arms. I held her against me as I let the warm rays drench my skin.

Chapter Twelve

CATRAIN

I lay naked in the bed, still panting from the things Thorne had just done to my body. Pleasures like I'd never imagined coursed through me with every touch. Maybe it was the strong, inexplicable connection we shared, or maybe it was that he was a vampire and that made him an incredible lover, but what I'd been told would happen when a man and a woman got together was nothing compared to what happened when I was with Thorne.

"You are so beautiful." He kissed his way back up my body, collapsed beside me, then pulled me against him.

With a sigh, I pressed my head into his chest and slung my arm over his toned stomach. I fit perfectly under his arm like he'd been made just for me, and me just for him.

The sun had just set, and Thorne and I had spent the entire day walking around the estate in the sun and sneaking back to his room hour after hour for more of the touching and kissing I couldn't seem to get enough of. Each time we made love, it seemed our connection deepened, and each time it became harder to accept that things with him were only temporary. Next week I'd have to pull myself from his side and force myself back to my island for a life he could never be part of. But I tried not to think about that and instead relished every second we got to spend together.

"Well, shit," he mumbled against my hair. "The sun went down. I wasn't ready to stop enjoying it for the day."

"It will rise again tomorrow, and we'll spend all day outside by the pool again."

Thorne let out a sigh and hugged me tighter. "As much as I would love nothing more than to spend the day at the pool with you, Aiden, and Emilia, I promised you I'd show you more of the world while you're here. And there is a lot more to this world than just our estate."

"I'm happy here." I shrugged and kissed his chest. "I'm happy right where I am."

"Well, I think we could be equally happy *and* show you some wonders of the world. I think we need to go on a vacation."

"A vacation? What's that?"

"A vacation is a getaway from your regular life. We can go somewhere warm and sunny so I can soak up the rays while I can, and somewhere unlike anything you could have imagined. Maybe something tropical. There's nothing like the Caribbean in Scotland."

"I don't even know what that means." I laughed.

"Which is exactly why we need to go somewhere so you can see it. Get dressed."

He kissed my head and whooshed out of bed, dressing faster than I could process.

When he stood fully clothed at the foot of the bed, I furrowed my brow. "Slower next time. I want to soak in every inch of that body while I can."

His deep, infectious laughter flooded the room, and he

lifted the bottom of his shirt, giving me a peek of those incredible abs. "Better?"

"Much." I grinned, then got up and pulled on the comfortable soft dress Emilia had lent me after we'd left the pool.

"Come on. The rest of my family should be up by now, and we need to tell them the news of the sunlight curse. Then you and I are leaving on vacation."

He took my hand and tugged me down the hall behind him, his excitement palpable as he called for his family to meet us in the living room. They all arrived in seconds, taking their places in the chairs I'd noticed they had seemed to claim as their own.

"Catrain! You're still here!" Annella smiled. "I thought you went back last night."

"That was the plan." I looked at Thorne to finish the rest.

"Last night, I went to take Catrain back to her island where she'll ascend at the end of the year to take her mother's place… and powers. Since she'll be spending the rest of her life there, I convinced her to stay with me for one week and let me show her some of our world."

"Very cool!" Mark grinned. "You're gonna love it."

"And there's more," Thorne said with his growing smile. "Catrain already has some pretty cool magic." He looked at me with a glint in his eye, and I knew he was referring to the way I seemed to glow with every orgasm. "She won't get full strength to remove our curse until she takes over for her mother, but after Catrain heard what really happened to our clan, she has agreed to lift the sunlight curse from us as soon as she takes power."

Their eyes widened one by one as they glanced between each other.

"Are you saying we'll be able to go in the sun again?" Lothaire asked.

"Yes." Thorne smiled wider. "Next year, our entire family will no longer have to hide from the sun."

"Holy shit," Grizella said.

"Oh my God!" Mark squealed. "I couldn't have picked a better time to be a vamp! Wait." He held up a finger. "I'm family, right? Please tell me I'm part of the family and get the curse lifted."

"You're family," Aiden said with a nod. "You'll always be family."

"Oh, thank God." He slumped back. "I'd have just died if I still had to live in the dark and you bastards got to play in the sun."

"Thank you, Catrain," Lothaire said, and his sincere eyes met mine. "You have no idea what this will mean to us."

"I'm so sorry for what happened to your people," I answered. "The story has been warped through the generations, and there was no mention of the horrible fate that befell so many of your clan. You have my apologies, and I'll do everything I can to make sure you don't suffer anymore."

"And," Thorne cut in and lifted his hand to show the ring. "For one week, Catrain has enchanted my ring to block the sunlight curse. Guess what I did today?"

He waggled his eyebrows as they waited.

"I hung out at the pool with Aiden and Emilia!"

"No shit?" Annella's mouth fell open.

Mark joined her in the stunned gesture. "And you're not crispy as fuck!"

"He used sunscreen." Emilia laughed.

"That's incredible," Grizella said as she shook her head. "What was it like?"

They all turned to him and watched as he smiled and sighed. "It was incredible. I can see now why Aiden fought so hard to be human again. I'd forgotten how amazing it was to stand in the sun."

"And next year, we'll all be able to, right?" Mark asked.

"Yes. I promise," I said. "My mother will never change her mind about you and already regrets helping Aiden. She'll never help the vampires again, but soon I'll be the one with the power. I know that you aren't the monsters we'd always thought you to be."

"But that means you have to go back?" Mark asked.

Those words twisted my gut into knots, but I nodded. "Yes."

"That sucks." He puckered his lips and pulled a face. "It'd be fun to have you around."

Knowing my days with Thorne were numbered felt like the sweetest poison. "I have a duty I must fulfill."

"We'll miss having you around," Emilia said. "But I understand. And we appreciate you helping the rest of the family get to come back out in the sun with Aiden and me. Maybe someday you can sneak off the island and join us for another margarita pool party."

I nodded but knew the reality of my upcoming life meant I'd never return or see them again.

"I hate to cut this short," Thorne said as he slipped his arm around my waist. "This ring loses its juice in only six days, and I want to enjoy my life in the sun with this woman. As much as I love you all, I don't want to waste another minute of it chatting with you arses I've seen every day for over six centuries… and will be seeing daily for centuries more."

Aiden chuckled and shook his head.

"I'm taking Catrain on a vacation. I just texted the pilots to get ready, and we're heading out soon."

"Ooh!" Mark beamed. "Where to?"

Thorne furrowed his brow. "I'm not sure yet. Somewhere tropical. Any suggestions?"

"Oh!" Emilia sat forward. "Bora Bora! It's where Aiden and I went. It's the most peaceful island, and you can rent out all the over-the-water villas and have the place all to yourselves. So romantic."

Aiden and Emilia shared a sweet smile, but Thorne shook his head.

"It sounds incredible, but Catrain is going to spend the rest of her life on a quiet, secluded island. I want beaches and tropical, but I need somewhere with a city she can experience and mountains and rainforests she can explore. I want her to see as much as she can before she goes back."

"Easy." Mark snorted. "O'ahu. You've got everything you need there. Gorgeous beaches, hot clubs, tropical waterfalls, and, oh!" He grinned. "Ziplining. Do it. Do it."

"O'ahu?" Thorne rubbed his chin. "I haven't been there."

"It's awesome. Aiden sent me there for my birthday a few years ago."

"I did?" Aiden's eyebrows rose.

"Yep," Mark said matter-of-factly. "Well, I mean, I booked and planned the trip, but I put it on your credit card."

"Ah." Aiden laughed. "Well, I hope you enjoyed your present."

"I did." Mark grinned. "You'll love it, Thorne. Catrain will too."

"It's beautiful," Grizella added. "I mean, I've never seen

it in the sun, but it's gorgeous at night. Lothaire and I have been twice."

"I want to go to O'ahu!" Emilia turned to Aiden. "Can we go?"

He stroked her hand and smiled. "Of course, baby. Anything you want."

"Me, too! I'm coming!" Mark clapped.

"Same!" Annella joined in his excitement. "I could use a vacay after being locked in that dastardly cage for days. A brief reprieve before I hunt down those bastards from Clan Lennox and part them from their heads."

Thorne held up his hand as Lothaire and Grizella nodded their agreement. "Hell no. Sorry, but not this trip, guys. This trip is just me and Catrain. Another time we can all go as a family."

A cumulative grumble passed between them.

"I get it," Emilia said. "You don't need to drag all of us on your romantic getaway. You two have an amazing time, and we'll see you when you get back."

"But next time, we're *all* going to Hawaii." Mark pointed his finger at Thorne.

"I promise," Thorne agreed. "Next time."

"When do you leave?" Lothaire asked.

Thorne looked down at his phone and smiled. "They'll be ready by the time we get there, so right now. Annella? Can you pack Catrain some clothes and suits she can wear?"

"On it!" Annella flashed out of the room, and a few seconds later she appeared at my side, holding a brown and tan bag. "Everything you need is in here. Clothes, suits, makeup, hair stuff. Thorne can take you shopping for anything I missed when you get there, but this should pretty much cover it."

"Thank you," I answered, a bit stunned as she shoved the bag in my hand. It was impossible for me to process what lay in store for me, and I couldn't begin to imagine what this O'ahu place was like. But from the smile on Thorne's face, I knew he was excited to show it to me.

"We'll be back in six days," Thorne said quickly, then took my hand and tugged me to the door.

They all called their goodbyes, and I followed Thorne out to the garage. He held the door for me as I climbed into the Bugatti.

He flashed over into the driver's seat and started the engine. "Ready?"

"I don't even know what I'm supposed to be ready for." I laughed as I settled back.

"Do you trust me?" He arched a brow.

After a long pause, I nodded. "I do."

"Then hang on, baby, because we've got an adventure ahead of us."

With a smile that split his face in two, he tore out of the garage. My stomach dropped with the speed we hit, and I loved the exhilaration of the quick twists and turns of the car. We sped down the roads until we reached something he called an airport. He parked the car and hurried to my side, taking my hand as he helped me out.

"Your private jet awaits." He waved his hand over the huge, strange metal object.

"Wait a minute." I stuttered to a stop as I looked at it. "Does this mean we have to fly?"

Thorne chuckled. "Of course. Why else would I have brought you to an airport? Airports are where planes take off and land."

"I didn't know what an airport was!" I argued and backpedaled toward the car. "I don't want to fly."

"Shit. I forgot you're scared to fly. Catrain," he soothed as he stopped me by tightening his grip on my hand. "You will be fine. I promise. Planes are very safe… safer than that car, in fact."

My heart pounded in my chest as I sucked my lip between my teeth. Everything in this world was new to me, but the thought of flying scared me more than I could comprehend. It seemed so unnatural. So dangerous.

But also as exciting as the man staring at me with those mesmerizing eyes.

"Trust me," he said, and the look in his eyes coaxed away some of my anxiety. "I will never let any harm come to you. I swear it."

With a gentle tug on my hand, I let him pull me forward. One slow step at a time, I followed him to the plane. Two men in suits stood on either side of the stairs, and they gave him a sharp nod as we passed between them. Thorne led me up the steps and into the plane. Everything inside looked meticulous and clean. White leather covered all the chairs and the couch, and a red-haired lady greeted us with a smile.

"Welcome back, Mr. Mackay." She stepped aside and gestured to the large chairs near the back.

Tentatively, I followed Thorne and sat down next to the window where he guided me. I couldn't remember a time in my life I'd been as terrified as I was while I sat down and followed her instructions to strap myself in.

"If you think the dirt bike and the Bugatti are fun, you're gonna love this," Thorne whispered as he reached over and took my hand in his.

His confidence comforted me. Something in his eyes made me believe it when he said he'd never let harm come to me. Deep down, I knew he never would.

A few minutes passed, and the plane rumbled even louder than the car and the dirt bike. Thorne noticed me tense up, and his grip around my hand tightened.

"It will get loud and a little bumpy, but it's all normal. Just look out the window. It's amazing when we take off."

The plane started moving, and for a moment, I thought about screaming for them to stop. For a moment, I wanted to jump off and run back to the safety of my island.

But one look at Thorne, and I knew I didn't want to miss a second at his side… or miss out on the new world he was so excited to show me.

"Look!" He pointed out the window as the plane raced down the runway.

My eyes widened as I saw the ground drop out from beneath us, and with it, my stomach did too. Each second that passed lifted us higher and higher, and as terrifying as it was, it was equally exhilarating.

Flying.

I was flying.

In my wildest dreams, I never thought I would fly like a bird, and yet here I was soaring higher and higher over the moonlit landscape below.

I stared at the flickering lights of the city, getting smaller by the second. "It's beautiful."

"You're beautiful," he whispered into my ear. "Thank you for trusting me. We've got a long flight and a couple stops before we get there. We're going to get to see the world below in the daylight. It's something I've never seen either, so we can explore it together."

I loved knowing that even though everything was new to me, some of this was new to him. It was a world we could experience together.

With a sigh, I settled my head back onto his shoulder and stared out at the incredible sights below me.

The plane made a screeching noise as it touched down. This time it didn't scare me like it had the first time we'd landed to refuel in New York. Thorne hadn't been lying when he'd tried to explain the size of the city. He'd taken me for a quick tour while the plane refueled and switched pilots, and I couldn't keep my mouth shut the entire time we drove around in the back of a cab.

The lights. The colors. The people. The buildings that stretched so tall into the sky I thought I'd break my neck trying to look up at them.

It had been incredible, and I couldn't even imagine what Hawaii would be like after seeing something like New York. The world Thorne lived in amazed me with every turn.

"Welcome to Hawaii." Thorne waved a hand toward the window as the plane slowed to a stop. "Beaches, clubs, luaus… it all awaits."

I squinted against the bright sun when they opened the door to the outside. Thorne reached into the bag and pulled out a pair of sunglasses for me and slid them into place, then put on his own mirrored sunglasses. Hand-in-hand we walked out into the warm, salty air, and two beautiful women with sun-kissed skin and flowing black hair greeted us with wide smiles and necklaces made of the most colorful flowers I'd ever seen.

"It's called a lei," Thorne said as he ducked his head while they slid it over his neck. "It's part of their traditions. Go ahead. Let them put one on you."

I mimicked his bow and waited while they slid the lei

over my head. When I stood up, I thanked them for the beautiful flowers. A long black car pulled up in front of us, and a dark-skinned man wearing a black suit stepped out. My eyes widened at the sight of him, and Thorne noticed my shock.

"Have you ever seen a person of color?"

I shook my head.

"Everyone on your island looks very similar, but out here, the world is full of people of every shape, size, and color you can imagine."

I couldn't stop staring at the way his bright white smile contrasted with his skin.

"Like the rainbow," I said as I smiled. "People out here are like the rainbow."

Thorne laughed and nodded. "Exactly. And there's no need to be alarmed when you see people of different skin tone, size, or shape. You'll see it all here."

Excited to see what other kinds of people lived in this world, I followed Thorne to the backseat of the car.

"Aloha!" the driver said as he opened the back door. "I'm Mika. I'll be your driver for your stay. Anywhere you want to go, just say the word, and I'll be ready."

"Nice to meet you, Mika." Thorne grasped his hand and shook it. "I'm Thorne and this is Catrain. We've got a few days here, and we want to see it all."

"Then I'm just the man to drive you." His smile widened as we slid past him onto the black leather seats.

"Do you have the address for our resort?" Thorne asked when Mika climbed into the front seat.

"I do. You have the private villa, correct?"

"That's correct," Thorne answered as he slid his arm over my shoulder.

"Enjoy the ride and we'll be there soon."

The car pulled out, and I stared out the window in awe at the sights moving by.

"Look how blue the ocean is!" Thorne pointed out the window. "I've never seen it in the sun. Isn't it incredible?"

The aqua blue water rolled in waves up onto the sand, and several men on long boards glided across the top of them.

"Those are surfers," Thorne said when he noticed my eyes tracking them. "We may have to try that. Something else I've never done."

"Yes. I want to try everything. It's amazing." Tears burned behind my eyes from the emotions engulfing me on the inside. In all of my life, I'd never imagined how incredible the world could be. How diverse and magnificent the sights, sounds, and the people. After a lifetime of seeing the same faces and places, the beautiful scenery stretching out in every direction overwhelmed every one of my senses.

"Do you like it?" Thorne asked as I craned my neck up at the strange trees lining the road we drove on.

"I love it." I turned to him, swallowing down the lump in my throat. "Thank you. Thank you for making me come with you."

"Thank you for trusting me. I just want you to be happy, Catrain. Always."

He wiped a tear from my eye and slid his hand under my chin, lifting my lips to his for a soft kiss. If only he knew how happy he made me… and how devastated I was that after this week with him, I'd never know happiness like this again.

Chapter Thirteen

THORNE

The warm sun drenched my skin while I lay on top of my surfboard, waiting to catch the next wave. Catrain floated next to me, and the way her toned, tattooed body shimmered in the sun had me struggling not to climb on her board and take her right there. Sex on a surfboard may prove difficult, but I was seconds away from trying to figure it out.

"Here comes another wave!" she called, and like it had every minute since we'd arrived, her smile lit up brighter than the sun.

Closing her eyes for a moment, she chanted, and the wave grew taller as it hurtled towards us, gaining speed as it approached. Catrain wanted everything bigger and faster, so she'd learned how to control the water and create even larger waves with her magic. With the wave the size and speed she wanted it, she grinned then paddled faster to get in position when it arrived.

I exhaled a pained sigh as she drifted farther away, then with one powerful push, I propelled my board to her side.

We hopped up onto our feet in unison and laughed as the wave rose under us and sent our boards careening toward the shore. Considering we'd only had two lessons yesterday, it was amazing how quickly she'd picked it up. My vamp skills made most physical tasks easy for me, but Catrain's years of training as a warrior made her a natural athlete, surprising even our instructor with her quick study.

"Shit!" Catrain called as she lost her balance. I saw her control the wave beneath her with magic as she tried to salvage her ride, but she'd already tipped too far. With flailing arms, she struggled to stay upright, so I veered my board toward her and snagged her around the waist just before she fell.

I held her body against mine as we rode the last of the wave together, her laugher echoing around us until we lost momentum and toppled into the water together.

We popped up in the surf, laughing and wiping the saltwater from our eyes.

"I almost had it to the end!" She laughed as she slapped the water in frustration.

"So damn close, baby." I reached out and pulled her up against me. Her body pressed against mine, and she softened in my embrace.

"Hi," she said as she smiled against my lips.

"Hi," I whispered back between kisses. "Are you having fun?"

Her arms tightened around my neck as she nodded enthusiastically. "Yes. I love it here. I love the beach, the trees, the flowers, the people, the food. Oh, the *food!* You are really missing out. You'd love it too if you could."

Maybe I would love the food if I could eat it, but there was one thing I knew I loved with every fiber of my being, and it was right here in my arms. It took every ounce of my considerable strength to keep from spitting it out each time I opened my mouth, but knowing our time together had an expiration date, I decided not to complicate things even more. So instead, I just kissed her each time I wanted to say, "I love you."

The number of kisses I'd given her the past two days since we'd arrived had left her lips red and swollen.

And I kissed her again.

"Want to go another round?" she asked as she broke apart our kiss. "I can make an even bigger wave then race you to the beach."

I arched an eyebrow. "You do realize I'm a vampire, and I could run around this island several times, come back out with my surfboard and still beat you to the beach, right?"

She laughed loudly, and it warmed me in the core of my soul.

"Good point. Well, then let's just go again for fun."

"Actually, we have an appointment this afternoon."

"An appointment? For what?" She furrowed her brow.

"It's a surprise. And you're gonna love it."

The lines in her furrowed brow deepened as she pursed her lips together.

"Seriously. You. Will. Love. It," I said, punctuating each word with a kiss. "Trust me. I haven't let you down yet, have I?"

Her lip twisted tighter, but then she shook her head. "No. You haven't."

"Then come on."

I tugged her toward the beach, and we paddled in side by side. After we arrived on the shore, I texted Mika to pick us up. With towels tied around our waists, I put a surfboard under each arm, and we strolled up the beach to the parking lot.

When we got there, Mika had already arrived and leaned against the limo wearing a hot pink floral Hawaiian shirt. After he'd dropped us off at our villa the day we'd arrived, I'd told him there was no need for formal suits as long as he was our driver, and he'd been wearing nothing but Hawaiian shirts ever since.

A trend I'd jumped on myself and now owned six of them after Catrain and I went shopping yesterday.

"Have fun?" he asked while he opened the door.

Catrain's face lit up as she climbed into the back. "We had the best time!"

"You know where we're going?" I paused before I followed her, and he nodded.

Mika shut the door behind me, and I climbed in beside Catrain and pulled her into my arms. He followed the roads away from the beach and onto the highway, taking us to the north end of the island.

When we arrived, he parked the car and let us out.

"See you in a few hours," I said as I took Catrain's hand in mine.

"I'll be here catching up on my reading." Mika lifted up a novel and smiled. He settled back into the car and put on his reading glasses as we walked away.

"Where are we going?" she asked as we headed toward the main building.

"You'll see." I continued keeping the secret. Partly because I wanted it to be a surprise, and partly because I knew she'd say no if she knew.

"Welcome!" A tall Hawaiian man with a bald head and an enormous grin opened the door. "I'm Ori. You must be Thorne and Catrain."

"We are." I shook his hand, then slid my sunglasses onto my head as we stepped inside.

"Pleasure to meet you both." He shook Catrain's hand as she looked around, trying to figure out what we were up to. "Since you booked all the tours this afternoon to be solo, we can get started whenever you're ready. First, we'll get you fitted with your equipment, give you a rundown of the basics, and then we can hop in the ATV and get started."

"Sounds great, man. We can't wait."

"Can't wait for what?" Catrain asked as she looked out the window at the vibrant farmlands surrounding us.

"Ziplining." I grinned.

"What is ziplining?" she asked.

Ori's eyes saucered as he looked at me and chuckled. "Oh, boy."

"You're gonna love it," I promised as I waggled my eyebrows at her.

Ori laughed and shook his head, then gestured for us to follow him in. As he fitted us for equipment and explained the safety basics, Catrain started to grasp exactly what it was I had planned for her.

"No way!" she argued as he strapped the blue helmet onto her head. "I'm not *flying* without a plane! I barely wanted to fly *in* the plane!"

"It's very safe. Lots of straps and safety regulations in place." I slapped her on her ass that the harness only amplified. "Trust me. I'll keep you safe. Have I let you down yet?"

With a scowl, she shook her head.

"Then come on." I slid my arm around her shoulder and guided her to the ATV Ori had parked out front. We hopped inside, and she let out an exasperated sigh as she accepted her fate.

"You'd better not get me killed."

"Never." I kissed her nose as Ori drove us off in the ATV.

When we got to the first line and climbed the stairs to the top, Catrain shook her head when she looked at the expansive drop below.

"I can't!" She stepped away from the edge. "I'll fall!"

Stepping her away from Ori, I whispered in her ear. "I'm an immortal vampire. I will make sure you're safe. Not that you'll need me… you're a badass witch. You've got this, baby."

I watched the resolution flicker in her eyes as she exhaled a breath and gave me a sharp nod.

"Quick before she changes her mind!" I laughed as I tugged her to Ori.

He hooked up our harness to the side-by-side lines, and we each stepped up onto the boxes. When I stepped onto mine and looked out, the views stretched out in front of me took my breath away. The world in the light looked so vibrant and colorful.

Almost as beautiful as the woman standing beside me.

"Whenever you're ready," Ori said.

"On three." I gave her a reassuring smile. "One, two… three."

We pushed off together, and she screamed as we sailed down the line. After a few seconds of sheer terror in her eyes, it transformed into pure exhilaration. Her screams turned into laughter, and as we sailed across the lush green canopy below, she looked over at me and smiled.

"Told you you'd love it!" I called to her.

"This is incredible!" she called back, and her smile widened even more, though I wouldn't have thought it possible.

The two of us passed over trees and fields below, and when I looked out at the horizon, I could see the beautiful ocean glistening in the falling sun. I wished the zipline would go on for miles so I could continue taking in the beautiful scenery… and the beautiful woman flying beside me. But it came to an end, and we slowed down as they caught us and pulled us to the platform. Catrain waited to get unhooked, then launched herself into my arms.

"It was incredible! And so beautiful! Did you see the ocean? It was right over there!"

Her excitement invigorated me even more as she bounced in my arms.

"Can we do it again?"

"There are seven more lines to go. Just wait until we hit the half-mile long one."

Her excited squeals made me laugh harder, and before I knew it, she dragged me across the sky bridge to the next line.

The cold, fierce warrior I'd met on the beach was nowhere to be seen as we continued zipping side by side. Instead, the woman flying across the sky with me radiated joy from every inch of her. Her laugh. Her smile. The way her eyes lit up when they took in the incredible scenery below us… and when they'd lock with mine.

Magic.

And not the kind that let her hold fire in her hands, knock a vampire on his ass with sparks, or glow blue when I'd bring her body to heights she'd never known.

This was the kind of magic that existed between two people in love.

Deep, undeniable, unbreakable love.

And for the first time in my life, it had happened to me.

We landed on the last platform and waited while they unhooked us from the line. Catrain still vibrated with excitement and energy and wanted to go again, but the sun would set soon, and the tours would close for the evening.

"You can always come back," Ori said as we descended the steps with him.

The moment the words came out of his mouth, the happiness that hadn't left her face since we started this tour dissipated. Sadness replaced the joy in her eyes, and she dropped her gaze to the ground.

"You know what, Ori," I said as I stopped at the base of the stairs and glanced off to the highest mountain top in the distance. "Why don't you go back without us. We'll walk."

"Walk?" He shook his head. "It's a long walk and can be dangerous. It's safest if you just ride back with me."

I stared deep into his eyes and spoke slowly. "Drive back by yourself. We had a wonderful time, and our driver came and picked us up. You don't need to worry about us."

Ori nodded slowly and climbed onto the ATV and drove away.

"What did you just do?" Catrain asked as she watched him go.

"I used my influence to send him away. There's something I want to do. But you gotta trust me again."

"Again?" She arched a brow.

"Yep. You ready?"

With a soft laugh, she shrugged. "I'm all yours."

All yours. Just thinking she was mine made my heart feel like it soared on its very own never-ending zipline, but then remembering she belonged to another felt like it'd fallen off the line and plummeted into the rocks below.

Trying to force the thought of her in the arms of another man from my mind, I pulled her up against me. "Don't be scared. You may get dizzy when I'm done, but you'll feel better in a few moments."

"What are we—"

I didn't let her finish. I took off at vamp speed, holding

her in my arms. The trees and fields flew by in an instant until I skidded to a stop at the top of the tallest mountain. Catrain wobbled in my arms, but I held her close while I waited for her to catch her bearings.

"Whoa," she breathed as her teetering stopped.

"Fun, huh?"

"Yeah," she answered, but she still sounded disoriented. "Okay, now I feel sick."

"Give it a little time for your body to re-acclimate. I've got you."

After a minute, she looked up and smiled. "I'm better. And we need to do that more often."

Chuckling, I released my tight grip. "I knew you'd like it. You sure do have a need for speed, Maverick."

"Maverick? What is that?"

"A movie reference. *Top Gun.* It's just someone else who loves to go fast like you. We'll rent it tonight."

"I loved racing the ponies on the island, but I never really knew what speed was until I met you. And you're right. I love it." Her blue eyes sparkled as she waggled her eyebrows.

"Now that we're up here, I thought we could slow down a bit and watch the sun set from the best view on the island." With the wave of my hand, I gestured to the incredible landscape stretching out in every direction.

Catrain finally took her eyes off me and smiled when she looked at the panoramic view of the ocean. "It's beautiful."

"Sit," I said as I settled into the grass. She sat beside me and pressed her head into my chest as I wrapped my arm around her shoulder. The sun started its descent into the ocean, and we sat quietly and watched it.

"Does it make you sad to see the sun set?" she asked.

With a sigh, I answered, "Yes. Which is funny, because for centuries, I'd count the seconds until it went down. Now I don't want to miss a minute in it. Hell, I'm ready to go to Norway where they have months the sun doesn't set. In fact, we have a home there because usually we go during the Polar Night, where the sun doesn't rise for months." I laughed. "Funny how different my life will be after you lift the sunlight curse."

A curse that would only lift once she left my life.

"But I'd still choose to live in the dark and not have you go back."

Silence settled between us, then she pressed deeper into my arms. "I don't want to go back," she whispered. "But I have to."

I pressed a kiss against the top of her head. "I know."

"How am I ever going to live without this?" She gestured to the gorgeous sunset illuminating the world around us. "Without you?"

My heart squeezed in my chest as I clenched my eyes shut.

I wanted to beg. Plead. Throw myself at her feet and beseech her to stay with me.

But I'd promised to respect her decision, and I knew no matter what I said, she'd still have to go. Instead of saying what I wanted to say, I just squeezed her tighter and said, "I know, but you'll do what you must."

With a long exhale, she nodded her head.

"At least you don't have to think about me with another woman. I'm done. I'm going to be a bachelor yearning for you until the end of my days. It's me who has to live with the knowledge you're married to *Uradech*." I scoffed, then immediately regretted my words.

"It's not that I *want* to marry him," she said as she

turned up to stare at me. "I would *never* choose to marry him. And I'll never love him."

"Why do you have to marry him? Can't you just rule alone and pine for me as a single witch forever? I'd sure feel better if I didn't have to think about you married to another man. We'll both be miserable and alone. Right?" I tried to lighten the somber mood I'd created.

"I have to." She looked away. "It's a deal we made with their bloodline after the pact with the vampires fell through. His tribe moved to the island and took on the role of our protectors. In exchange for their service, one of their family gets to marry the leader of our tribe and rule at our side."

Her words felt like a punch to the gut.

Her protectors?

I knew what the protectors of their tribe were… the ones who came after us.

The ones I thought were extinct.

The ones I thought *we* made extinct.

"Wait," I stuttered. "Are you trying to tell me he's a werewolf?"

I didn't think it was possible to hate the man more than I already did, but knowing he was the vile creature I had thought I eradicated from this world six hundred years ago made my blood start to boil.

"Yes." She nodded as she kept staring at the ocean. "Uradech's bloodline all carry the shifter genes."

Opening and closing my mouth like a fish, I tried to process this blow to my sanity. "But how can that be? We killed them all."

She lifted a shoulder and let it drop. "Not all of them."

"Holy shit. We thought they were all dead."

She peeked over her shoulder at me. "You thought we were all dead too."

"True story." I chuckled, then it petered off as I started to process what she'd said. I furrowed my brow and lifted a finger. "Wait a minute. If your leader has to marry a werewolf, then that means your father was a werewolf. So, does that mean *you're* a werewolf?"

Lucky for my already strained sanity, she shook her head.

"My father was a werewolf, so I do have the werewolf bloodline. But because I'm a Pict witch and the heir to the throne, we don't turn. It only takes one parent with the werewolf gene to pass it on, so our ancestors worked it into the magic that created werewolves that it wouldn't affect the leader of the Picts. It ensures there is no way the wolf line could find a way to overpower the Picts and rule."

I exhaled a deep breath. "So, no wolfing out for you?"

She sucked on her cheek. "Nope. No wolfing out for me."

"This is so mind blowing. I can't believe werewolves are still alive. Annella is gonna go wild when I tell her. She hated those fucking things. I swear she took out half of them herself."

She scowled as she turned to look at me. "Why would *you* hate them? We created them to protect us from you. Then you went and wiped them out."

My eyes bulged. "Is that what you were told?"

The judgment in her eyes faltered, and she answered with less confidence. "Yes."

Snorting, I shook my head. "They weren't created just to protect you; they were created to *eradicate* us. My clan was just going about their business when a pack of very lethal werewolves hunted us down. They killed some of us, we killed some of them, but we were highly outnumbered at the time. After they killed our Chieftain, Lothaire inherited the position, and we retreated and hid out for awhile while we regrouped. But they were incredibly adept at tracking us. But jokes on them… we could make new vampires, and they couldn't make new werewolves since they can only be born as one. Once we realized we were at risk of extermination and that they couldn't turn more werewolves, we turned hundreds of humans into vampires to help us fight back. In fact, the only reason there are so many vampires today is because we were forced to create an army to fight them. It worked though, and we eradicated them." I rolled my eyes. "Or *thought* we did."

Catrain sat silently for a moment, then shook her head. "Once again, our history tells a very different story. I had no idea they hunted you down. No wonder you wiped them out."

"It was survival of the fittest… and it turns out the original Pict protector model was the winner." I lifted my chin.

She chuckled quietly. "They are very powerful. Far more powerful than humans, and as powerful as vampires, but with several safeties built-in."

"What safeties?"

"As long as the pact is intact, they cannot kill anyone on my island. It's built into the magic that they can never turn on us. And of course, they can be killed by Pict magic… unlike vampires. They aren't immortal and live a normal lifespan, and as you know, they can't turn other humans into werewolves and multiply."

"You're saying your people learned their lesson after they created us." I laughed.

"I suppose they did." She joined me.

Our laughter petered off, and I exhaled a long sigh. "So, when are you marrying the dog?"

"He's not a dog." She looked at me and rolled her eyes.

"And it's not like I *want* to marry him. It was the agreement that was struck. They become shifters who protect us, and in exchange—"

"He gets to marry you," I breathed, finally understanding.

"I cannot break the treaty. It could trigger a war."

"When?" I asked again, noticing she'd avoided the question.

A soft breeze lifted her hair. "We marry under the next full moon."

My heart stalled in my chest. "That's less than two weeks away!"

She sat silently. "It's part of the tradition. We need to be married before I take power to ensure we keep up our end of the pact."

Jealousy and rage ripped apart my insides, but I waged a war to tamp them down.

"Maybe you can just say no. So what if they want to wage war? They can't hurt you, right? Just kill them all with a lightning bolt and run off with me. Or hell, let me and my family loose on your island, and we'll finish the job we started. It's been centuries since I've had werewolf blood in my mouth. I'm not going to lie… it's a bit of a delicacy."

Even though I said it in jest, I secretly hoped she'd answer with "Okay." Instead, she just laughed softly and shook her head.

"If we break the pact, the safety of not being able to harm a Pict disappears. They could wipe us out if they wanted. And we're not going to kill them all. They are part of my tribe now, and it's my duty to marry him."

I couldn't bear to talk about her with another man for a second longer, and I knew I'd never convince her to deny her duty. "I know it is. I'm sorry I brought it up. We're not supposed to be talking about the future while we're here. Just you and me enjoying every second together while we can."

"And I am." She slid her hand across my jaw and lifted her lips to mine. "So much."

When her lips touched mine, every nerve in my body fired. She slid onto my lap, straddling me as she deepened our kiss. I raked my hand through her hair and pulled her tongue into my mouth, working open my shorts button with my free hand. Our passion exploded as she ground against my hard cock while I pulled it out of my shorts.

"Take me now," she whispered in my ear before she nipped it.

We'd forgone condoms once I'd explained vampires couldn't procreate, and for the first time in my life, I cursed that my immortality made me unable to father children. The primal animal clawing its way out of me wanted to implant one inside her belly and claim her as mine. Create something with the love for her that incinerated me from the inside.

She slipped her underwear off to the side and lifted her dress. When her wet heat slid over my throbbing cock, I moaned and pressed my hips against hers. She lowered herself down my shaft, and I growled into her neck as I buried myself inside of her. With panting breaths, she writhed on top of me until I was calling her name on repeat, and her body glowed with the blue light I was sure they could see from the ships docked in the ocean below us.

After her colors faded, she collapsed against my chest, and I wrapped her up in my arms.

All I wanted to do was say, "I love you" over and over, but instead, like I'd done every time the words wanted to escape, I kissed her again.

Chapter Fourteen

CATRAIN

The gentle crash of the waves on the shore added to the fire-lit dinner atmosphere at the beachside luau. Other tourists dripping in vibrant colors and leis filled up every table around us, and the dancers kept us entertained through every course.

"You are missing out so much," I said with my mouth full of lobster. "This is amazing. I know I'm supposed to be eating the traditional pork with everyone, but I've been eating wild hog my whole life. There's nothing like this on my island."

Thorne leaned back in his chair and twisted a clean fork in his fingers. "Aiden couldn't stop raving about the stuff. I can't even imagine what that crusty little thing tastes like." He wrinkled his nose.

"Better than blood, I'm sure." I rolled my eyes.

"Ah. Don't knock it 'til you try it."

"Pass."

"Well, you may not like drinking blood, but you

certainly would love having me drink *your* blood. It's supposed to be orgasmic. Better than sex."

It seemed impossible to imagine anything better than sex with Thorne, but for a moment, I wondered what it would be like. As quickly as the thought popped into my head, I shook it back out. My mother was certainly prepared to skin me alive for spending time with a vampire, but to let one drink my blood? She'd probably drop dead on the spot if she found out—the ultimate abomination.

"You're thinking about it, aren't you?" His eyes narrowed, and the light of the tiki torch burning beside our table seemed to ignite the mischief more.

Heat flushed to my cheeks as I shook my head. "No. No way."

"Just say the word, and I'll make you glow so many colors you'll look like a disco ball."

Even though I didn't know what a disco ball was, the warm heat in my cheeks cranked up to scalding.

"Can I get you another piña colada?" our server asked, interrupting our silent stare-off.

"Yes, please," I said to him quickly after clearing my throat. "I would love one."

With a gracious smile, he took my empty glass and left.

"You're still thinking about it, aren't you?" Thorne leaned forward, closing the distance between us.

I opened my mouth to argue but couldn't find the words… the words to lie.

A satisfactory smirk pulled up one corner of his lips as he sat back in his chair.

"Do you still have bags of," I whispered the next word, "*blood* left, or do you need to get more?"

"I packed plenty. More than enough for the trip. But

that doesn't mean I don't like dessert." He waggled his eyebrows.

"Stop!" I laughed. "I would be disowned. It would be the biggest insult to my people to let a," I whispered again so the other guests at the luau wouldn't hear, "*vampire*, feed on me. You're supposed to be my mortal enemy."

Thorne flicked his wrist. "Minor detail."

"You just keep your fangs in your mouth."

"But I don't need to keep my," he leaned forward and whispered, "dick in my pants, do I?"

With the slow shake of my head, I said, "That you definitely don't need to do."

Just thinking about being with him again already had the blood pumping through my veins and making a beeline between my legs.

The hula dancers started again on stage, and a man twirling fire caught my attention.

"Bet you could give them a run for their money. I know how well you can shake your hips, and you don't need a fire knife to twirl fire. You can just use your hands. You could make a good living as a hula dancer."

"Stop." I laughed. "I can shake my hips, but not like those girls. They are incredible."

I turned again to watch the talented women rolling their hips in a way I wanted to try on top of Thorne later.

"I'm glad we did this," Thorne said. "Even though I can't eat or drink all the luau food, it would be a crime not to go to one when in Hawaii. And since tonight is our last night, it's important you got to see this."

Our last night.

I glanced down at his ring, noting the slow fade of color. Like sand slipping through an hourglass, our break from reality dwindled as well. This had been the most incredible five days of my life, and my stomach twisted in knots knowing it had to end.

"I'm glad I saw it too. It's really incredible learning more about their culture. It's beautiful. My tribe has traditional dances as well, but nothing like that."

"Yeah? You have dances?"

"Yep." I shoved another bite of lobster in my mouth.

"You going to show me later?" His eyebrow rose.

"Maybe." I smirked, then picked up an oyster and let it slide down my throat in one swig.

Thorne bit his fist and cringed. "God. You're killing me. It's equal parts disgusting and seductive. I can't decide what I should be feeling when I see you slide those things down your throat."

I laughed as I set down the empty shell. "Delicious."

"Yes, you are."

I felt his foot on my leg under the table and narrowed my eyes with a smirk. "Are you going to let me finish my dinner, or are we going to have to sneak out of here back to our villa?"

Twisting his lips, he shrugged. "Can you eat faster?"

I lifted another oyster shell and pressed it seductively to my lips, then retrieved the oyster with my tongue. Thorne's eyes saucered as he watched me suck it into my mouth and finish with a lick of my lips.

"I'm so grossed out and so turned on right now, I don't even know what to do with myself."

For the millionth time since I met him, I laughed. When the server returned with my piña colada, I could barely thank him between fits of hysterics.

"You need to drink that, and then you need to do that thing with your tongue to something other than that disgusting oyster."

I lifted my glass in a cheers and smiled. "With pleasure."

We made it five more minutes until I put the cherry from my drink in my mouth. Thorne tossed a wad of cash on the table and yanked me into his arms. As we made our way through the resort, he stopped and slammed me up against a palm tree. It dug into my back, but I didn't care about the pain. The pleasure of his tongue inside my mouth numbed any discomfort in the rest of my body.

His hand slid along my thigh, working its way up my little black dress, but stopping just short of where I needed his fingers to go.

"Someone's coming," he whispered in my ear and removed his hand, leaving me panting for more.

A strolling couple passed by and greeted us with a knowing smile, and we watched them walk hand-in-hand into a building with loud music pouring out the doors as they opened.

"What's going on in there?" I asked as Thorne dragged me by the hand toward our villa.

"Sounds like a dance club."

I tugged him to a stop. "What's a dance club?"

He paused, then shook his head with a laugh. "Fuck. I did promise to show you everything, so I guess I can keep it in my pants a little longer and introduce you to the wonderful world of clubbing."

"Clubbing?" I asked.

"Dancing. You'll love it. Come on."

Even though I didn't know what to expect inside, and I was dying to rip off his clothes again, the sounds of laughter and upbeat music excited me as we started toward it. I'd already seen so much since I'd left my island. The city, lights, shops, restaurants, so many different looking people, and so many trees and flowers I'd never imagined existed.

So far, every time Thorne promised me I'd love something, he'd been right.

The closer we got, the louder the music grew, and I felt it thumping inside my chest, just like I'd felt the drums when we'd dance around the fire at home. But this music was different. It had so many rich, complex sounds I'd never heard before. Like the stuff I'd heard on the car radio, but so much more intense. As we reached the door, the colored lights flashed and flickered and lit up the darkness.

"Ready?" Thorne asked before he pushed open the door.

I nodded and grabbed his hand.

The loud music and lights assaulted my senses when we stepped inside, but it was anything but unpleasant. People stood on a stage playing instruments while colored lights flashed all around them. Mobs of people danced in front of them, moving together to the beat of the music.

"Not like your dancing at home, is it?" Thorne shouted into my ear, which was necessary due to the volume of the crowd and the music.

"No!" I called back. "Nothing like at home. It's amazing!"

"You want a drink before I get your ass out on that dance floor?"

I smiled and nodded.

"Piña colada again?"

I nodded faster. Since I'd tried one on our second night, they'd become my new favorite.

"Stay here. I'll be right back." After a quick kiss, he disappeared into the crowd.

Closing my eyes, I swayed back and forth while the music moved my body. As the song sped up and the crowd pulsed along with it, I started to wish that I'd skipped the drink and headed straight for the dance floor with Thorne.

"Like this song?" a deep voice whispered into my ear.

I spun to see a man standing behind me. He rubbed a small green square on the tip of a long stick. It resembled the fighting spear I'd left at home. As I studied the stick, I noticed his gaze working its way up my exposed legs.

Instead of answering him, I just narrowed my eyes and turned away back toward the band.

"You wanna play pool?" he asked, leaning too close to my space again.

"No," I answered quickly and scanned the crowd for Thorne.

"Aw, come on, hottie. Don't be like that. Come have a drink. Maybe a dance."

"No," I said more sharply and spun to stare him down. "Go away now."

"You don't have to be such a bitch," he snapped back.

"Leave me alone. Now." I narrowed my eyes.

He ran a hand through his dark hair and scoffed. "Damn, girl. You need to loosen up. Maybe a good fuck would do the trick."

My mouth fell open at the crude words, but before I could respond, I felt something touch the inside of my thigh. His green eyes met mine before I looked down to see his long stick lifting my skirt.

"This will settle you down."

Rage reverberated inside my chest in place of the music, and with one swift move, I dislodged the stick from his hands, spun it with the skill I'd honed since childhood, and landed six blows to his head and body before swiping his legs out from under him. The small crowd around me laughed and cheered as I placed the tip of the stick against his forehead and pinned him to the ground.

"Don't touch me. Ever."

When I removed it, he had a dark green spot in the center of his head.

The group of men he'd been with laughed as they pointed at their downed friend, and not one of them offered him any help back to his feet.

"Damn, girl!" a dark-skinned woman next to me cheered. "I saw what he did! Hell to the yeah! Screw that douchebag!"

She held up her hand, and I remembered seeing people do it on the beach the other day, so I slapped my palm against hers.

"You are one badass bitch!" She laughed as she kicked the guy still lying on the floor before heading out to the dance floor. When I turned back around, Thorne stood smiling, holding my piña colada in his hand.

"I leave you alone for one minute." He shook his head and glanced at the man still struggling to get up off the floor.

"I handled it." I shrugged and took the drink from his hand.

"Damn straight you did, baby. And I don't think I've ever been this turned on."

"What about now?" I asked with an arched brow as I slid the cherry between my lips.

His mouth slackened as I finished pulling the stem out of my mouth.

"If you keep this up, we aren't going to make it onto that dance floor."

I took a long swig of my drink and slid my arm around

his waist and whispered in his ear, "Take me dancing now, and I'll do that thing with my tongue later."

Thorne growled in my ear, "You're killing me, woman," then pulled me to the edge of the dance floor. "You gonna show me those dance moves or what?"

His seductive eyes encouraged me as he spun me out onto the dance floor. With one sharp pull, he yanked me against his chest and started moving with me to the music. The smell of alcohol and sweat flooded the air and only enhanced the sexually charged energy around us.

We moved together to the music, sweat beading on my skin as I danced with him, grinding our bodies together in a way that made me want to rip off his clothes and take him right here on this dance floor. He spun me around, pulling my back against his chest as he moved my body against him. His breath brushed across my ear as he took it between his teeth. It ignited the already burning inferno inside me.

When his lips brushed across my neck, I closed my eyes and pressed my head back into his shoulder. His arms tightened around my waist, and I could feel his rock-hard cock pressing into me.

But that wasn't the only thing I wanted inside me.

"Bite me," I whispered, barely able to believe I'd uttered the words.

"What?" he said as he slowed our movements.

"I want to feel it. I want to feel what it's like to have you drink from me. Do it."

His already heavy breathing sped up as he pulled me tighter against him. "Are you sure?"

I spun around and looked into his eyes, making sure he could see the intent in mine. I rose on my toes and brushed my lips against his, then sucked his lip between my teeth. When I let go, I whispered, "Drink from me."

A fire I'd never seen lit up in his eyes as he stared into mine. "Not here. Come with me."

He pulled me off the dance floor and out the door of the club. We kissed our way along the beach back to our villa, stopping along the way to tear at each other with a passion I'd never imagined possible. When we reached our private beach, Thorne pushed me up against a tree and held my face between his hands as he kissed me so deeply I struggled to breathe.

"Are you sure?" he asked as his lips worked down my neck.

"Yes. Do it," I panted.

His cool hands slid up my thigh and rubbed across my damp panties as his tongue drew lazy circles around my neck. My heart pounded faster as I waited for the pain that would come when his fangs slid into my skin. But instead, I felt his finger dip beneath my panties and move over the spot between my legs that had me ready to explode with a rainbow of colors.

"Ready?" he asked, and I heard the pop of his fangs.

"Yes," I breathed, as he continued working circles around the place between my legs I hoped he'd never stop touching.

Searing pain burned through my neck, and I gasped as he slid his finger inside of me at the same time as his fangs. The pain from his bite dissipated in seconds, and soon a pleasure like I'd never imagined replaced it. I felt our bodies connecting as he drank my blood, the world around me spinning out of control. I didn't even notice him undo his pants, but I felt him slide inside of me as his fangs penetrated me even deeper.

I cried out from the intensity of the pleasure… a pleasure I never wanted to stop.

His hand tightened around my head as he pulled himself even deeper into my neck and my body. He wrapped his arm under me and lifted me against him. I wrapped my legs around his waist and let his powerful thrusting pin me in place to the tree. As my body reached the pinnacle of heights only he could take me to, I cried out his name and let the waves of pleasure wash over me. The air around us glowed red from the new light I emitted as Thorne pushed inside me one last time. With our bodies still locked together, he held me tight against the tree.

"What was that," I panted as he slid his fangs out of my neck, pressing a soft kiss to the spot his teeth had just been.

"I don't know," he said while he struggled to catch his breath.

"Is that normally what it's like?" I asked as he slid out of me. We collapsed into the sand and lay side by side.

"Not for me, it's not." He pressed a hand to his head and blew out a long breath. "It's never been like that for me. That was—"

"Incredible."

"Yes. Incredible." I touched the spot on my neck, shocked to find the wounds had already healed. "I can't even feel a bite mark."

"My saliva heals the wounds my fangs make."

Still spinning from the sensations I'd just experienced, I let out a deep sigh. "I felt like we connected. Like, *really* connected. I can't even explain it."

Thorne rolled over and ran his fingers across my face. "We did connect, Cat, because we *are* connected. It was different because we're different. It was different because…"

He drifted off for a moment and then leaned up and kissed my lips. But as I kissed him back, he broke it off and shook his head.

"No. Fuck it. I'm not going to stop myself from saying it anymore. It's different because I love you, Cat. I love you more than I ever knew a man could love a woman. I love you with my heart, my soul, every fucking molecule in my body. And I'm going to love you for all of fucking eternity. Literally. Because that's how long I'm going to live… and love you. You can't go. You can't. I know you love me, too. I can feel it."

He pressed my hand to his heart as I fought the tears burning behind my eyes.

"Tell me you don't feel this love between us."

"I can't, Thorne," I started, but the lump in my throat stopped me from saying more.

"Yes, you can! Fuck!" he shouted as he leaped to his feet. The force of his words startled me. He grabbed a handful of hair as he paced in front of me. "I know I promised not to do this. I know I promised to just spend this one week with you and say goodbye, but I can't, Cat. And I don't know how you can either. Fuck your fucking commitment. What about *me?* What about *us?* Please. Don't make me live without you."

He dropped to his knees and took my hand in his. "Stay with me. Stay here. Travel the world. Drink the piña coladas. Fly on the ziplines. Become a pro surfer. Dance with me for the rest of our days. We'll do whatever you want every single day. Always your choice. Every fucking day. There's so much more I want to show you. So much more you need to see. I don't even care that having you stay means the sunlight curse doesn't get removed. I'd live for eternity in the dark again as long as you're with me. Please, Cat. Stay with me."

The dam holding back my tears broke as I started to sob. Of course, I loved him. I'd known it since the first time our lips had touched. But what I wanted didn't matter. It couldn't.

"Thorne. I do love you. I do," I started and saw the hope flicker in his teary eyes. "But I can't stay."

The light in his eyes disappeared behind a cloud of sadness.

"I can't. I'm so sorry. I can't."

It was impossible to look at him and still tell him no. The tears poured down my face as I jumped up and raced off down the beach. I didn't even know where I was going, but all I knew was that I needed to get away from Thorne before that look in his eyes killed me… or coaxed me into throwing away my destiny and my duty to my people. I tore down the beach, leaving a trail of sand flying behind me, hoping that he wouldn't come after me and steal away the last of my senses.

Or hoping he would.

But when I finally stopped running and turned around… he wasn't there.

I collapsed into the sand and pressed my head to my knees and sobbed away all the anger and despair I had, knowing that the life that awaited me was one where I'd never see him again.

Chapter Fifteen

THORNE

I paced along the length of our six-bedroom villa while I watched the sun come up over the horizon. Catrain had run off hours ago, and now that she hadn't returned, I regretted not going after her. What if something had happened to her, and I'd let my self-pity and anger push her right into harm's way?

At first, I'd thought she needed space, and so did I, but now that the hours had ticked by, fear replaced the rage that had consumed me at the thought of losing her. Unable to stand the wait any longer, I decided to try to hunt her down. For once in my life, I wished I had a werewolf with me that could follow her scent like the dogs they were. Or a Pict witch to locate her with a spell. But the Pict witch I needed was the very one missing. Instead, I just needed to use my heightened senses to listen for her as I raced around the island.

I opened the door to bolt out but stopped when I saw her staring back at me, her eyes red and swollen from the tears she must have shed all night.

"Christ. You're safe. I thought something happened to you."

I yanked her into my arms and held her against my chest. When she returned the embrace, I let out a sigh. "I'm so sorry I did that. We had a deal. I went back on it. Please forgive me, Catrain."

"There's nothing to forgive. I knew that we wouldn't be able to part easily, and I came with you anyway and set us both up for torture. I shouldn't have come, but I needed to be with you. It was selfish of me, and I made this so much harder for us both."

Pressing my chin on the top of her head, I shook my head. "No. You were right to come. I'm glad I got to spend this time with you and that you got to see the world. Does it hurt like hell I'm gonna have to say goodbye? Yeah. More than standing under the noon sun without my ring. And it's going to feel like being burned to death for years to come, but it was worth it to have you just for a little while. I promise you it was."

"I'm really going to miss you, Thorne. I hope you know that. I hope you know that if I had a choice, it would be you. It would always be you."

When she looked up, I saw the lazy tear slide down her flushed cheek. I wiped it away with my thumb and leaned down to kiss her soft lips.

"No more tears. We have a few hours left before we have to head to the airport. What do you say we hit the surf one last time?"

With a sniffle, she smiled. "I would like that."

Even though it felt like my heart and soul were being ripped from my body and shredded into a million pieces, I pushed through the pain and slapped a smile on my face.

"Come on, baby. I'll race you."

With a flash, I whisked out the glass patio doors overlooking the ocean. Catrain hadn't even taken a step before I stood grinning on the beach, holding two surfboards I'd snagged from the villa's shed.

"Cheater." She laughed. "I need to put my suit on. I'll be out in a second."

"Slowpoke," I teased.

The rays from the rising sun sparkled across the ocean like millions of little diamonds. It was something I wouldn't have noticed when I was a human, but now that I'd been centuries without seeing the beauty of it, it was something I'd never stop appreciating. I glanced down at the ring and saw the blue had faded even more, signaling the end of my days in the sun.

At least for now.

In a few months, when Catrain took power, we'd all be able to walk in the sun again. Watching sunrises with my family would almost certainly become a new tradition. The thought of sitting on the cliffs near our home watching it come up with each of them soothed the pain of knowing that Catrain wouldn't be there to watch it with me.

A little.

But even with the slight balm, the pain remained almost unbearable.

"Ready," Catrain said, and I turned around to see her approaching in the little black bikini I wanted to tear off her.

The full weight of the pain rushed back with a vengeance.

Instead of dropping to my knees and begging her to stay once again, I forced a smile. "Let's go."

We paddled out side by side, sitting on our boards as we waited to catch a wave. When she worked her magic to ensure the perfect one approached, I saw the light reignite in her eyes.

"That's a good one!" She started paddling with it.

"Don't fall off!" I teased as I paddled beside her.

When the wave reached us, we hopped up onto our boards. Her wet blonde hair trailed behind her as she maneuvered her board on top of the wave. She looked over, and her smile lit up her whole face.

That.

That was why the pain awaiting me when we parted would be worth it.

Having been the one person in her life to bring that smile to her face reminded me why I'd set myself up for a heartbreak greater than any other man had endured.

Catrain would spend the rest of her life trapped on an island married to a man she'd never love, but it would be the memories I gave her that would make her smile in the night. Memories of me. Our kisses. Our laughter. Of the one week she got to be herself.

A week with the man she'd always love.

The wave broke and sent us both toppling forward with it. We emerged together, and her laughter echoed across the water.

"Again?" she said with her eyes lit with excitement.

"Anything to make you smile."

With my words, her smile grew. We climbed back onto our boards and paddled back out, catching wave after wave until it was time to pack up and go.

Mika arrived and helped us carry our bags to the car. The joy that had been on Catrain's face all morning while we surfed slipped away as we climbed into the backseat. She stared out the window in silence as we made our way to the airport, the beautiful scenery no longer making her smile.

"You okay?" I asked as we pulled into the airport.

"No." She shook her head and looked at me. "I'm not. I'm never going to be okay, but it doesn't change what I have to do."

I had no words to offer her comfort because I couldn't find them for myself either. Instead, I just kissed her.

We boarded the jet and settled into our seats, silence the only sound besides the roar of the plane as we took off and left our little paradise behind.

Chapter Sixteen

CATRAIN

Thorne parked the Bugatti in the garage and pressed his head back into the leather seat. "We're back."

My body ached from all the travel, but not as much as my heart did knowing what would happen tonight.

The color in his ring had worn off an hour ago, meaning we had to part before the sun came up in only five hours. Tonight, he would drive me back to the island.

"You want to come in and say goodbye to everyone?" he asked, looking over at me with blue eyes weighted with so much sadness it physically pained me inside.

"I do. Is that okay? Do we have time?"

"As long as we leave in the next hour or so, we'll have time to take the dirt bike back and…" He drifted off. "Say goodbye."

Swallowing over the lump in my throat, I nodded.

"Come on."

He flashed out of the car and opened my door. I relished the coolness of his skin as he took my hand and led me into the castle.

"We're back," he called inside.

One by one his family appeared in the entryway, each hugging us with a warmth that still surprised me.

The monsters I'd been led to believe didn't exist in his family.

The betrayers.

The ruthless slayers of the werewolves.

The bloodthirsty killing machines that I'd spent my whole life hating.

Instead, the people wrapping their arms around me and squeezing me tight were a family I would give anything to join.

They cared about each other. Fought for each other. Would die for each other.

Not unlike the family waiting for me at home. The one where this impossible choice meant sacrificing my own happiness.

"Well? Was I right or was I right?" Mark said as he let go of my shoulders. "O'ahu was a winner, wasn't it?"

"It was amazing," I answered.

"Perfect choice, Mark." Thorne clapped him on the back.

"Zipline? Did you do it?" He looked between us expectantly.

"Hell yeah, we did." Thorne grinned. "Took a little convincing to get Cat up there, but once she started, it was almost impossible to get her to stop. I have a feeling she's going to be trying to rig up zip lines across her island."

They all laughed, and I joined them. "I love it. To think I was so scared to fly when I got here, and now all I want to do is soar across the sky over and over again. The views were incredible."

"And you should have seen this girl on a surfboard."

Thorne blew out a slow whistle. "Seriously. She could go pro with a little more practice."

"I've never tried it," Mark said. "But I have spent a lot of time watching surfing, because *hello* hotties. There's something about a dude on a surfboard that just—" He bit his lip. "Yum."

He wasn't wrong. I'd been mesmerized watching Thorne's shirtless, toned body maneuvering that board across the waves. Just the thought of it made me want to drag him upstairs for one last roll in the sheets.

"I'm so happy you had fun," Emilia said.

"Me too," I answered, shaking the thoughts of Thorne on top of me from my mind.

Or at least trying to.

"Is it going to be hard to go back now?" Aiden asked, and I saw the exchange between him and Thorne.

"It's going to be impossible," I admitted.

They stared at me in silence, and each one glanced at Thorne who just dropped his gaze to the ground.

"I hope you all know how much I have come to care about your family. I'm so sorry for all the misplaced anger from my tribe. I swear to you that I will set things right when I take over as their leader. And I will lift the sunlight curse as soon as I am able. After the first of the year, I'll find a way to send word. You can all come to the island, and I'll perform the spell."

"Thank you, Catrain. It means the world to us," Lothaire said.

"So, this is it?" Emilia frowned. "You're just going back, and we'll only see you one last time when you remove their curses?"

"I wish it could be different." I pursed my lips into a tight smile.

"Any chance you could try to run a locator spell on Leeya and that shit brother Leith before you go?" Annella asked. "I still haven't gotten my payback yet."

"Unless you got a possession of theirs while we were gone, unfortunately, I still can't help you out there."

"Worth a try." Annella clucked her cheek. "But don't worry. I'll find them anyway."

The intensity in those fiery blue eyes of hers erased any doubt that she would find them… and I pitied anyone on the receiving end of her wrath.

"We'll miss you, Catrain," Aiden said before pulling me in for a hug. As he pressed me against him, he whispered in my ear, "I know Thorne, and I know he loves you. And he always will. He'll never stop waiting for you if you ever change your mind, you will always have a place with us."

Tears burned behind my eyes as I nodded into his shoulder. "Thank you."

When he released me, each one of Thorne's family gave me one last hug, and I fought the tears that would go on for eternity if I let them free.

"Goodbye." I waved as I joined Thorne at the door. "Take care of yourselves. I'll send word in a few months."

They stood together in the door, each waving as they bid me goodbye.

Thorne closed the door, shutting them behind it. We walked in silence back to the garage.

He pulled out the dirt bike and smiled. "Want to drive?"

Even though I wanted to feel the excitement of driving the dirt bike one last time, the tears in my eyes blurred my vision too much to navigate the dark countryside.

"I'll just ride behind you," I answered softly.

As if he understood, he pressed his lips into a thin smile and jumped on the bike. "Hop on."

I climbed up behind him and wrapped my arms around his waist, pressing my face against his muscular back. Each time I touched him, my body buzzed with feelings I hoped I'd always remember. Feelings I knew I'd never feel again after we said goodbye.

Thorne started up the bike, and I held on tight as we tore out across the countryside. It looked so similar to the first time I'd been on this bike with him, but this time we were going in the opposite direction. I tried to soak in the sights of my surroundings, and the feel of Thorne in my arms, as much as I could until I saw the familiar tree on the outskirts of the lake that would be my home for the rest of my days.

When Thorne slowed the dirt bike to a stop, I bit my quivering lip and swallowed back down the tears.

"We're here," he said as he hopped off. When he turned around and offered me his hand, I saw the pain in his eyes.

"Thank you." As I clasped his fingers, the familiar sparks traveled between us, and I tried to burn that feeling into my body, hoping I could relive it over and over for the rest of my years.

"So. This is it." He blew out a puff of air. "I can't believe it's over."

"Neither can I." I squeezed his hand, then felt the tears break loose.

"Hey, hey," he said quietly as he pulled me into his arms. They enveloped my body as he pulled me against him. "You're going to be fine. Me? Not so much. But you? You'll be okay."

"I'm so sorry I can't stay. You know I want to."

With a heavy sigh, he squeezed me tighter. "You sure your mom won't let me move to the island and stay with you? I mean it. I'll live on that island for eternity and never leave if she'll let me be with you. I swear to God I'll be the best damn protector she's ever seen. I'll put those stanky ass werewolves to shame."

I laughed through the tears and shook my head. "She'll never allow it. If I thought for a second she would, I would drag you across the lake in that boat."

"I know you would." He kissed the top of my head, and I squeezed my eyes shut tight. "And if you ever change your mind, I will always be waiting for you. Always. I love you, Catrain."

The power of his words seeped into my soul and tore at my heart.

"I love you, too. Always."

He sighed again. "Then I guess this is it."

"This is it."

"But I'll see you again in a few months, right?"

"Yes." I nodded as I looked up into his eyes. "I promise I'll remove the curse. I'll send word."

"But I won't be able to do this, will I?" He slid his fingers under my chin, leaned down, and kissed me. It reignited the fire I'd been struggling to put out.

"No," I whispered as I leaned up and kissed him again.

"That's too bad," he whispered between kisses. "Because I'm going to be thinking about it when I see you again."

"I will, too. I'll always be thinking about this."

I kissed him again and held it even longer.

"I hope Uradech knows you'll be thinking about me even when you're with him." Thorne kissed me so hard my knees wobbled beneath me. But his strong arms kept me upright as he finished his assault on my senses.

As he slowly pulled his lips from mine, he left me panting in his arms, desperate for more.

"Change your mind," he said as he pressed his forehead to mine. "You still have time."

I closed my eyes and leaned into the weight of him. "I will always love you, Thorne."

Feeling my resolve slipping with each moment in his arms, I knew I would never leave him if I didn't go now. I rose on my toes and kissed him one last time, the salt of my tears mingling with the taste of his lips. Without another word, I broke us apart and rushed to the boat we'd left on the shore. With a quick push, I got it into the water and climbed over the edge.

Sobs wracked my body as I dug the paddles through the soft waves, forcing myself to stare at the water instead of looking up at him. But as I moved off the shore and settled into my rhythm, I made the mistake of looking up one last time. Thorne leaned against the tree, his arms crossed over his chest as he watched me go. With a slow lift of his hand, he bid me goodbye as I disappeared into the fog, and out of his life forever.

Chapter Seventeen

THORNE

"Another?" the bartender's deep voice interrupted my spiraling thoughts as he pointed to my glass.

I pushed it forward, keeping my eyes glued to the worn spot on the countertop.

His massive tattooed forearm slid into my line of sight as he took my glass away. When it appeared again a few moments later, I grunted my thanks and took the thick red drink disguised as a Bloody Mary. As we did at most clubs we frequented, we handed them our bottles of blood to keep cool and influenced bartenders to think it was special Bloody Mary mix and not to notice any of our vampire quirks. Once poured into the opaque glasses we brought along with us, and topped with a few garnishes, even the nearby patrons didn't notice the unusual beverages. It was a trick we'd learned centuries ago, and one that I intended to make the most of tonight.

Tonight, I needed blood.

Lots and lots of blood.

The last four nights sitting alone in my room unable to

sleep all day and running through the countryside at night to blow off steam hadn't erased an ounce of the agony Catrain's absence had left inside me.

Not. One. Bit.

In fact, each day we spent apart seemed to increase the already unbearable anguish.

Annella, Aiden, Emilia, and Mark had dragged me out to this club tonight, hoping perhaps a night of distraction could ease some of the pain.

It didn't.

I tossed half a glass of blood down my throat, then slammed it back on the bar.

"Easy, tiger," Annella said as she slid into the stool beside me. "You're gonna break that glass. Or the bar."

"Good," I grunted.

"You wanna dance? Maybe even get some fresh blood? We could pick out a nice girl for you to take a few sips of."

Just thinking about drinking blood from someone other than Catrain made my stomach twist into a never-ending knot. It only reminded me of the pleasure I felt when I drank from her, and the way her body responded to my touch as I slid my fangs inside her neck.

I picked up the glass and slammed the rest of the blood.

"Damn." Aiden blew out a slow whistle as he took the stool on the opposite side of me. "You're gonna blow through all those bottles of blood before the hour's up."

"I know," Annella agreed. "I was just suggesting maybe some fresh off the vein would help him perk up a bit."

"That's not a bad idea." Aiden scanned the sweaty bodies on the dance floor.

I followed his sweeping gaze and noticed Emilia and Mark dancing together in the center of them.

Aiden jutted his chin to the left side of the DJ's stage.

"What about that red-head? I can see her jugular from here."

"I don't want to drink from anyone," I mumbled as I pushed my glass forward.

The bartender appeared again and asked if I wanted another.

This time I looked up and locked up with his intense green eyes. "Just keep 'em coming, man."

He nodded his head, and a piece of his dark, wavy hair fell in front of his eyes. He pushed it out of his face as he took my glass. Before he could get it off the bar, Annella caught him by the wrist and stopped him. When he looked at her, she gave him her signature seductive stare.

"Hey, hot stuff," she crooned as she curved her full red lips into a smile that would make the Cheshire cat green with envy. "What's your name?"

"Owen," he answered as he leaned closed to her.

She traced her long fingernails across the tattoos that climbed up his forearms and wrapped around his biceps that were bigger than my head. This massive dude had to stand a couple inches above Lothaire. He looked like he should have been a bouncer instead of a bartender.

Or maybe a WWE wrestler or an MMA fighter. Hell, maybe he was, and this was just a part-time gig. If it weren't for my vamp powers, there's no way I'd ever pick a fight with a guy his size.

Annella twisted a piece of her long, auburn hair between her fingers. "Hi, Owen. My friend here needs to slow down on the Bloody Marys. How about you give us a few minutes?"

His pupils dilated as he stared at her, and I couldn't decide if she was influencing him, or if he was just attracted to her.

Likely the latter based on the sound of his heart speeding up as he raked her body with a heated gaze.

"Of course," he answered. "Just let me know when you're ready for one."

She blew him a little kiss as she released his hand, and it brought on a bright white smile that contrasted his olive skin.

"Holy fuck is he hot," she whispered as he walked away. "I wanna climb him like a tree."

Aiden laughed, and normally I would have too, but this time I just kept staring at that damn spot on the bar.

"You okay, man?" Aiden asked, bumping me with his shoulder.

"No," I answered honestly. "Far fucking from it."

"Hey, Nella? You want to give us a minute?" Aiden twitched his head toward the end of the bar.

She kissed my cheek. "Of course. Love you, boo. Hey, Owen," she called to the bartender she couldn't stop making eyes at. He turned to look at her, and she pointed to the end of the bar. When she met him there, she whispered something in his ear, and he followed her into the stockroom. No doubt she was going to have a little fresh blood herself… or knowing Annella, a little something more.

Aiden reached over the bar and grabbed a glass and a bottle of whiskey before plucking the bottle of blood from the ice bin. He filled up my empty glass with blood, and poured whiskey in his, then clinked them together.

"Welcome to the broken hearts club, brother."

"Fuck this club," I growled and took a long swig of my blood.

"It's the worst club in the world, and I should know. I used to be president of it."

Scoffing, I nodded. "I remember it. Well. In fact, it's the

whole reason I've kept my ladies at arm's length. Losing Isobel almost killed you, man."

"It did," Aiden answered. "But I survived. And now I have Emilia. It doesn't feel like it, but you are going to be okay again."

"It doesn't feel like it right now."

"It never does."

I took another sip of my blood. "Would it be wrong to say that it would be easier if she died?"

Aiden's eyebrows stretched to his perfect hairline. "Whoa."

I shook my head. "I'm not saying I want her dead. God, no. I'm just saying it would be easier if she'd been taken from me like you lost Isobel and not that she left me by choice. Easier if I didn't have to walk through this world knowing she's still out there, but I just can't see her… and to picture her in the arms of that fucking *werewolf*."

That last mental image made me want to shove my hand inside my head and rip out my brain, so I didn't need to picture him having his way with her.

"I'm still shocked that werewolves are out there, and more shocked that she's marrying one. I can't even imagine what that feels like."

He placed a hand on my back as I slowly shook my head. "Like having my heart ripped out and left to burn in the sun for all eternity."

"Are you sure you can't convince her to come back?" He propped his hand on his chin.

"I'm sure." I scoffed. "I literally got on my knees and begged. Me. Begged, Aiden. Not my proudest moment."

"Being in love isn't about being proud. It's about being willing to do anything, *anything*, for the woman you love. There's nothing I wouldn't do for Emilia. Nothing."

"I *would* do anything for her. Hell, that's why I shut the hell up and let her get on that boat and leave me. It's what she wanted. Trust me, I thought about influencing her to stay with me, or trapping her in Hawaii and saying the jet was broken. Forever. Especially when I found out she's supposed to get married… tomorrow." I growled. "It took everything I had to put her back on that plane. She's never gotten to make her own choices though, so for once in her life, I wanted her to be in control. And she chose to go back… to marry him."

"But did she?" Annella said as she reappeared at my side. "Sorry, I was eavesdropping."

"It's fine. I tell you everything anyway."

"She didn't *choose* it, Thorne. She did what she's been trained to do since birth. She followed the only path she's ever known. That's not a choice. I saw the way she looked at you. Her *choice* would have been you."

"Concur," Aiden added with a knowing nod. "That girl is head over heels in love with you."

I glanced back and forth between the two of them. "So, what are you saying? I did the wrong thing?"

Annella snorted, and Aiden just shrugged and took a sip of his whiskey.

"Seriously? I did the wrong thing letting her go?" I looked back and forth between them.

Aiden set down his drink and looked me in the eyes. "All I'm saying is that if you love a woman, you will do *anything* for her happiness. If you think she's happier where she is, then you stay the hell out of her way. But if you think she's happier out here with you…" He arched a brow. "Then you do whatever the hell you have to do to get her that happiness. Have you done *everything* in your power to be together?"

"I thought so." I shrugged. "What's left? Kidnap her?"

"Men." Annella slapped me on the back of my head. "What is the one thing standing in your way?"

"Her mother," I grumbled.

"And have you talked to her mother?" Aiden asked.

The minute he said the words, I realized I *hadn't* done everything in my power. I'd begged Catrain, but I hadn't begged her *mother*… the one making all the decisions.

"Fuck. I just assumed she'd shut it down."

"And she very well might," Aiden said. "But you won't know until you try, will you? If it were Emilia, I would fight for her until the ring was on her finger… and probably even long after that."

"So, you're saying I should go to the island and beg her mother?" I asked them both.

They nodded in unison.

"What if she won't let me back on the island?"

Annella shrugged. "Then you'll be able to say you tried everything in your power."

"So, basically, I'm an idiot." I shook my head.

"Dude." Annella pressed her hand on my shoulder, and her strength surprised me. "Your woman is about to marry a *werewolf,* and you're sitting here pining. A. Were. Wolf." She cringed and shuddered. "No woman should have to endure those smelly beasts… especially not the woman you love. Go to the island and beg her mother… you have to try. And if that doesn't work, then take out that fucking werewolf and any others you find on the island. Or better yet, let me."

She waggled her eyebrows, and it caused me to chuckle.

"You do have a reputation for slaying werewolves. Didn't the wolves used to call you 'The Slayer' or something?"

"Damn straight they did." She grinned proudly. "A name I earned… and a name I'm proud of."

I puckered my lips while I pictured her decimating Uradech with the skill I'd seen her use to take out countless wolves. "Maybe I *should* sneak you onto the island with me and let you rip."

"Now that I know I missed some and they're still alive?" She arched a brow. "It's all I can think about. Well, that and killing Clan Lennox. Damn, my kill roster is filling fast."

Aiden and I laughed as she stole my cup and took a drink.

"What time is it?" I asked as I fumbled for my phone.

"Three in the morning," Annella said, pointing at the digital clock behind the bar.

"Fuck. I won't have time to get to the island, talk to her mom, and get back before sunrise. Damn it! Why can't my ring still be working?"

"What time does she marry him tomorrow?" Aiden asked.

"I'm not sure. All I know is she said they marry under the full moon. So, it's gotta be at night."

"Then you get home, and the minute the sun goes down, you get your ass back to that island and fight for your girl."

"Thank you," I said as I looked between them. "I guess I needed a kick in the pants."

"You need a kick in the dancing pants!" Mark said as he bumped his hip into me. "Come on! Dance floor. Now."

Emilia shimmied next to him and slid onto Aiden's lap.

The bartender passed us, and Mark's eyes tracked him as he went by. "He's fucking gorg."

"He's stupid hot… and taken." Annella smirked with a glint in her eyes.

"Gah. Already, bitch?" He crossed his arms and peeked at the bartender again.

"Yep. And his blood is some of the best I've ever tasted."

The bartender passed by and slid a napkin in front of Annella. When she saw the phone number on it, her ivory skin flushed an unnatural shade of red.

"Call me," he said with confidence before walking away.

"Are you blushing?" Emilia laughed.

"No!" Annella argued, but the flush of her cheeks deepened to crimson.

"Stop the presses. Do you *like* him, like him?" Mark asked.

"No." She rolled her eyes, but Mark kept staring at her.

"Okay, maybe." She shrugged. "I thought I was just going to drink his blood quick, but he was actually really sweet."

"Well, would you look at that." Aiden grinned. "Annella's actually smitten."

"Fuck off," she said and flipped us the bird. "I just think he's stupid hot, really nice, an amazing kisser, and his blood tastes fabulous."

"So, you're saying you're smitten." Emilia laughed.

"A smitten kitten," Mark teased.

"Why are we even talking about me?" Annella changed the subject. "The thing we *should* be talking about is that Thorne has been a whiny bitch, and he's going to go fight for Catrain tomorrow."

Mark and Emilia squealed and clapped their hands in unison.

"You are? Yay!" Emilia cheered. "What can we do to help?"

"Nothing," I said, then slammed the last of my blood. "I

just need to get home and get ready, because the minute the sun goes down tomorrow, I'm off."

"That's our boy." Mark patted my shoulder. "You go get your girl."

My girl.

Damn straight she was. And it was time I fought like the warrior I was to make her mine again.

Chapter Eighteen

CATRAIN

"Hold still," Alpia said as she stuck another flower into the braid in my hair.

"I'm bored." I drummed my nails on the wooden arm of the chair I'd been sitting in for the better part of the afternoon. Preparing for my wedding ceremony had been an entire day of traditions. Bathing in a special floral oil, having my body painted in traditional wedding designs, wearing the decorated leather dress passed down for generations, and now this ridiculous floral hairdo.

After returning to the island and enduring a week's worth of wrath from my mother, this felt more like punishment than tradition. I'd already been locked up in my hut every minute I wasn't at her side, but I'd take that any day over sitting here getting primped for my wedding. Solitude in my hut had been a welcome reprieve from the scowls and glares she impaled me with every chance she got. The silence was a retreat from the barrage of angry words her sharp tongue had spit at me. I'd heard it all.

I was a disappointment.

Ungrateful.

I'd broken tradition.

Luckily, she didn't know that my little "adventure to the mainland" had been far more than that. I hadn't just saved one of the vampires she hated so much, I'd fallen in love with one.

Or if she suspected, she didn't say a word about it… probably too horrified to admit her heir had broken one last tradition and not saved herself for marriage, instead giving her most precious gift to the man that made my mother's blood boil.

Day after day, I listened to her preach about how selfish I was and how I'd disappointed her and our ancestors. But her words fell on deaf ears because as she berated me for my "childish mistake," all I could hear was the sound of Thorne's laughter, the crash of the waves beside our villa in Hawaii, and his soft breathing as he'd hold he against him when we'd sleep. My body may have been back on our island, but my mind was still with the man I loved.

After days of strange looks from the tribe and the scoldings from my mother, things had finally started to return to normal… as normal as they could be with my wedding coming up.

My wedding that was *tonight.*

Alpia tugged my hair as she tightened the braid. "It's your wedding night. You're supposed to be enjoying all this pampering."

Rolling my eyes, I shook my head, but she grabbed it and stopped the motion.

"Quit. Moving."

"Are you done yet?"

"You're worse than a child." She stuck another flower into the braid wrapping around my head like a crown.

She wasn't wrong. I hadn't exactly been a willing participant all day, and not just because I hated all the fuss. Every step farther in the process was one step closer to the aisle where Uradech would be waiting.

One step closer to being the wife of someone other than the man I loved.

Thorne.

The vision of his face assaulted my mind again. His laughter rang in my ears, and my skin burned as it remembered his touch. Closing my eyes, I let myself remember the taste of his lips as he kissed me that last time.

"Done," Alpia said as she stepped in front of me.

I held Thorne's vision in my mind for another moment before I opened my eyes and looked up at her.

"You look so beautiful, Catrain. Uradech will die when he sees you."

I rolled my eyes and shook my head before pushing out of the chair.

"Seriously?" Alpia scoffed. "You're really going to keep up the attitude even though you're about to marry the strongest, most handsome warrior on the island, and then get to ascend to the leader of our clan? Why are you acting so selfish?"

"Selfish?" I snapped as I spun around.

Her blue eyes that looked like mine widened as I stepped forward to face her.

"Why would I be jumping for joy right now? I am giving up everything I want for my people. *Everything.* That actually makes me the opposite of selfish."

Instantly, the irritation in her eyes dissipated as she dropped her gaze to the ground. "I'm sorry," she replied, losing the unnatural attitude in her voice and resuming her normal dulcet tones. "I didn't mean to upset you."

Seeing her submitting to me without a fight caused a mixture of guilt and irritation. Just like every other person in our tribe, even my own little sister had been taught never to argue with me. The heir to the throne should be respected at all times. And because of it, until Thorne came into my life, no one had ever expressed what they truly wanted to say to me.

"Don't." I shook my head. "Don't apologize to me because it's what you've always been told to do… what *everyone* has been told to do. If you have something to say to me, then say it."

She peeked up from the floor but lowered her eyes again.

"Alpia," I took her hand and led her over the bed at the side of the room. She followed my lead and sat beside me. "I shouldn't have snapped at you."

"I shouldn't have questioned you," she quickly answered.

"Yes. Yes, you should have. You're absolutely right. I have been acting terrible. And you're my sister. You're supposed to tell me when I'm acting like a spoiled child."

"You have a lot of pressure right now, that's all." She finally looked up.

"I do." I blew out a sigh. "But that's no excuse for treating you so poorly. I know you're only trying to help."

A soft smile curved up her pink lips. "I just want you to be happy, Catrain. I want everything perfect for your big day. Uradech will make a fine husband. The finest…" She drifted off, and I saw pain flash in her eye.

A pain I recognized because it was the same as my own.

The pain of longing for a man that could never be yours.

"Wait a minute." I reached over and lifted her chin with my hand. "Do you have feelings for him?"

Her eyes widened as she shook her head and dislodged it from my grip. "No! He is your betrothed and has been since before I was born. I cannot have feelings for him."

But I saw the truth in her eyes.

Chuckling, I lifted her head again. "Alpia. Please, I'm begging you, for once in your life, be honest with me. Don't tell me what I want to hear… tell me what's in your heart. I promise you I won't be angry."

Her lip quivered as a sheen coated her eyes. "I can't."

"Yes, you can. We're family. We're sisters. We should always be able to be honest with each other. Support each other. Love each other."

I remembered the connection between Thorne and his siblings, the one they briefly shared with me, and I wanted so badly to feel that again. I wanted to have it with my own sister instead of having her treat me like a superior to be catered to.

With a gentle squeeze on her hand and a soft smile, I said, "If you love him, you need to tell me, Alpia. I never want to do anything to hurt you, and I can't marry the man that my sister loves."

She just looked away and shook her head. "He's your betrothed."

"He may be my betrothed, but I don't love him… and I never will."

"How can you not love him?" she asked as she turned back to face me. "Uradech is incredible. He's so handsome, strong, kind…" She stopped herself from going on when she saw the smile growing on my face.

"You *do* love him."

"No!" She shook her head so hard I thought it may pop off.

"Yes, you do. And do you know how I can tell? Because I love someone else, too, and I recognize that look in your eyes."

"You love someone else?" She gasped. "Who?"

"If I tell you, will you be honest with me about Uradech?"

She bit her lip, then nodded.

"I'm in love with Thorne."

"The *vampire*?" She practically shrieked.

"Shhhh…" I lifted my finger to my lips, then nodded my head. "Yes."

"But he's a *vampire,*" she whispered. "You can't be serious! He's a bloodthirsty monster!"

I shook my head and smiled. "He's not. In fact, none of his family is. They are kind, wonderful people. All the things we've been told about them have been lies. The betrayal of the pact came from our people. The werewolves hunted *them* down. All these centuries of hatred toward them has been completely misplaced. And Thorne is the most amazing man I've ever met. I love him with all of my heart and always will."

I told her more of the stories of what had really happened all those centuries ago, and about the love that had grown between Thorne and me. A love I knew I couldn't live without.

When I finished, she just shook her head and said, "Wow."

"It took everything I had to force myself back here to marry Uradech and take our mother's throne. It's not what I want. At *all.* What I want is a life with Thorne."

"That may be so, and it sounds like he's more than

worthy of your love, but Mother would never allow it. Never." Her eyes widened.

With a heavy sigh, I flopped back on the bed. "I know."

Alpia leaned back with me, and we lay side by side, staring at the thatched ceiling.

"I do love Uradech," she finally whispered. "With all my heart."

I rolled my head over and met her teary eyes. "I'm so sorry, Alpia. This must have been torture for you getting me ready for a wedding to the man you love."

"It's not fun," she admitted. "But it's our duty. It's your duty to marry him, and my duty to watch you. Uradech and I can never be."

"Does he share your feelings?" I stroked my fingers through her ebony hair.

She shrugged. "I think so. He's always coming around doing nice things for me, and I catch him staring at me all the time. And when I turned eighteen, he told me he loved me and tried to kiss me. Of course, I told him he was your betrothed and slapped him."

"Why didn't you tell me this?" I bumped her with my elbow. "I'm your sister!"

She shrugged. "Because he's supposed to be your husband. It didn't matter how we felt about each other."

"It *does* matter. It matters to me. It's one thing to force myself to give up the man I love, but I'm sure are hell not going to do the same thing to you. I could never live with myself, marrying the man my sister loves. I'm calling off the wedding."

"You can't call off the wedding!" She sat up straight.

"Can't I?" I sat up with her.

"It's tradition! You have to!"

"I'm so sick of tradition. What about free will? Evolution? Adapting to changes? The rest of the world out there has changed and moved forward, but we are here on this island stuck in the same cycle. Over and over and over again. Why can't we change it? Why can't we start a new tradition?"

"Because of the pact with the werewolves, that's why." She lifted her eyebrows. "If we break it, they can kill us all. The pact says that they get to marry the leader of our clan."

"Then you be the leader."

"What?" She gasped.

The moment I said the words, I felt the weight of my lifetime of forced duties lifting from my shoulders. As the seconds ticked by, I became even more convinced that this was the right choice.

My choice.

"You have always been better suited to the position than me. I've never wanted it, but you..." I took her hand in mine. "You have always been the better choice to lead our tribe. You're kind, fair, strong, and you love your life here on the island... a life you can spend with the man you love. Let me step aside, and you marry Uradech and ascend the throne."

"We can't! It's never been done before! The eldest daughter ascends... that's how it's always been done."

"Then we start a new tradition. Today. I'll tell Mother I'm abdicating the throne to you, and you can marry Uradech and take over."

"She'll never allow it!"

"I will not marry your love." I shook my head and sighed. "And I will not give up mine."

We sat and stared at each other for a long moment, and I saw the pained look in her eyes, giving way to one filled with happiness.

"You would really step aside? Are you sure? I can't ask you to do that for me."

"You're my sister. I would do anything for you. This is the right choice… the right choice for *both* of us, and for our people. Will you accept?"

Tears filled her eyes, and she nodded vigorously than tossed her arms around my neck and held me tight.

"Yes! More than anything, yes! I would love nothing more. Thank you, Catrain. I love you so much."

"I love you too."

Her grip around me loosened as she sat back, and our worry-filled eyes met. "What do you think Mother will say? What if she doesn't think I'm worthy?"

"No one is more worthy. At first, she will fight me on this because she lives her life never breaking tradition. But there are times to change tradition… and this is one of them. I'll convince her."

"Okay," she said as she chewed her lip… the same nervous habit I had.

The door to the hut opened, and Calita popped her head in. "They're ready."

Alpia and I shared a worried look before I lifted my chin and straightened my shoulders. "Come on, Alpia. Let's go tell Mother the new plan."

She held my hand as we started out the door. Even though it was nighttime, the shadows of the trees swayed in the sand underneath the full moon.

Alpia tugged me to a stop. "Wait. If you're going to be with Thorne, does that mean you're leaving the island?"

I met her concerned gaze and shook my head slowly. "I'm not sure. I know Mother will never allow him to come here, but maybe when you're ruling, you can lift the rules and allow us to come back to the island to visit."

"Anytime," she said and pulled me in for a hug. "If you say he's a wonderful man, I believe you. You will always be welcome here… and so will he. Even if he has to sleep in a cave."

I sucked the air through my teeth, remembering the promise I'd made him and his family. "About that. Once you have full powers, I'm also going to need you to lift their sunlight curse."

Her eyes widened as I gave her a wide sheepish grin.

She laughed and tossed an arm around my shoulder. "We'll figure it out. But first, we have to convince Mother to even let us do this."

"You just let me handle her." I slid my arm around her waist, and we started down the beach toward the ceremony site that awaited me… and my mother.

Alpia and I rounded the corner of the beach, and I saw all several hundred members of our tribe gathered around the fire crackling in the sand. They formed a half-circle around it and the wedding arch towering above it.

The wedding arch Uradech stood under.

My mother stood at his side, and when she saw us coming, she quieted the chattering crowd by raising her staff. Alpia and I shared a worried look again, but I squeezed her hand tighter and walked with purpose toward my mother.

She started the traditional chant to announce the bride, so I hurried my steps and dragged Alpia along with me.

"Mother, we need to talk," I said as I approached her.

The wrinkles on her face deepened as she scowled at me, no doubt upset I'd already broken the tradition of not speaking during the ceremony.

"Silence," she said, then went back to the ceremony.

"Mother," I said more firmly. "I need to talk to you."

She spun around and impaled me with a look. But this time, instead of slinking beneath it, I straightened my shoulders and held her condemnatory stare.

"Now."

Her eyebrows rose to her hairline as we stared at each other while the tribe murmured their confusion. I glanced at Uradech and noticed his gaze wasn't fixated on me at all. He stared at my sister with the same love in his eyes I saw when Thorne looked at me.

How had I not seen it before? Now that I knew about their affection, it seemed as clear as the Hawaiian waters that they loved one another.

"You dishonor the ceremony," my mother started, but I stopped her by lifting my hand.

"Please. Walk with me."

Alpia's grip on my hand tightened, and her quick breathing stalled out as she held her breath.

My mother and I stood locked in a staring match for several long moments before she lifted her chin and stepped to my side.

I tried to comfort Alpia with a quick smile, then let go of her hand and stepped away from the crowd with my mother.

"I know it is tradition for the eldest child to ascend the throne," I said as I started walking at her side, "but I have something to tell you."

We had only made it several paces away when I heard a voice I would recognize anywhere calling my name through the mist.

Thorne.

My mother's eyes widened as she and I spun to stare into the fog. Thorne paddled his boat toward us, calling my name as he called into the abyss.

"What is he doing here?" she snarled. "He is not allowed."

What *was* he doing here? We'd agreed he wouldn't return. Yet there he was calling my name as he searched the fog. Even though the timing couldn't have been worse, I didn't want to be without him any longer.

"Mother, please. Let me grant him entrance."

She spun and grabbed me by the shoulders, her eyes narrowing with the intensity of her demands.

"If he comes, he dies." She pointed to the full moon hovering above us, and I knew what she meant.

The werewolves could shift into wolf form at any time, but their powers grew with the moon. The fuller the moon, the stronger they were. Under a full moon, a werewolf was much more powerful than a vampire… even an original one. Even a single wolf could take down Thorne. Uradech and his three younger brothers combined would lay waste to Thorne at my mother's command.

"Mother, please," I begged. "I know you don't approve, but I have a plan. Just let me give Thorne entrance, and I'll explain the whole thing to you."

"No. He is forbidden."

"Mother!" I shouted. "Enough! You cannot control me any longer. This is *my* life, and I choose Thorne. I love him, and you will *not* kill him."

Fury burned inside her eyes at my disobedience, but I didn't care.

Not anymore.

All I cared about was being with Thorne again, and I couldn't stand to be away from him another minute.

I waved my hand over the fog and released it as I held her gaze.

Chapter Nineteen

THORNE

When the fog lifted, I saw Catrain and her mother staring each other down on the beach. Behind them stood hundreds of their tribesman, with Uradech at the center beneath a floral covered arch.

The wedding.

Was I too late?

Had it already happened?

Panic that I'd already lost her, and desperation to see her once again drove me on as I dug the paddles into the water and pushed. The little wooden boat sailed onto the shore and skidded to a stop.

"Catrain!" I called as I hopped out and ran toward her.

"Stay there," she commanded, and the serious tones of her voice advised me to listen. I slowed to a stop and watched the altercation between her and Liùsaidh.

"You chose this," her mother said. "Remember that."

"Mother," Catrain warned. "If you'll just let me explain what I have planned, I think you will agree with my decision."

"Uradech!" Liùsaidh called across the beach.

"Mother," Catrain ground out. "Don't."

Unsure what they were arguing about, I looked back and forth between them. Liùsaidh slowly looked toward me, and her eyes burned with centuries-old hatred that would have incinerated me if it could. She held my gaze while she commanded Uradech, "Kill him."

"No!" Catrain shouted, then tore across the beach toward me, calling, "Go! Get in the boat! Get off the island! Now!"

Before I had a chance to respond, I glanced at Uradech and watched as he narrowed his eyes and lowered his head. The same hatred that had burned in Liùsaidh's eyes now lit up his.

Even though I'd seen my fair share of werewolves centuries ago, I'd never watched one change. They'd always been in wolf form when they attacked us. I stood in awe as I watched Uradech drop to his knees, his body morphing before my eyes until he took on the form of the giant wolf I hadn't seen in five hundred years.

When his transformation finished, the giant black wolf looked at me, lifted its lips, and snarled.

"Thorne! The full moon! He's too powerful! Get in the boat and go!" Catrain called again as she made it to my side.

"No," I growled as I locked with Uradech's bright green eyes.

If I left now, she would marry him tonight, and I would lose her forever.

I decided right there I would rather die than give up the fight of making her mine… because she was mine. And I was hers.

Always.

"This ends now." I popped out my fangs as Uradech charged towards me.

"Thorne!" she begged, but it was too late.

I flashed across the beach, colliding with his giant, muscular body and sending him rolling across the sand. He leapt back on his feet with a snarl, tearing back toward me with white fangs glinting in the moonlight.

The loud snap of his jaws echoed in my ears after he launched at my head but missed with my well-timed spin. I connected a well-placed kick to his stomach that sent him sailing across the beach, skidding to a stop before he hit the water's edge.

Uradech rose, and his roar vibrated through my chest.

"Stop! Both of you! Stop!" Catrain shouted.

"Kill him!" her mother screamed over her.

The hatred burning in Uradech's eyes told me he didn't need any other encouragement from his leader. He charged at me again, and I lowered my head while I waited to meet him. As he leaped into the air again, I swung my fist intending to lay him out with the power of my blow. But his quick dodge missed my strike, and instead of sending him flying, he tackled me to the ground. As his huge body pummeled me into the sand, I remembered why we'd had to create an army to defeat them.

They were as strong as us.

And under this moon… stronger.

His powerful jaws snapped next to my head as we rolled across the beach. Even my strongest blows didn't dislodge him as he tumbled to a stop on top of me. For a moment, I wondered if I'd made a mistake in challenging him. Maybe I'd just condemned Catrain to a life without me… a life married to the hairy beast whose weight drove me deeper into the sand.

I saw the back of his throat as his open mouth closed toward my head… and one snap of those jaws would remove it. I caught his neck with my hand and held the weight of him as he snapped and snarled at me, his hot breath scorching my nostrils. As I held him off, I glanced over and saw Catrain standing on the beach. Her hands moved to her mouth as tears filled her blue eyes.

"Thorne," she whispered.

Uradech dug his feet into the sand, trying to get the leverage to break my grip on him–the one thing stopping him from ending my immortal life. But as I looked to Catrain one last time, I felt the strength I needed to defeat him moving through my body. He may be stronger than me in this moonlight, but he wasn't fueled by the power of love that coursed through my veins.

I wouldn't fail.

I couldn't.

Failure meant Catrain would spend her life at his side, instead of a life at mine.

Never.

With a powerful thrust, I pushed his heavy body off me, sending him flying into the wedding arch. It crumbled from the blow, sending pieces of wood and flowers collapsing on top of him.

When he emerged from the pile, he shook the rubble from his body, then lifted his lips in a snarl as he locked back onto me. As Uradech tore toward me, I braced for impact. But before he reached me, Catrain's sister jumped in front of me. Uradech threw himself to the side to avoid colliding with her, landing in the sand with a thud.

"Stop, Uradech! Please!" she begged.

The giant wolf lifted his dark body from the ground,

and his glowing green eyes searched hers as he heaved heavy pants.

"You need to listen to me," Alpia begged, stepping toward him with open hands. "Please don't hurt him. Please. I'm begging you, Uradech. End this now. He doesn't deserve to die. Stop this fight. For me."

Uradech's penetrating eyes moved to me before drifting back to hers. After a long pause, he lowered his head and stepped in front of her. I watched in awe as his body morphed again, and soon the man stood in front of her.

"Thank you," she said as she tossed her arms around his neck. "Thank you."

Catrain raced to my side and launched into my arms. I caught her around the waist and pulled her against me.

"Catrain. I'm so sorry I came back, but I couldn't let you do it. I couldn't give you up."

"I couldn't do it either," she whispered into my ear as she held me tighter. "I love you, Thorne. I choose you. I'll always choose you."

The power of those words seeped into the deepest part of my soul and flooded it with love and light like I'd never known.

I grabbed ahold of her face and consumed her with my kiss. Just like when I'd drank her blood, I felt our bodies connecting… our souls merging. I could have stood there on that beach kissing her for the rest of eternity, but Liùsaidh slammed her staff into the ground, and we all spun to look at her.

"I said kill him!" she snapped at Uradech, who glanced at Alpia, then lowered his eyes to the ground.

Catrain slid from my arms and took her sister by the hand. Together, they approached their mother.

"No one needs to die, Mother. If you'll just give me a chance to explain, we have a plan."

Liùsaidh didn't answer as her daughters approached her.

Catrain reached her first. "I am giving up my right to the throne."

The tribe who watched silently all gasped along with Liùsaidh.

"You can't!" Liùsaidh screeched. "The tradition—"

"I know the tradition," Catrain cut her off. "But I'm making a new tradition. I don't want the throne. I don't want to marry Uradech." She pulled her sister forward. "But Alpia does. She loves him, and she will make a much better leader than I would. Alpia is the one who should marry Uradech and take your throne."

Liùsaidh looked between them, and after a moment, shook her head. "It's not how it's done. The eldest ascends."

Catrain stepped forward and slipped her mother's hands into hers. "I know that's how it's always *been* done, but that doesn't mean we can't change… adapt. This isn't what I want, mother. I know that hurts you, but it's true. You want a ruler who *wants* to rule, not someone forced into the throne. Alpia is the right leader. She will take care of our people and our traditions the same way you would. It should have always been her."

Liùsaidh stood silently, then glanced over to her youngest daughter.

Alpia lowered her eyes to the ground and stared at her bare feet.

"This is what you want?" Liùsaidh asked her.

Alpia lifted her head and looked to Uradech. His eyes lit up the way mine did when I looked at Catrain, and he nodded his head as he smiled.

"Yes. This is what I want," Alpia said. "I promise I won't let you down, Mother. If you'll just give me a chance, I will make you so proud."

Liùsaidh twisted her lips as she looked to Uradech. "Do you agree to this? You must agree to ensure our pact remains intact."

"Yes," he answered quickly. "Yes, I agree. I will marry and rule with Alpia."

Alpia's face lit up like a thousand suns as she smiled at him, and he returned the warmth with his growing smile.

Liùsaidh looked to Catrain and impaled her with a heated stare. "There is no going back if you decide to do this." She glanced to me. "If you choose *him* over your people."

"It's not about him. I've never wanted this. Never. I have dreaded this day my entire life, but only now I realized I have a choice. I choose my happiness. I choose Alpia's happiness. Uradech's happiness. I choose what's best for our tribe. And yes," she paused and looked at me, "I choose Thorne. Alpia should reign, and I agree to give up my claim to the throne."

"Then it is done." Liùsaidh bowed her head and stepped forward toward the tribe. "Let it be known that the heir to the throne is my daughter, Alpia. She will wed Uradech under the next full moon."

The shocked faces of the tribespeople started to soften as they saw the joy between Uradech and Alpia.

"Does anyone oppose this union?" Liùsaidh asked them.

They glanced between each other, all answering with the same shaking heads.

"Then let it be decided. Alpia, come."

Alpia hurried to her side, and together they stood in front of the tribe.

Liùsaidh tapped her staff in the sand. "Bow to the new heir."

One by one, they lowered themselves to the ground. I glanced over to see Catrain watching with tear-filled eyes and that smile I'd missed so much.

When the tribespeople rose, Liùsaidh pulled Alpia in for a hug and kissed her on the cheek. After she let go, Alpia raced to Uradech, and he caught her in his enormous arms.

I walked over to Catrain, and she spun to see me.

"Did you just pull it off?" I asked as I stopped in front of her.

"I think I did." She grinned.

"And this means you can be with me?" I asked, still struggling to believe the new reality.

A reality that meant I got to spend my life with the woman I loved.

"Yes," she answered with a smile, then arched an eyebrow. "As long as you still want me, that is."

Instead of answering with words, I snagged her around the waist and folded her backward with the power of my kiss. She lay suspended in my arms as I tried to kiss away all the pain and agony I'd been in since I'd said goodbye. Tried to kiss her so hard she'd never question her place at my side again.

When I knew she struggled to breathe, I softened my kiss and peppered several small ones on her lips. "Does that answer your question?" I asked with a smile.

"Question answered." She laughed.

I pulled her back to standing, keeping her pressed against my body where she belonged. We turned to her mother, whose narrowed eyes didn't hold the same joy as her sister's.

"Now, you go." Liùsaidh pointed to the boat.

"What?" Catrain asked, stunned.

"He is banished. He must leave now."

"Mother," Catrain started, but Liùsaidh lifted her hand.

"Their kind is an abomination and are not welcome here. He goes, and you choose. Him or us."

Catrain's lip shook, but she sucked it between her teeth and lifted her chin high. "Fine."

Taking my hand in hers, she started toward the boat.

"Stop!" Alpia called, then raced over to us. She grabbed Catrain and held her hand tight as she spoke to her mother and her people. "Everything we have been told about the vampires has been a lie."

The tribe murmured their displeasure, but like the leader she was destined to become, she ignored them and went on. "Our history is twisted, and it's time we treated the Mackay clan with the respect they deserve… and that includes Thorne. He is a bloodsucker because we made him one when we cursed his family for breaking a pact *we* broke first."

She told the story of what really happened to our clan as the tribesman and Liùsaidh listened closely. "We killed half of their clan. And then we cursed them. The only monsters here are us, and I intend to right that wrong. I am the heir to the throne, and let it be known that when I ascend, Thorne and his family will always be welcome here. Always."

When she finished talking, Catrain threw her arms around Alpia's shoulders. The two sisters stood locked in an embrace while Liùsaidh looked on.

They broke apart, and Alpia turned to her mother. "She's going to be with him one way or another. You have the power to put aside your prejudices and embrace your daughter and the man she loves, or you can banish him from this island and possibly lose her forever. The choice is yours, Mother. But I choose to accept him and embrace him as one of our own."

She put her hand on my shoulder, and I looked down at her and smiled. "Thank you, Alpia. I appreciate you saying so. Just make sure the light-tight cave is ready for when I return, and I'll bring Catrain to visit you as often as she wants. I promise."

"You'll always be welcome." She rose on her toes and hugged me. "Well, once I'm in charge you will be," she added as she glanced at her mother.

Catrain wiped a tear from her eye and mouthed "thank you" to her sister.

Liùsaidh stood silently for several long moments, then let out a sigh and tapped her staff on the ground. "Come."

Catrain and I glanced between each other, trying to determine which one she meant.

With a roll of her eyes, she pointed to both of us. Catrain took me by the hand, and we walked together to where her mother stood.

"I do not approve of you with a bloodsucker." Her penetrating gaze passed between us.

"I know, Mother. But if you'll just give it some time, you'll see that he's not a monster like we were led to believe. None of them are."

She shook her head and pulled a face. "As long as he drinks human blood, he will always be monster to me."

Catrain chewed on her lip and nodded. "I understand. But I love him, Mother. I hope someday you'll find a way to accept him for what he is."

"I will not." Liùsaidh looked at me, piercing me with those gray eyes. "No bloodsucker will be with my daughter. I forbid it."

"What?" Catrain and I echoed.

Liùsaidh closed her eyes and lifted her hands. They glowed blue as she held them over me. Her immense powers surged through my body, and it felt like my blood boiled in my veins. The pain searing through me dropped me to my knees, and I heard Catrain screaming my name and begging her mother to stop. As the pain reached unimaginable depths, I clawed at my exploding head and rolled in the sand, desperate to make it end. When I didn't think I could withstand even another second, the intense pain vanished as quickly as it had started.

"What did you do?" Catrain shouted at her as she dropped beside me. "Thorne? Are you okay? Thorne!"

Too stunned to answer, I just rolled over onto my back and struggled to catch my breath.

"What did you do to him, Mother?" Catrain demanded as she kneeled over me. "Tell me! What did you do?"

Liùsaidh looked down her nose at us. "I returned his original powers. No daughter of mine will be with a bloodsucker. Now he doesn't need to drink blood again."

My original powers?

Stunned at the words I'd just heard, I looked down at my hands. They looked the same, but as the pain left my body, I realized everything inside me felt completely different. I felt like I had after the first time I'd transitioned over six hundred years ago. And for the first time since then, I felt hungry… and not for blood.

"Are you saying—" I whispered as I rose. "Are you saying I'm the way I once was? I can eat food, go in the sun, and live an immortal life?"

Liùsaidh gave a sharp nod of her head.

"I can't believe it," Catrain whispered as she lifted her hand to her mouth. "You… you're like Aiden now."

It was almost impossible for me to comprehend that I'd no longer have to live in the dark and survive on blood. I'd be able to enjoy a life at her side, tasting the foods she loved and sipping on piña coladas with her. The joy surging through me erased the last of the pains from the spell.

"Thank you, Liùsaidh," I said as I crawled to my feet. "Thank you so much. I'll never forget this kindness."

She pursed her lips and arched an eyebrow as she looked away. Even though I knew it killed her inside to help me, and she wouldn't be welcoming me anytime soon, I tossed my arms around her and hugged her tight. She struggled against my embrace but gave up and stood still while I squeezed her a little tighter.

"I promise I'll take care of her," I whispered into her. "Always."

Her stiff body softened with the words, and I felt her head nod against my shoulder. Before she changed her mind and dropped me with a lightning bolt, I released my grip on her and stepped back to Catrain's side.

"Thank you, Mother. I love you so much." Catrain pulled her in for a hug before letting go and slipping her arm around my waist. "Alpia really will be a better leader. And she and Uradech are going to make you the most beautiful grandbabies."

Alpia and Uradech glanced at each other, a pink flush traveling across Alpia's cheeks as she stared up at him.

"You go now," Liùsaidh said, gesturing to the boat.

Catrain glanced at it, then looked back at her mother. "Will I be welcome back?"

Liùsaidh nodded. "Always, child."

With a wide grin, Catrain tossed her arms around her mother one last time. She then hurried to her sister, squeezing her tight before moving to Uradech.

"Take care of my sister," she warned with a finger in his face.

"I love her. I'll always protect her," he answered with a smile. "Thank you for doing this for her. For us."

"I'd have done it sooner if I'd known how you two felt about each other. I wish you both all the happiness in the world."

"Hey, none of these long goodbyes," Alpia said. "I'm getting married next month, and you're going to be here."

"I wouldn't miss it for the world." Catrain kissed her sister on the cheek.

"Go on. Go back to the world and ride that dirty bike, or whatever it's called." Alpia gave Catrain a little shove. "I've got things under control here."

"I'll see you soon," Catrain said with a wave and jogged back to me.

When she arrived in front of me, I offered her my hand, and she took it with a smile. I helped her into the boat, then pushed it away from the shore. After I climbed in, she settled between my legs and leaned her back against my chest as I paddled us away.

"Did you bring the dirt bike?" she asked as she peeked up at me.

"Of course." I paddled faster.

"Good. Then I'm driving." She smiled.

Pausing from my paddling, I leaned down and kissed her. My whole world shifted when our lips touched, and I knew the feeling would never go away.

"Paddle faster," she whispered against my lips. "I need a piña colada."

Laughing, I pecked her one more time and shoved the paddles back into the water, surging us toward shore.

Chapter Twenty

CATRAIN

As I sat beside the pool soaking up the sun, Emilia filled me in on the movie she and Aiden had watched last night.

"Gah. I can't think of the name. Baby!" she called to Aiden as he walked toward us carrying two drinks. "What was the name of that movie we watched last night?"

"Shit. I can't remember. It was on Netflix, so I'll look on my phone." Aiden walked in between our lounge chairs and placed a drink on each side. "Piña colada for you. Margarita for you."

"Thanks, love," Emilia said, then she sat up and kissed him.

"My favorite. I lov—" Before I could finish my sentence, a big splash of water slammed into my face. I closed my eyes against the assault, but when I gasped, I got a mouthful of pool water. After spitting it out, and wiping the water from my eyes, I opened them and looked for my assaulter. The tiny droplets of water on Thorne's skin glistened in the late afternoon sun as he grinned at me from the pool.

"Hey!" I shouted at him. "What the hell? You ruined my drink!"

"Get in here with me!"

"Oh, Thorne. Your ass is in trouble." Aiden laughed as he saw my eyes narrow.

"Damn straight, it is." Arching an eyebrow, I stared at him while I lifted my hand as the sparks crackled between my fingers.

"Oh, shit!" Thorne shouted as he flashed out of the way before my bolt slammed into the water where he'd stood.

He appeared at my side and caught my hands, holding them tight against my body while he pressed his forehead against mine.

"Nice try. I'm almost back to full speed though, so you're gonna need to get faster than that."

With a quick kiss on my nose, he flashed away again.

Emilia doubled over with laughter and shook her head. "You've got your hands full with that one."

Wringing the water from my hair, I sighed. "He's in trouble later when I can catch him."

"I don't doubt he is." Aiden laughed as he slid onto the chair behind Emilia. She lay back against his chest as he wrapped his arms around her.

"You done trying to shock me?" Thorne called from the house.

"Only if you bring me another piña colada, because this one is full of pool water!" I called back.

A few moments later he appeared at my side. In his hands he clutched a fresh drink, complete with extra cherries. "Truce?"

I took the drink and twisted my lips, then shrugged and said, "For now."

Thorne mirrored Aiden's position and slid in behind

me. I leaned back against him and sighed when his fingers drifted across my bare midriff.

"We still cooking brats on the grill tonight?" he asked Aiden.

"I've got some fresh links in the fridge. Maybe a couple burgers, too."

"With cheese," Emilia said. "Cheddar."

"You got it, baby."

"You know what I still need to try?" Thorne said before he leaned forward and took a sip of my piña colada. After he finished with an "ahh," he sat back and said, "Lobster. I still haven't tried that."

"Oh! So good!" My eyes widened as I remembered the sweet, buttery taste.

Emilia and Aiden nodded their agreement.

"I'll order some tomorrow," Emilia said. "We can have a New England lobster boil!"

"I have no idea what that is, but if it involves lobster, I'm in." I laughed.

"You'll love it."

I didn't doubt I would. I loved everything out here in this world. The last three weeks since I'd returned had been filled with more fun and excitement than I'd ever imagined. Thorne had been eager to try all the food with me, and it was wonderful experiencing all the new flavors with him... for both of us. He'd made it a point for us to try something new every night, and we'd made our way around restaurants all over Europe.

We spent the rest of the afternoon by the pool until the setting sun cooled the air. Aiden, Emilia, and Thorne didn't need to worry about the cold, but I didn't have their immortality powers, so I had to hurry inside when I started to catch a chill. Thorne followed me upstairs, and joined me in the shower, causing me to glow blue before I could even get the conditioner out of my hair.

We dressed and headed downstairs for the barbeque. Aiden met Thorne out by the grill and handed him a beer while I went to the firepit crackling beside them and sat with Emilia. The moment the sun dipped beneath the horizon, the rest of his family appeared at our side.

"Have fun in the sun, my Funky Bunch?" Mark slid into a chair beside me.

"Yes. We had a blast, Marky Mark," I answered.

"I miss you for afternoon margaritas," Emilia said with a pout. "We used to have so much fun."

He puckered his lips. "I know. No more margaritas for me though…" He looked at me and waggled his eyebrow. "Unless we can convince your sister to do to all of us what she did to Thorne?"

I sucked the air through my teeth. "I'll work on it. I promise. She will be able to lift your sun curse for sure, but I'm not sure if she'll be able to do what my mother did to Thorne. But I promise I'll try my best."

"You rock," Annella said as she slid onto the other side of me. "But no pressure. I'm okay drinking blood for eternity if that's what we need to do."

Mark rolled his eyes. "That's just because you've got that new bartender dude with the 'golden blood' or whatever the hell it is. The rest of us would still like a cocktail if we could."

"How's that going?" Emilia asked her.

Annella flushed pink like she did every time someone brought up Owen. "Good."

"Did you," Mark made a circle with his fingers and stuck his pointer finger in and out of it, "yet?"

"God, Mark!" Emilia slapped him on the shoulder as we all laughed.

"God, Mark is right." Annella swatted him on the head. "And no."

"Seriously?" Emilia and Mark echoed.

"What's up with that, you smitten kitten?" Mark asked. "I thought you wanted to climb him like a tree. You've been out with him three times and still haven't done the dirty?"

Annella shrugged. "I don't know. It's not that I'm opposed to doing it by any means, I mean hello, look at him. Even his muscles have muscles. But he wants to take things slow. You know, kissing and holding hands and stuff. All the making out and buildup is actually pretty hot."

"I think that's so sweet," Emilia smiled.

"So, you're just dating him? Like dinner and stuff? No hanky panky?" Mark furrowed his brow.

"Yeah. You know, *romance*. He takes me to dinner. The movies. Long walks through the city. We talk. It's pretty incredible, actually."

"No sex, but you drink his blood. How romantic," Mark teased.

She sucked the air through her teeth. "Yeah. I know that's not typical date stuff, but I can't not have a few sips when I see him. That shit tastes amazing. I just influenced him not to remember any of my vampy stuff. It works."

"Well, I'm really happy for you," I said. "He sounds like a great guy. I can't wait to meet him."

"Soon." Annella smiled. "I think he and I will be ready to take things to the next level soon, and I'm hoping maybe after your sister lifts our sunlight curse. It's always been impossible dating humans and never seeing them in the sun, but now knowing that may be over soon, I think I'm ready to give dating one a try. If it keeps going well, I'll bring him home to meet my crazy family."

"I promise I'll behave." Mark held up his fingers in scout's honor.

"No, you won't," Emilia and Annella said in unison, then burst into laughter.

"What's so funny?" Thorne asked from the grill where he and Aiden pushed the meat around on the flames.

"Nothing!" I called. "Just Mark being Mark."

"Makes sense." He lifted his beer and laughed.

Grizella and Lothaire joined us around the fire, and I sat back and listened to their stories, admiring the laughter and love between this family. Knowing I was part of them warmed me more than the flames sending sparks up into the air.

Thorne, Aiden, Emilia, and I had our dinners, which turned out surprisingly well since Aiden and Thorne burned the burgers, but they salvaged them by scraping off the charred outside. After we finished eating, Thorne took me by the hand and led me away from the group.

"What are we doing?" I asked as he tugged me to the garage.

"You'll see." He opened the garage door and pulled out a brand-new red dirt bike.

I grinned when I saw it. "Is that for me?"

"For us. I finally returned the one I 'borrowed,' so I bought us a new one."

"I love it!" I slid my hand over the shiny paint.

"Want to go for a ride? We need to test it out."

"Yeah! Can I drive?" I asked as he climbed on.

"Later. First, I need to take you somewhere. Hop on."

I didn't hesitate and climbed on behind him. My heart

fluttered when I pressed my body against him. I knew this feeling I had for him, this love I had for him, would never falter. In fact, it seemed to grow stronger every day. Not once did I question the choice I'd made to be with him, and I knew I never would.

I belonged with Thorne. Always.

We scooted across the countryside, and I recognized the familiar trail. When we reached the top, he hopped off and held out his hand.

"I know this place." I smiled as I took it. "The cliffs."

"Come on." He pulled a blanket out of the storage on the back of the dirt bike and led me to the edge of the cliff.

After he laid out the blanket, we sat down beside one another. I lay my head on his shoulder and sighed.

"I love you, Thorne. And I love our life."

He slipped his arm around me and pressed his chin on top of my head. "I love you more than anything in the world, and I'm going to love you for eternity. Thank you for choosing me. Choosing us."

"We were never a choice." I looked up at him. "We were destined to be together. And we always will be."

"I'm really glad to hear you say that." Thorne lowered his lips to mine, kissing me deeply as I listened to the waves crash below. When I opened my eyes, I saw the moonlight glint off a giant diamond ring he held in front of me.

"Oh, my God," I gasped as I looked up at him. "Is that? Are you?"

His blue eyes flickered with mirth as he smiled.

"My whole life, I avoided falling in love… and avoided the pain that would come with losing it. It wasn't worth it to me until you. Ever since we met, I've realized that there is nothing more terrifying, nothing more painful, than being without you. I don't want to spend another minute of my life without you... however long that may be. I love you, Cat. And I will choose the risk of losing you over the certainty of misery without you every day. Every single day. I'll love you when you're old and gray. I'll love you when you need me to carry you to the dirt bike. Or I'll love you for eternity if you choose to become immortal with us when your sister does the spell."

The words stopped my heart as I considered them. I'd be lying if I said I hadn't thought about it, but being a Pict witch, I wasn't even sure if it was possible. And I hadn't dared ask my mother about it. She already had too much to process with me abdicating the throne and running off with a vampire. But with Alpia ascending soon, I knew that she would help me become immortal if that's the life I wanted.

"You don't need to decide about immortality now. I'll love you no matter what. I'd rather spend a short life with you than none at all. But immortality or not, will you make me the luckiest man on the planet? Marry me?"

Tears slipped down my cheeks as I nodded my head. "Yes. Yes!"

I tossed my arms around his neck and covered his face with kisses.

"I love you, baby," he whispered in my ear as I held him. "And I always will."

"Good. Because I'm not going anywhere. Ever."

"Ever?" He sat back, and his eyes sparkled as much as the diamond. "Does that mean you'll become immortal?"

"Yes. My answer is yes. One human lifetime with you could never be enough. I don't want to leave you. Ever. I love you, Thorne."

Thorne took my hand and slipped the ring on my finger,

then took my face in his hands and kissed me so deeply I didn't think I'd ever come up for air. If immortality meant kisses like this for eternity, then there was nothing I wanted more.

Thorne and I belonged together… always.

Next in the Immortal Hearts Series

vinci-books.com/EternalLight

She loved him. They turned him into a weapon.

Annella Mackay is a legendary vampire warrior. Owen was never meant to matter—until her enemies murdered him and he rose again. Now a werewolf-born hybrid, he's losing control, and Annella must save him… or destroy the man she loves.

Turn the page for a free preview…

Eternal Light: Chapter One

ANNELLA

The speakers pumped out the music from the band, flooding the club with sounds that made everybody on the dance floor pulse and move to the beat. Normally, I'd have been out dancing in the center of them, but dancing hadn't brought me to the club tonight.

I placed my chin on my hand and tracked the gorgeous bartender with my eyes. When he picked up the whiskey bottle from the drink well, his inked forearm swelled, and with it my desire to have it wrapped around me.

He lifted his head as he poured the liquor into the shot glass, and those emerald green eyes collided with mine. The look inside them sent my stomach into its own kind of dance routine.

A dance routine only Owen could inspire.

After over six hundred years on this planet, I'd never met a man that made me feel the way he did. The feelings he created in me felt primal and raw… not unlike the way he looked.

Owen towered over everyone with his incredible height,

and tattoos covered the massive muscles on his arms. I could only imagine where else on his impressive body they traveled. Paired with his dark wavy hair and rugged beard, he looked dangerous.

Primitive.

Wild.

He looked like a man I wanted to tame, but a man I knew I never could.

No. I hadn't come to the club tonight for dancing. I'd come for Owen.

He gestured to my Blood Mary… because I'd influenced him into thinking liquor filled my glass instead of blood.

"You need another?" he asked, his deep gravelly voice rolling over the words.

Even his voice turned me on–floating over me and leaving every cell crackling with electricity.

"Need another… kiss? Don't mind if I do." I arched an eyebrow, and he matched it.

A smirk lifted his full lips before he angled his ripped body toward me. His substantial height made it easy for him to clear the bar with a slow lean. Each second felt like torture as I waited for his lips to reach mine. When they did, my world flipped upside down as he slid his tongue inside my mouth.

My heart rattled faster against my ribcage while he kissed me slow and sensual. The rough pads of his fingers traced my jawline as he pulled me in even deeper. I relished every second in the ecstasy his kiss and his touch brought me, but before I'd had my fill, he pulled away. I almost jumped the bar and launched into his arms, desperate for a little more.

"Miss me while I was gone?" he asked as he held my hungry gaze and slid the shot glass he'd filled down the bar. It landed directly in front of the man who'd ordered it.

"Cool trick! Thanks, man!" the guy called to Owen before downing his shot.

"Maybe," I answered as I twirled a piece of my long, auburn hair around my finger. "Did you miss me?"

"Maybe." He matched my cool response as his half-smirk grew.

"Just maybe?" I arched an eyebrow.

He leaned forward and brushed another soft kiss against my lips. "Okay. Maybe more than maybe."

I sighed into his kiss and grabbed his t-shirt, knotting it tight into my fist as I deepened it.

I wanted more of him.

All of him.

And I was ready to throw our old-fashioned courting out the window and jump his bones right on the bar.

I'd met Owen here a couple months ago on a night out with my family. After a hot make-out session and a few sips of his blood in the stockroom, he'd asked me on a date. I'd accepted, of course, because hello… he's gorgeous. But also, he'd made me laugh and had turned out to be surprisingly sweet for a guy who looked like he could crush a person's skull without breaking a sweat. Instead of just a quickie and a meal, I'd felt something click between us… a connection I'd never felt before.

Though the sexual chemistry between us could burn this entire country down, instead of my usual routine of a quick roll in the sheets and an even quicker goodbye, we'd ended each one of our three dates with only a goodnight kiss.

Long, hot, sensual kisses that left me reeling for days.

After our third date, he'd gone out on tour with his band and left me here for a month with my lust multiplying by the second. Now that he'd returned home and texted me to come see him, I didn't think I could even wait until his shift ended before I unleashed the pent up sexual frustration he'd created in me.

Even though I truly enjoyed this new experience of romance and dating, and dating a *human* no less, the longer I went without feeling him inside me, the more I craved him.

It was intoxicating. A sweet torture–and I savored every second.

A torture that had gone on long enough. A torture I was ready to end.

We continued our silent stare-off as I sucked my lip between my teeth. "What time does your shift end?"

"By the time we're done serving and cleaning up, I won't get out until five in the morning," he answered.

Fuck.

Five in the morning meant we wouldn't have time to do much of anything before the sun came up. There were plans to have the Pict witches lift our sunlight curse in the new year, but until then, I'd need to continue avoiding the sun's rays.

"Can you get off early? Like now?" I considered using my powers of influence to make him quit his job so I could have him all to myself tonight if he said no. I'd already been influencing him to not notice me drinking his decadent blood on our dates, but I knew forcing him to quit his job was probably not very good dating behavior.

Another look at those lips, and I still considered it.

"I just got back after a month off. I don't think my co-workers would go for it." He chuckled.

Double fuck.

"So, you're saying I just have to sit here and watch you

pour other people's drinks all night?" I stuck out my lower lip in an exaggerated pout.

"Would watching me all night really be the end of the world?"

He walked away, and I soaked in every impressive inch of his massive frame. The broad shoulders and wide back. His perfect round ass I wanted to bounce a quarter off. That face that looked rugged and rough, but beautiful as well.

He glanced over his shoulder and caught me ogling the goods and smiled. "Told you it wouldn't be the end of the world."

I didn't even try to conceal the fact I'd been mentally undressing him. There was no hiding the passion in my eyes, and I loved that he was bold enough to call me out on it.

Hot. As hot as the man himself.

The bar business picked up, and Owen and his two co-bartenders picked up with it. I sat at the bar for the better part of an hour watching him sling drinks with style. Even more than his bartending show, I enjoyed watching him flat-out deny every other woman who came up batting her eyes.

And there were plenty.

Each time a beautiful woman tried to entice him, his eyes drifted to me when he answered her and sent her packing. If there was any way to be more turned on by a guy, I'd never known it.

"You still good over here?" he asked as he took a break from the customers still waving money his way. "Anything I can get you?"

"I think you know damn well what you can get me," I answered unashamedly. I'd given up being prudish centuries ago.

Owen laughed, and it drowned out the din of the crowd. "Damn, Annella. You're killing me, girl."

"Seriously," I said as I leaned closer. "You need to take off the rest of the night. Let's go hang out. You can tell me all about your tour."

When he shook his head, a piece of his dark hair fell in front of his eyes. He tucked it behind his ear. "My tour involved riding on a bus with a bunch of sweaty dudes, playing live music every night, and thinking about you every minute I was gone."

Thump, thump, thump.

There went my damn heart again.

"You thought about me?" I tried to keep my voice sexy and cool, but it rose several octaves anyway.

"I haven't stopped thinking about you since I saw you sitting at this bar the night we met."

Thump, thump, thump, thump.

There. That was the sweet side of this sexy, powerful man that continued tipping me upside down. For every second I wanted to treat him like a sex toy, I also wanted to get to know the man who could say things that made my six-hundred-year-old heart feel like a teenage girl with a crush the size of Texas.

"Seriously, Annella. I would kill to get off early and spend some time with you. But I'm stuck here all night. How about this? I'll get off at five and take you out for breakfast. There is this twenty-four-hour diner all the late-night servers congregate at, and it's a pretty fun party. We'll have bacon and waffles, drink some coffee while you tell me more about what you were up to all month, then go for a stroll and watch the sun come up. Then maybe we can go back to my place."

The twinkle in his eye almost erased the knowledge that

I couldn't do any of those things. I couldn't eat food, I couldn't drink coffee, and I *definitely* couldn't watch the sun rise.

At least not yet.

Even though I wanted to say yes… God, did I want to say yes… I shook my head.

"I'm afraid I'm not a morning person. How about tomorrow night we go out?"

"I'll take you whenever I can get you," he said. "Tomorrow night it is."

My unnaturally childish smile split my face as I tried to twist it back into the sultry one I'd mastered over the centuries. But as he leaned in for a kiss, I lost the battle and embraced the smitten kitten look he continued coaxing out of me.

After a quick kiss, he leaned back and scanned the bar filled with customers still vying for his attention… the attention he'd given to me and me alone. I caught the glare from the blonde several stools down who'd done her best for the past ten minutes to attract his attention with her over-inflated breasts—and failed. I held her eye contact while I smirked, then took a sip of blood.

Mine.

The rock band that had been playing all night came back from their break, but when the lead singer took the mic, it didn't turn a single eye from the show Owen put on behind that bar. Charming, charismatic, and sexy as all hell. He held the attention of everyone in the area.

"We're back from our break," the lead singer said into the microphone. "And we saw that one of our favorite bassists is back from his tour across the pond in Ireland. What do you all say we get Owen Hunter up here to join us for a song?"

The crowd went wild, and all eyes turned toward Owen. Chuckling, he shook his head while he shook a martini shaker. But the crowd urged him on more, and one of the other bartenders gave him a shove. His gaze drifted to me for a moment before he smirked, handed off the shaker, and raised his hands in submission.

Owen walked out from behind the bar and weaved his way through the crowd. The blue lights illuminated his incredible frame as he stepped up onto the stage. When he picked up the bass guitar and took his place in front of the microphone, I was certain I could hear my panties rip.

"Thanks for inviting me up here, guys," Owen said into the microphone. "It's good to be back in Scotland."

The crowd cheered again.

He whispered something to the lead singer, who passed it through the rest of the waiting band.

"This song goes out to a special girl in the crowd tonight."

Thump, thump, thump, thump, thump.

His green eyes locked with mine as he lifted his lip in a half-smirk. "This one's for you, Annella."

If I hadn't been dead already, I'd have died again.

When he started plucking the strings on his bass and crooning into the microphone, I nearly melted into a puddle from the heat scorching me from the inside out. The gorgeous man on the stage mesmerized me, commanding the attention of everyone in the building but staring only at me.

While he sang the song about the woman who controlled his heart, those eyes stayed locked onto mine. And I couldn't have looked away even if I'd tried.

Owen commanded me in a way I'd never thought possible.

I'd spent my life as one of the most powerful people on the planet, but underneath his smoldering stare, I felt powerless… an emotion I didn't even recognize.

And one I enjoyed because he made me feel something new and exciting.

After he finished up the song I never wanted to end, the crowd cheered again as he walked off the stage. People clapped him on the back as he made his way back to the bar… and back to me.

Instead of going behind the bar again, Owen walked over to me, stopping in front of my stool. My breath hitched in my chest as I looked up at the beautiful man towering over me.

"You like the song?" he asked as he leaned closer.

Words refused to form on my tongue, the one that wanted to be back in his mouth, so I just nodded my head and bit my lip. I bit it so hard I tasted my own blood.

"Good. I'll give you a private concert later," he whispered as he leaned down and brushed his lips against mine.

I sighed into his mouth as I wrapped my arms around his neck and pulled him in for a kiss so deep I worried I'd hurt him with my vampire strength. But he didn't flinch against the power of my passion, instead sliding his arms around my waist and dipping me backward on my stool. When we finally broke apart, he sat me back upright and gave me one last kiss before heading back behind the bar, leaving me stunned and senseless.

I spent the next two hours watching him like I was the president of his fan club… and I may as well have been.

A sexy rockstar. A sweet romantic. A powerful, primal man who set my soul on fire.

I'd slap on a button with his sexy face on it and wear that shit with pride any damn day.

That realization shocked me.

I was Annella Mackay…

A restless wanderess. A lethal warrior. An immortal vampire. A woman who'd never belonged to a man in her life… and never wanted to.

Owen glanced over at me and smiled.

Until now.

Eternal Light: Chapter Two

ANNELLA

"So then what happened? You just kissed him goodbye and left?" My friend Mark, one of the newest vampire's in our clan, asked from his perch at the foot of my bed.

I rolled onto my stomach and rested my head on my forearms. "Yes. It was torture, but I couldn't stay another minute. I wanted to go back to his place so bad, but it's not light tight. Even going at full vamp speed, I barely made it back here before the sun went up."

"Fucking sunshine getting in the way of a good lay. Been there, sister. It's not fair."

"Not fair at *all.*" I sighed. "I've never wanted anything in my life as much as I want to find out if what those eyes promise is legit… what those *kisses* promise."

"Gah!" He grabbed a handful of his perfectly styled blonde hair. "I can't even imagine!" Mark rolled over and went face to face with me. "*I'm* dying, and it's not even happening to me. On the one hand, it's so freaking hot that you guys are holding out and letting that sexual tension build because the release will be explosive when it happens. On the other hand, it's like enough already! Jump his freaking bones!"

"My thoughts exactly." I sighed. "And I'm definitely at the jump his freaking bones stage now —enough of the waiting. I can't take it anymore. We're going on our date, and I'm jumping his bones."

"Do it. Jump those freaking bones, sister."

He held out his hand, and I gave it a slap.

"Oh," I added. "I'm gonna stay over at Owen's for the night, then head to our apartment just a few blocks away before the sun comes up. That way, I'll be able to stay in bed with him until the last moment, then just pop down the road to our apartment and get out of the sun. It will only take me a few seconds to get there."

"So, you're saying not to worry, and you aren't kidnapped again if you don't come home tonight."

Until a couple months ago, that would have been a joke. As an immortal vampire, we didn't have to use the buddy system like a normal human woman. I was a vampire… an apex predator. And as one of the original vampires, I was an apex predator *of* the apex predators. We were stronger, faster, and more lethal than any other vampire who came after us. But a couple months ago, Clan Lennox, a clan who wanted to take power from my brother Lothaire, the leader of all the vampires, had got the jump on me and took me prisoner.

Luckily, with the help of Catrain, a Pict witch my friend Thorne went to for help, my family tracked me down and saved me.

Saved me. Ugh. Just the thought I'd needed rescuing boiled the blood in my veins. I may be the most petite of my clan, but I'd garnered a reputation for being the deadliest of the originals. My fierce reputation among the vampires only grew each year along with my legend. Then Clan Lennox got ahold of me, and I worried they'd tarnished six hundred years of being the baddest bitch around. I was more determined than ever to remind the rest of the clans just who they'd messed with.

I wanted to make an example of Clan Lennox, but they'd gone into hiding after their plan to kidnap me and kill Lothaire failed. I'd been hunting for Leith Lennox, their leader, and his sister Leeya ever since. If they wanted a war–they'd have one.

And I never lost.

"One of these days those fucking Lennox's will have to rear their heads. And I'll be waiting to lop them off the minute they do."

His brown eyes widened. "Samesies, girl. I'm still pissed off that Gregor seduced me to distract me while they took you. The nerve! I don't care if he's a hot Scot, I'm gonna make him pay for using me."

The night they had taken me, Mark had been out dancing with me, but met a handsome Scottish vampire named Gregor. Mark thought he'd met the perfect man, but it turned out that Gregor had just been keeping him busy while they hit me with a UV light and took me down in the alley.

"Every single member of Clan Lennox is dead. No one comes after Clan Mackay and lives to tell about it. No one." I tightened my eyes into tiny slits.

"I'm new to this whole 'slaughtering our enemies' thing, but I'm right there with you, girl. Those bastards almost killed you. They need to go buh-bye."

When I'd been taken and held in that cage under the

UV lights that weakened me to the point of near-death, it had been the first time in centuries I'd actually feared for my life. It wasn't since the werewolf wars six hundred years ago that I'd felt the cold fingers of death scraping against my skin.

Back then, we'd realized the werewolves equaled us in strength and were even stronger under a full moon. We'd also been outnumbered. They'd been created by the same Pict tribe who'd created us, and their one goal in life had been to eradicate us.

And they'd almost succeeded.

But we had one advantage on our side. We could create new vampires.

When we fed someone our blood and killed them, a couple hours later, they would awaken. After enduring a painful few minutes of transformation, they emerged as a vampire. Werewolves could only be born. In a matter of days, we created an army to turn the tables and eradicate the beasts instead.

And I'd led the war against them, slaying countless wolves until we'd destroyed every last one of them.

Well, almost every last one of them. We found out when Thorne met Catrain that a few werewolves still existed on the island where she and her tribe still lived. Since magic protected it, they'd managed to survive there undetected.

But the rest of those fucking wolves? Wiped from this planet.

Just like I planned on doing to Clan Lennox.

No one got to terrorize me and live to tell about it.

No one.

"You guys in there?" Emilia called from the other side of the door.

"Yes! Come in!" I called back.

The door opened, and Emilia flashed to the bed and landed right next to Mark. Her expectant blue eyes blinked at me. "Well? How was it?"

Mark lifted his hand and stopped me from talking, then rolled over and faced her. "Quick recap. After Owen texted he was back, she went to the bar, they had a super hot greeting kiss, then she had to sit there and watch his rough and rugged sexy ass bartend all night. But lots more kisses between slinging drinks. Then he got up on stage and sang to her—"

Emilia's eyes widened, emphasizing the hopeless romantic my brother Aiden, her fiancé, had turned her into. "He sang to her? He sang to you?" She spun to look at me.

"Yeah. He sang to her. Like a rockstar serenade in front of the entire club," Mark answered and got her attention back. "Long story short, they ended on a hot kiss, and she's seeing him in two hours. And tonight, they are finally doing it. It's business time."

"Oh my God, I'm dying for you!" Emilia squealed and bounced in place. The movement made the long chestnut waves of her hair bounce. "I think it's so romantic that you guys waited, and that he sang to you. He really sang to you? Up on stage?"

With a girlish sigh that never should have come from a woman like me, I rolled onto my back. "You guys. He looked so hot up there. All rockstar shaggy hair, tattooed bad boy… but the way he stared at me while he sang about the girl who controlled his heart..." I drifted off.

"Epic. Oh my God. So freaking epic," Emilia sighed.

"What are you wearing tonight?" Mark asked after a long pause.

"I don't know," I answered, then flashed over to my

closet. "It's like nothing is good enough. On the one hand, I'm thinking sexy rocker chick like this." In seconds, I whipped on some torn jeans and a sexy black shirt that dipped to my navel."

"Hot. Very hot," Mark said, and Emilia nodded.

"Or I could go more sexy elegant." I whipped on a black dress that accentuated every one of the admirable curves I'd inherited from my mama.

"Ooh. Pretty." Emilia nodded.

"Another excellent option," Mark agreed.

"Which one? Or should I pick something else? I don't want to look too desperate, but I also want to make sure that there is no way he can make us hold off one more night."

"Oh my God." Mark placed a hand over his mouth. "Our Annella is nervous. *Nervous* about her date with a boy."

"Aww," Emilia crooned as they bumped their shoulders together.

"Shut the fuck up," I snapped but started laughing.

They were right. I *was* nervous. A new emotion I hadn't felt in centuries… just add it to the list of new feelings Owen continued evoking in me.

"Everyone meet me in the family room," my oldest brother Lothaire called from somewhere in the castle, and we all perked an ear toward the sound. "Now."

I switched out of my dress and back into my regular clothes, then flashed down the stairs with Mark and Emilia. Emilia flew to Aiden's side and slid onto his lap. Mark went to his chair nearest Lothaire and his gorgeous raven-haired wife, Grizella, and I sat near Thorne and his new fiancé, the Pict witch, Catrain.

Catrain's tribe had made us immortal over six hundred

years ago… and her tribe had cursed us, causing us to survive on blood and hide from the sun. But since we'd found their tribe this year, they'd removed the curse on my brother Aiden, and our friend, and honorary brother, Thorne. Both of them, along with Aiden's fiancé Emilia, enjoyed all the original perks of immortality but could eat food, drink cocktails, and play in the sun.

When Catrain's sister took over for her mother in a couple months, the mother who still hated our kind, she'd promised to remove the sunshine curse on my entire family. I counted the days until I could go in the sun and not have to race back for cover when the sun came up.

It meant more time with Owen.

As excited as I was to have the curse removed, I hoped she'd find a way to do more than just lift the sun curse… I hoped she could return us to our original powers and make us all immortal with all the perks enjoyed by Aiden, Thorne, and Emilia.

"Thanks for coming down," Lothaire started.

"What's up, Lothaire?" Thorne asked as he slid an arm around his little blonde witch. His hand wrapped around her tattooed arm as he squeezed her tight.

Lothaire rubbed a hand down his beard, and his amber eyes narrowed as they swept across us. "Clan Lennox has resurfaced."

Rage pumped through my veins, replacing the lust Owen had filled them with.

"Where?" I growled.

"Leeya was spotted in Glasgow last night."

"Glasgow?" I asked, stuttering over the simple word. "I was in Glasgow last night."

"I know," Lothaire said, concern brewing in his eyes.

"Do you think she was hunting Annella?" Aiden asked.

Ice-blue eyes, the same color as mine, flicked to me as they filled with worry.

"Where was she spotted?" Thorne's rugged, shadowed jaw tightened as he waited for the answer.

"Outside the same club."

"Shit," Mark spit. "So, she was hunting Annella."

My eyes narrowed as I digested how close my enemy had been. They narrowed more that she had the audacity to hunt *me*. It was me hunting *her*.

"It seems that way," Lothaire said. "So, until we figure this out, we all need to stick together and stay close to home. We need to work as a clan to find them and get rid of them for good."

It shouldn't have been what popped into my head when our lives were on the line, but a pain of sadness twisted up my gut that I wouldn't be able to see Owen tonight.

After all the waiting and anticipation, it seemed we'd need to hold out even longer.

"No one travels alone right now. They managed to capture Annella with a UV light, and she's far stronger than them," Grizella said, and her emerald green eyes warned each one of us to heed the advice but fixated on me. She knew how much I looked forward to seeing Owen again. "That means none of us can assume we can outfight them. We don't know what they're up to, and we aren't taking any chances. We stick together."

"I understand," I answered as the rest of my family nodded in agreement.

I didn't like it, hell, I hated it. But I understood. And I wouldn't put myself at risk for abduction again, and my family at risk having to rescue me.

"Did anyone get a piece of her clothing, hair, personal effects, anything?" Catrain asked.

As a Pict witch, she could perform locator spells as long as she had a personal item to track. It was how she'd found me when I'd been taken.

"No. Nothing," Lothaire answered. "A couple vampires loyal to Clan Mackay spotted her, but they didn't approach."

"Damn," Thorne huffed.

"If you can get anything of hers or Leith's, I am happy to run a spell to find them."

"We'll keep trying," Aiden answered. "And in the meantime, we need eyes all over Glasgow. If that psycho Leeya is back, then her brother must be nearby."

Aiden had dated Leeya years ago, and she'd developed an obsession for him that almost took the life of his new love, Emilia. Along with Leeya's brother, who wanted to harvest humans like cattle, the two of them had turned into a massive headache for our family.

A headache it was time we eradicate.

"I've already sent word out to all the vampires in Glasgow to watch for them. In the meantime, we just need to be ready to move out at a moment's notice. Thorne and Aiden, since you can walk in the sun, I think we should plan on having you two do some daytime searches of the city. Just check some of their old haunts."

"I'll help too," Emilia said.

It was easy to forget to include Emilia in these things because until a few months ago, she'd been a human. Now she had the same powers we'd had when we first became immortal… the same powers shared with Aiden and Thorne.

"Thank you, Emilia."

"I'll go too, of course," Catrain said.

She didn't have our immorality or the speed, strength,

and fangs that came with it, but she had some powerful magic that proved very handy in knocking vamps down on their arses. And with her skills with weaponry, she was an incredible asset to our family.

"Let's wait a few days and see what our contacts find out," Lothaire said, "but if they don't locate them, we'll all head to Glasgow and start hunting. Annella, Mark, Grizella, and I can work at night, and the rest of you use your perks of day walking to hunt in the sun. We aren't letting them get away this time."

I'd already been motivated to reap my revenge on them before, but now that they stood between me and Owen, a new fire to kill them all burned inside me.

The knocker on the main castle door slammed against the old wood several times. We all spun toward the sound.

"Are we expecting anyone?" Mark asked.

"No," Lothaire answered as he pushed out of his chair.

We all flashed to the door, and when Lothaire opened it, a body crashed into our foyer.

"What the fuck?" Lothaire said as he sidestepped the body and glanced out at the emptiness outside. "Whoever knocked must have been a vampire because this guy certainly didn't do the knocking. Who the fuck is this?"

Lothaire's massive frame blocked me from seeing the body, so I peeked around him.

When my eyes locked onto the man laying at our feet, my hands flew to my mouth as I gasped.

"Owen!" I cried out, then dropped to my knees and pulled his limp body into my arms.

"Oh my God!" Emilia shrieked, dropping beside me. "Is he dead?"

I pressed my fingers to his neck, then listened for the beat of his heart.

The sound of silence nearly stopped my own.

"He's dead," I whispered, barely able to utter the words I couldn't believe were true. "He can't be dead."

Tears streamed down my face as heartache like I'd never known tore through my soul. I hadn't known him long, but I'd connected with him in a way I'd never connected with anyone in my life. And now he'd been ripped from me before we even had a chance.

"Holy shit." Thorne pushed his hands into his brown hair. "Who in the hell would kill Owen? Wait—"

His voice drifted off as he looked at me.

The agony wracking my body transformed instantly into a rage that burned hotter than the sun.

"Leeya," I ground out. "She saw me at the club last night, which means she saw me with him. Saw us kiss. Saw that he meant something to me. Killing him was a fuck you from that psycho."

Anyone who'd been in that club had seen the connection between Owen and me. Instead of starting a romance, I'd marked him for death. A pawn to be used to cause me pain.

And it had worked.

"Annella, I'm so sorry," Aiden said as he dropped to my side and pulled me into his arms. "We'll get her for this."

I'd already wanted her blood pouring down my face before, but now I wanted to make her suffer long and hard for it. I wanted to hear her screams while I ripped her body apart the way she ripped my heart apart by taking Owen from me.

"I'm going to kill that fucking bitch," I said between sniffles.

"We've got your back, baby." Mark lowered himself to my other side and wrapped his arms around my shoulders.

I couldn't stop staring at Owen. Staring at the gorgeous, powerful man with the beautiful voice now silenced forever. He'd been so full of life, so full of passion and power. Leeya had taken him from me, and I'd never felt the fires of rage and revenge burn hotter.

All the negative emotions in the universe wound through my heart and squeezed the hope right out of it. As Mark and Aiden sandwiched me into a hug, I looked once more at the lips I'd never get to kiss again.

The lips that just… opened?

With a jolt, Owen inhaled a sharp breath, and my shocked gasp inflated my own lungs.

"Jesus, fuck!" Mark shouted as he fell backward.

I struggled to release the breath trapped in my chest as I heard another inhale of air fill his lungs. I looked up to his eyes, and saw them open wide, shocked, and searching his surroundings.

"Where am I? What happened?" he asked as he inhaled another breath.

His confused green eyes searched the faces of my family all hovering over him, then slid to a stop when they landed on me. "Annella?"

"You're alive?" I whispered with a trembling lip.

I didn't wait for his answer or give an answer I didn't have. I just flung myself forward and kissed his lips over and over, then fell forward onto his chest and sobbed into his t-shirt. His arms wrapped around my body as he held me tight.

"What's happening. How did I get here?"

I wanted to answer him, but I still couldn't form words over the lump in my throat.

I'd thought I lost him. I'd thought Leeya had ripped him

from my life forever, but somehow, someway, he came back to me.

"I'm Lothaire, Annella's brother," Lothaire said. "I'm sure you're confused. We are too. What is the last thing you remember happening?"

Wiping the steady stream of tears from my eyes, I sniffled and sat back on my heels. Owen stared at me with the same confusion I shared.

He'd been dead. I was certain of it. Wasn't I? Or maybe Leeya hadn't killed him after all. None of it made sense.

"It's okay," I said to him. "You're safe here. Tell us what happened, and maybe we can help you figure this out."

Owen sat up but still looked dazed and confused. As he opened his mouth to speak, he slammed his eyes shut and fell backward on the floor. His howls of anguish flooded our castle, and his writhing sent me tumbling backward.

Thorne caught me in his arms and pulled me out of the way. Shock mirrored through the faces of my family as we watched Owen writhing in agony at my feet.

An agony I knew well… and one I hadn't felt in six hundred years but had seen many times since.

The agony that came when you awakened from death and transitioned into a vampire.

"Is he… turning?" Aiden asked, confirming my suspicions.

"Yes," I whispered. "I think he's turning into a vampire."

"Why the hell would Leeya turn him into a vampire and send him to us?"

"I don't know," I answered.

After several minutes of agonizing pain, he collapsed into a heap on the floor, his transformation complete.

"Owen, you're okay." I slid to his side now that his thrashing had ended. "Everything will be okay."

"What happened to me? What the fuck is going on?" he grimaced as he rolled up to his knees.

I glanced around at my family and exhaled a sigh. "This will come as a huge shock, and there is no easy way to say it, so I'm just going to rip it off like a band-aid."

"Annella. Tell me what the hell is happening."

"I'm not sure how it happened, but you just transitioned into a vampire."

"What?" he growled.

"I know. It's impossible to think vampires exist, and you think I'm fucking with you, but I'm not. You're a vampire now."

"That's impossible!" Like a wild, confused animal, he launched to his feet and spun around, staring at us.

"It's going to be okay. I promise. I'll show you everything you need to know and explain it to you. Because," I paused and bit my lip, "I'm a vampire too. We all are."

His eyes widened as he looked at me.

"I know this is a shock. First, finding out that vampires exist, second that you're dating one, and third that you've become one. It's a lot to take in."

"I can't be a fucking vampire!" he shouted so loud it forced me back a step.

Lothaire stepped to my side, and it surprised me that even at his impressive height, Owen still had him by a couple inches. It was rare to see Lothaire look small, but Owen managed to pull it off.

"Easy now, Owen. Just take a deep breath and relax," Lothaire said.

Owen grabbed a handful of his hair and shook his head.

"This can't be happening. It's impossible. It can't be possible."

I stepped toward him and touched his shoulder, but he shook my hand off and spun to glare at me. "Don't fucking touch me, *vampire*." His lip curled in contempt.

The response set me back on my heels.

"Hey!" Thorne warned as he stepped to my other side. "Watch it. You're one of us now too. You need to calm the fuck down, big guy."

"I'm *not* one of you," Owen ground out as his furious gaze scanned us all.

"Dude, you're a vampire. And a vampire who is handling this pretty poorly. Being a vamp is actually really cool," Mark started, but Owen just narrowed his eyes.

"You're just in shock learning vampires exist," Emilia said. "I was shocked when I found out too. I was a human when I found out Aiden here is a vampire." She pointed at him. "But it's gonna be okay."

"I *know* vampires exist," Owen spit out. "I fucking hate vampires."

He knows we exist? What?

Humans had no idea of our existence… or at least that was what I thought.

"And I can't *be* a fucking vampire!" Owen shouted.

"I'm feeling so judged," Mark whispered.

"Owen," I soothed, trying to push down the anger at his dramatic reaction to me. "You're just really confused right now. It's normal. How about we just sit down and take a breath for a minute? Whether you believe in vampires or hate them because of the things you've seen on TV or whatever, you're one of us now."

"I can't be!" he shouted, and I saw the betrayal flash in his eyes.

The disdain.
The horror.
"And why is that?" Thorne asked.
"Because I'm a fucking werewolf, that's why!"
We all gasped and took a step back.
What?

Grab your copy…
vinci-books.com/EternalLight

www.ingramcontent.com/pod-product-compliance
Lightning Source LLC
LaVergne TN
LVHW030918080826
845145LV00013B/2957